CRUEL MONEY

*Karen—
Bets are off!*

CRUEL MONEY

CRUEL BOOK ONE

K.A. LINDE

Copyright © 2019 by K.A. Linde
All rights reserved.

Visit my website at
www.kalinde.com

Join my newsletter to review free books and exclusive content!
www.kalinde.com/subscribe

Cover Designer: Sarah Hansen, Okay Creations., www.okaycreations.com
Photography: Yasmine Kateb, www.yasminekateb.com
Editor: Jovana Shirley, Unforeseen Editing, www.unforeseenediting.com

No part of this book may be reproduced or transmitted in any form or by any means, electronic or mechanical, including photocopying, recording, or by any information storage and retrieval system without the written permission of the author, except for the use of brief quotations in a book review.

This book is a work of fiction. Names, characters, places, and incidents either are products of the author's imagination or are used fictitiously. Any resemblance to actual persons, living or dead, events, or locales is entirely coincidental.

ISBN-13: 978-1948427241

ALSO BY K.A. LINDE

CRUEL
One Cruel Night
Cruel Money

WRIGHTS
The Wright Brother ✦ *The Wright Boss* ✦ *The Wright Mistake*
The Wright Secret ✦ *The Wright Love* ✦ *The Wright One*

AVOIDING SERIES
Avoiding Commitment ✦ *Avoiding Responsibility*
Avoiding Temptation ✦ *Avoiding Intimacy* ✦ *Avoiding Decisions*

RECORD SERIES
Off the Record ✦ *On the Record*
For the Record ✦ *Struck from the Record*

ALL THAT GLITTERS SERIES
Diamonds ✦ *Gold* ✦ *Emeralds* ✦ *Platinum* ✦ *Silver*

TAKE ME DUET
Take Me for Granted ✦ *Take Me with You*

BLOOD TYPE SERIES
Blood Type ✦ *Blood Match* ✦ *Blood Cure*

ASCENSION SERIES
The Affiliate ✦ *The Bound* ✦ *The Consort* ✦ *The Society*

Following Me

To 'The Dangerous Liaisons,'
May you continue to inspire future
generations with your brilliance.

PART I
IT ALL STARTED ON A BEACH IN THE HAMPTONS

NATALIE

1

Dear Natalie,

Here are the latest rejection letters from publishers regarding TOLD YOU SO. I will follow up with a list from Caroline of the remaining publishers who have the manuscript out on submission.

Regards,

Meredith Mayberry
Assistant to Caroline Liebermann
Whitten, Jones, & Liebermann Literary

Enclosed:

From Hartfield:

TOLD YOU SO has an interesting take on the value and cost of friendship. I enjoyed the journey the characters take and style of prose. But, unfortunately, that's where my praise ends. The heroine, Karla, was a caricature of bad judgment and a complete Mary Sue in every other regard. She's plain, ordinary, and not at all interesting enough to follow for 100k words. I felt Tina might have been a better lead, but it wasn't clear from the start whether the author was knowledgeable enough to convey the true depth of either of the characters. Perhaps the author should find a muse.

From Warren:

Natalie definitely knows how to tell a story and pull the reader in with a clever introduction. I just didn't find the characters relatable or the story high concept enough for what Warren is looking for right now. For us, we weren't completely sold on the genre, as it straddles the line between women's fiction and literary and thus, sits with neither.

From Strider:

TOLD YOU SO could have been great. Karla and Tina have so much potential, and the concept, while like several things we already have in our catalog, could have been brilliant. However, I never believed in their friendship, and the middle fell flat. The pace was slow, and for once, I was actually wishing there were a romance to break up the monotony. Maybe a more talented writer could have pulled this off.

"Fuck," I groaned. "I get the message."

I threw my phone on the cushion next to me. No need to torture myself by reading any more of *that*. I couldn't even believe my agent would send me those comments. Let alone on a Friday night before she left for the weekend. Even worse that it came through from her assistant with all those horrible notes about my writing.

Was this the writing on the wall? My agent was finally finding out that I was a hack. Two books and two years later with no offers and pile after pile of heartbreaking rejections. Maybe this was the end.

I stared around the beautiful Hamptons beach house I was vacation home–watching this fall. I'd been hired a month ago and shown up only three days prior, determined to finish my next manuscript. It was a dream come true to be here without any distractions—no parents or guys or anything. Just me and my computer screen.

Then, my agent had gone and dropped the biggest distraction imaginable on my plate. I glared at my screen.

Oh, hell no.

Hell. No.

I was not letting these letters set me back. Maybe TOLD YOU SO wasn't *the* book, but the next one might be.

No, I needed to cleanse myself of this bullshit. I didn't normally subscribe to my mother's New Age spiritualism. She spent her spare time reading about auras, staring into crystal balls, and divining from the stars. It was a running joke in my life at this point. But there was a time and place for everything. And, if I was going to get something done during the next couple of months, I needed to leave the past behind me.

I knew what I was going to do.

I was going to burn this motherfucker to the ground.

Okay, maybe a little dramatic. Even for me.

But, hey, this was on the publishers. Was it so hard to craft a kind rejection email?

It's not you; it's me.

Maybe we can just be friends.

Come on. I'd heard it all from guys. Publishers could have the decency to try not to break my heart.

Ugh, fucking rejection.

But a plan had already formed, and I wasn't going to back down now.

I set my laptop up next to the printer in the office library with a bay window overlooking the ocean. I'd planned to write at that window nook. And I still wanted to. I pressed print on the computer and left to raid the stocked Kensington family wet bar. I'd have to replace whatever I scavenged, but it felt worth it tonight.

I was only watching the house through the fall season. I'd gotten the job after watching my best friend's parents' flat in Paris last summer. Word of mouth moved me around the world from there. From Paris to Turks and Caicos to Aspen, and now, I was watching the mayor of New York City's summer home in the Hamptons. And the mayor had a damn good selection of alcohol.

"Jefferson's Ocean: Aged at Sea," I muttered to myself.

Good enough for me. I grabbed the bottle and went in search of everything else I needed.

Fifteen minutes later, I had the stack of papers, a packet of matches, and the bottle of bourbon. I hoisted a shovel onto one shoulder on my way out the back door. When I hit the sand, I kicked off my shoes, grabbed a fistful of my flowy dress, and traipsed across the beach. My eyes were cast forward, and I moved with a sense of determination. The sun had finally left the horizon, throwing me into darkness, which was good, considering I was about to commit arson.

When I reached the soft sand right before the waterline, I dropped my supplies and dug my shovel into the sand. The first shovelful was incredibly satisfying. I took out my frustration and aggravation on that hole. Driving into the sand like I could erase the words from my brain. The tension in my shoulders intensified as I dug until I hit the wet sand beneath, and then I tossed my shovel to the side.

I reached for the supplies, and with my foot on the pages so that they didn't blow away, I unscrewed the top of the bottle of bourbon and took a large mouthful. The liquid burned its way down my throat. I sputtered and then took another.

That made me feel steadier. More alive. I shuddered as the alcohol hit me and then put it aside before retrieving the most important part of all of this.

Pages and pages and pages.

Forty-seven pages to be exact.

Forty-seven perfectly polite, perfectly soul-crushing pages.

Every rejection letter I'd ever gotten in the last two years, including the latest batch my agent had just sent over.

My eyes skimmed over the first page before I balled it up and threw it into the pit. A smile stretched on my face as I tossed page after page after page in the sand. Forty-seven pages of kindling.

I grinned wickedly, ready to put all of this rejection behind me.

I snatched up the bottle of bourbon and liberally poured it on the pages, like adding milk to cereal. Careful to move the bottle far enough away so that it wouldn't blow up in my face, I snatched up the box of matches.

"This is for you," I called up to the moon. "My ritual burning, my offering of this energy. Just take it away and help me start over."

I struck the match against the box and dropped it into the pit. When the first spark touched the fuel, the papers burst into flames, sending a jet of flames up toward the heavens. I laughed and danced in a circle around the flames, already feeling lighter.

So, maybe this book wasn't the one. Maybe this hadn't changed the world. But maybe the next one…or the next one. And, even if it was none of them, I was a writer. I would never stop writing.

A weight dropped off my shoulders, and I tilted my head back toward the moon. I flung my hands out to the sides and did a poorly executed turn, tripped over my own feet, and landed in a heap in the sand. But nothing could stop the euphoria that settled in my chest. Who knew it would be so liberating to burn my rejection letters?

All I'd wanted was to change my luck and let the past go, but damn I felt like a million bucks.

The flames grew and grew, burning through the last two years of my life. And I rode the high as power threaded through me, leaving me drunk and not just from the bourbon.

Jumping back to my feet, I didn't even bother glancing down the beach. No one was in the Hamptons during the off-season. That was why I'd been hired to take care of the place during the interior renovation. Just last weekend, wealthy children of wealthy businessmen and wealthy politicians and wealthy celebrities had flocked to these beaches and overrun them at all hours of the day. But tonight, I was safe.

I wrenched at the bottom of my dress and lifted all the many layers of flowy material over my head. Tossing it into the sand, I unclasped my bra and discarded it as well. Then with a cry of triumph, I walked with my head held high straight into the ocean. The water was a bit frigid, and I shivered against the first wave that broke against my naked body. But I didn't care. I wasn't here for a swim. I was here for primal cleansing. Burn the negative energy and wash away the last remnants.

I dunked my head under the water and laughed when I breached the surface. This was what it was to live. This was what I needed to remember. Life went on.

The Kensington house was just another job. Just another way to make a living while I pursued my passion. One day, I would catch a break, but until then, I would be damned if I let those publishers bring me down. I'd put one foot in front of the other and make it work.

Confident that the ritual burning and impromptu skinny-dipping had done its job, I hurried back out of the water. My steps were light as air, and my smile was magnetic. Whatever spell my mother's crazy life-journey had cast over all of this nonsense, it sure seemed to work. Believe in anything enough, and belief would turn into reality.

But as I was tramping back up to the fire to collect my clothes, I realized with horror that I wasn't alone. And what was worse, I recognized the man standing there.

I never forgot a face. And definitely not *that* face. Or the built body. Or the confident stance.

No, even though six years had passed, I would never forget Penn.

Or what he'd done to me.

NATALIE

2

My dream and nightmare stood before me.

Clothed like a god walking off of a James Bond set with dark hair and midnight-blue eyes that flickered in the dying embers. Six years had only intensified his magnetic allure. The sharp planes of his too-beautiful face. The ever-present smirk, which sat prominent on those perfect lips. The coy glance as he slid his hands into the front pockets of his black suit pants.

I had been a girl then. Young, naive, and incredibly innocent. I'd thought him a man—bold, honest, emotive, and utterly larger than life. Now, as I looked upon him, I had no idea how I'd thought of him as anything but a rogue. The kind of man who could charm you with a glance and entice you out of your pants with a few pointed words. The sort of man I purposely walked away from now.

I'd never imagined I'd see him again. Never considered what would happen if I came face-to-face with him. But, now that I was, the words just tumbled from my mouth.

"What the fuck are you doing here?" I gasped.

He cocked his head to the side in surprise. An emotion I

was sure that he wasn't accustomed to. He was definitely the kind of man who liked his life in a certain order. People didn't surprise him. He didn't let people in his life enough for that.

"What am *I* doing here?"

His voice was just as I remembered it. Smooth as butter and deeply entrancing. I thought I'd made it up. Like no one actually talked like this. In my mind, I'd magnified everything he was and everything he'd done. But standing here, I was wondering if I had remembered him better than I gave myself credit for.

I braced myself for this conversation. I'd built steel walls up around my heart, mind, and body. I didn't let people in as easily. And I needed to prepare myself for his manipulation. Let the anger I'd harbored all of these years tear him down as he had once hurt me.

"That's what I said," I snapped back.

I'd finally reached him, and I scrambled for my dress. It was a floor-length white boho number that had more fabric than sense, which made finding how to get it on *incredibly* difficult under good circumstances.

These were not good circumstances.

I struggled with the dress and the layers of material, desperate to find the opening for me to slip my head through. As if it wasn't bad enough that I was seeing Penn again for the first time in six years, I had to do it completely naked.

Seemed fitting. That was the last way he'd seen me then, too.

"Yes, but you are the one who is out of place, skinny-dipping on this beach. Don't you know these are private residences?"

"I'm well aware."

I finally found the bottom to the dress and yanked it over

my soaking wet head. My long silvery-white hair was such a nuisance sometimes. If only I'd let my best friend, Amy, convince me to chop off my ass-length hair, but no. I had to have another weapon to make getting my dress on more difficult.

"And you're only supposed to have bonfires in preapproved metal containers." He glanced down at my makeshift fire. It had almost completely died out by now. "Not to mention, have at least a two-gallon bucket of water to douse the flames."

I rolled my eyes. Was he actually serious right now?

My euphoria from the ritual began to evaporate. Well, that hadn't lasted long.

With a huff, I ruffled the bottom layers, pulled my sopping wet hair out of the back of the dress, and then grabbed the shovel off of the ground. With a mighty heave, I covered up the dying flames with a heap of sand.

"There!" I spat. "Now, can we get back to what is important? Like what you're doing here after all this time."

He frowned, as if confused by my statement. And that was when it hit me.

He didn't remember me.

Penn had no *clue* who the hell I was.

Oh god.

I hadn't thought that this could get worse or more humiliating. Sure, I looked like a crazy person, burning soul-crushing rejection letters and then stripping nude into the Atlantic. But, now the guy I'd cursed for *years* was standing before me ... and he was staring at me as if I were a stranger.

Six years was a long time.

It was.

Most people might not remember someone that they'd had a one-night stand with from that long ago. I knew it was maybe a little irrational to be upset about it all. But, fuck it, I *was* upset.

You didn't have the most amazing night of your life with a total stranger and then completely forget that person! I didn't care who the hell you were. I didn't care how many times you'd had a one-night stand.

And it had been pretty clear that it wasn't Penn's first time—though it had been mine—but still, how could he have forgotten me?

"After all this time?" he asked.

"Never mind," I grumbled. "The real question is, what are you doing here? Do you live nearby? I thought this was the wrong time of year for the rich and entitled to be in the Hamptons. Memorial Day to Labor Day, right?"

I couldn't keep the snark out of my voice. No point in filling the bastard in on how I knew him. If he lived nearby, this was going to be one hellacious house-watching.

"Most people are gone. But this is my home, which is why I was wondering what you were doing here."

"This is *your* home?" I whispered, pointing at the house off the beach. "No, this belongs to Mayor Kensington. She hired me to watch it this fall. You can't possibly own that house."

He shrugged and then sighed. "I didn't think anyone would be here," he said, clearly frustrated at my appearance.

"But...but...why would you..."

Then, it dawned on me. My heart stopped. My jaw dropped. I released a sharp breath in disbelief.

"You're a Kensington."

He gave me a sheepish grin. "I suppose it's my family home."

"You have *got* to be fucking kidding me." I shook my head in disbelief.

I thought this ritual was supposed to cleanse shit from my life. Not bring in another issue. Fuck.

I could not deal with this right now. Not with my anxiety high from the rejection letters. I'd only been here three days. I'd thought this was a dream come true. Everything was pointing me to get the fuck out of Dodge. Because, man, what *else* was life going to throw at me? Everything always came in threes. That was what my mom had said.

"I can't," I said. I held up my hand to keep him from saying anything. Then, I grabbed the remaining matches and the bourbon, which he eyed curiously, and then stomped off with the shovel over my shoulder.

"Um...where are you going?"

"I don't want to talk to you," I told him.

I didn't care that I was being incredibly unprofessional. Or that I was probably ruining my chance at staying at this house. Not that I wanted to work for the woman who had *birthed* this asshole. But I just needed to get away. I needed to get away and decompress and figure out how to proceed. If I saw his gorgeous face and that come-hither smile anymore, I was likely to stab him with the shovel.

Penn didn't seem to listen though. He barged right up the beach after me. Heedless of the sand in his loafers or messing up his probably bajillion-dollar suit.

"Uh, you left this," he said, holding out my bra.

I squeaked, juggled my full load, and snatched it out of his hand. Just fucking great. It wasn't the first time he'd held my bra or anything, but, god, at some point, I had to catch a break. I had to.

"You're welcome," he muttered under his breath.

I had no intention of thanking him for anything. So, I kept my mouth shut.

"Are you going to tell me why you seem like you're ready to set *me* on fire?" he asked. He was calm—curious but calm.

I was a puzzle he needed to solve. He needed to be able to put me in a box so that he could figure out how to manipulate my emotions to his whim.

"No."

"All right," he said. But it only made him inspect me harder. "I really don't understand why you're mad. This is my house. I thought you were the one trespassing."

"Well, I'm not," I growled. "I got this job a month ago. And I had *no* idea that you were going to be here. In fact, I had no idea you were even a Kensington."

He peered at me inquisitively, as if he were memorizing the span of my face and the curve of my figure. As if he were about to take a test and was having a last-minute cram session to remember all the little things he already knew about me but promptly forgot. "Have we met before?"

I snorted. "Observant."

"And it was a bad meeting?"

I snapped my narrowed eyes to him.

He held his hands up. "Okay. Very bad meeting."

"The fact that you don't even remember is…" I trailed off.

"Bad?"

"Reprehensible."

"You know, you do look familiar. I thought you did this whole time."

I rolled my eyes skyward and then deposited the shovel back where I'd found it. Better to keep it out of arm's reach for the rest of this conversation. "Don't bullshit me."

"I wasn't."

"Sure," I said sarcastically.

I wasn't sure he knew how to do anything else.

"No, really, how do I know you?"

I shook my head. Hurt broke through the anger. Hurt that I hadn't let myself feel in so long. "If you can't remember, then I don't really see any reason to enlighten you."

Then, I reached for the door, but he stopped me in my tracks.

"Paris."

I whipped around in shock. He *did* remember. That bastard did remember something. But hurt was then immediately replaced with that boiling anger. That righteous, vindictive flame that shot through me every time I remembered my first time.

I yanked the door open and glared back at him. "That's right. We had one night in Paris. You wooed me, you fucked me, and then you ghosted!"

Pushing the door the rest of the way open, I stepped into the Kensington summer cottage. And I froze in place as four people turned to face me. Four people who had clearly heard me screaming at Penn and airing our dirty laundry.

Just…wonderful.

NATALIE

3

My face turned the color of a tomato.

"I…um…" I stammered, at a loss for words.

I looked like a hot mess, standing soaking wet in my sand-covered dress with a bottle of bourbon and my *bra*. They probably thought I was a lunatic. A madwoman that Penn had picked up outside when he went to check on the fire.

It was even worse that, whoever these four people were, they looked fabulous. Two men and two women clothed in tailored suits and cocktail dresses. Glamorous, confident, wealthy. It was evident in their dress and mannerisms and the way they let me stand there and gape like a fish out of water.

"I'm so sorry," I finally managed to get out. "I wasn't expecting anyone to be at the house tonight. I was hired by Mayor Kensington, but Penn informed me that he wasn't aware of that fact. Just as I was not aware that he had… friends with him."

Penn stepped over the threshold and inside. He kicked at

the sand on his shoes. Our eyes met, and my breath caught. He was even more stunning in the light. No wonder I'd noticed him in Paris, writing furiously in his notebook in the park by my flat. Or why I'd approached him at that party. Or why...I'd had that one-night stand.

"Why don't you introduce us to your friend, Penn?" the brunette girl asked coyly. She was tan, as if she had spent the summer on the beach, and wore a glittering emerald-green dress.

Strangely, she gave me Anne Boleyn vibes. I wasn't sure yet if that was good or bad.

"He doesn't have to, Katherine. I should be giving the introductions," the other girl spoke up. She was pale with a splattering of freckles and wavy dark red hair to her shoulders. Her black dress fit her like a dream, but she didn't seem as relaxed as the others. She was jittery, as if she'd had too much coffee. "This is Natalie Bishop. She's watching the house for the next two months."

"I...yes, I am," I said in confusion.

"Sorry," the woman said, stepping forward with an extended hand. "I'm Lark. Larkin St. Vincent."

My throat bobbed. And I'd thought the night couldn't get any worse. Here was the woman who had hired me.

I hastily put down the bourbon bottle and hid my bra before taking her hand. "Lark, it's so nice to meet you."

"It completely slipped my mind that you were going to be here this weekend. For some reason, I thought that you started next week. Since I handed this off to my assistant, I never saw you come into the office."

"So, you knew someone would be here and suggested it anyway?" one of the men asked. He was incredibly tall with smooth medium-brown skin and short-cropped hair. One look from his depthless dark brown eyes said he was as much trouble as Penn standing next to me. He knew the effect of his good looks.

I swallowed and glanced away.

Lark just rolled her eyes at him. "I didn't remember, Lewis. You can blame the fact that I haven't had a vacation in three years."

"That's your own fault," Katherine said.

The last guy just bobbed his head and said, "Yep."

"Stay out of this, Rowe," Lark said.

I saw this as my opportunity to get out of there. I looked horrible. This wasn't how I'd thought I'd meet anyone. "I'm just going to..." I pointed past them, down the hallway to the bedroom I'd been staying in the last two nights.

"That's probably for the better," Katherine said. "Did you fall in the ocean?" Her eyes cut to Penn's, and a smile grew on her pretty red-painted lips. "Did you push her in?"

Penn, who hadn't said a word up until that moment, finally spoke up, "I think we should allow Natalie a moment of privacy. On a good day, we're overwhelming. She shouldn't have to meet the crew like this."

My head whipped to the side. I was caught between anger and relief. Anger that he'd spoken for me. And relief that, dear god, I really needed to get the fuck out of there. It was way too much all at once. I didn't people all that well to begin with. I was better one-on-one. But standing where I was and facing down his incredibly attractive and put-together friends when I wanted to yell at him didn't help anything.

"Uh...yes. Privacy." I nodded and then stepped around his friends. "Nice to meet you all."

I raised my hand to awkwardly wave good-bye and realized a minute too late that it was the one that had been hiding my bra. My eyes widened in horror, and then I snapped it down to my side.

I opened my mouth to try to apologize for my behavior, but then I stopped and just fled down the hallway. I didn't owe anyone in there an apology, except Lark. And, really, what good would it do at this point? There was no way that I was keeping this job after she saw me like that. She would most definitely tell the mayor that I wasn't fit for the position. That whatever recommendation I'd gotten from my previous house-sitting job must have been fabricated. Because no one could have this many missteps and not be utterly incompetent.

THE ROOM I'd been assigned was a soft and luxurious guest bedroom with a white four-poster bed draped in a blue-and-pink-flowered duvet. It had an actual canopy on top. Everything was plush and inviting with a million and a half throw pillows of every variety imaginable and a rug so lush that my feet sank right into it. I was going to miss this room the most.

Only two nights in the down-feather bed, and it had already been the best nights of sleep of my life. I'd really been looking forward to another night in that bed. But, alas, it would not be.

I tossed my bra onto the bed with a huff, threw on a pair of shorts and an oversized T-shirt, and tied my hair in a messy bun on the top of my head. I kicked the sandy dress into a corner and then dragged the two suitcases out of the closet. I was a fast packer. Product of growing up as a military brat and traveling year after year after year to various locales the Air Force had sent us. As a vacation home watcher, I carried the entirety of my life in these two suitcases so that it was easy to move in. And, now, more importantly, out.

All signs had pointed that this was the perfect opportunity for me. Now, all signs pointed to run and run fast. I couldn't have been more awkward if I'd tried. I wasn't even that awkward *when* I tried. But something had just come over me. A cataclysmic reaction to being in Penn's presence again. My brain had shut off, and my mouth had opened. Ready to unleash on a relative stranger.

A stranger who was the son of my boss.

Who apparently was friends with the woman who had hired me.

I shook my head in exasperation as I unzipped the suitcase and pulled out the packing cubes. What had I even been thinking?

Of course, I hadn't been thinking. I'd just acted on impulse. Six years of pent-up anger had just unleashed.

I yanked open the first drawer and removed my clothes. This was such a fucking disaster.

Now, I had no idea what I was going to do for the rest of the year. This was a cushy job. Sit around and watch someone's house? Get *paid* to do that? Um…yeah, a no-brainer. But, without that, I'd probably have to go home. Back to Charleston. A month at home had been plenty to begin with. Between my parents constant arguing about my job and nagging about the lack of boyfriend situation and my perfect little sister, Melanie, starting her senior year of high school with the same guy that she'd dated since we moved to the town. I couldn't handle it.

I'd have to find another way. Maybe have Amy get me a job at the gallery even though she really didn't need the help. And maybe I could move in temporarily. Current boyfriend—Steve or Chuck or Tom or whatever his name was—probably wouldn't like that. They always thought they were the one until a few months later when Amy would kick them out because a new artist had come into town for her gallery. It was a recurring cycle. She loved artists. She somehow continued to settle for losers back home in the interim.

I needed to call her.

She'd freak out about Penn.

She was the one who had warned me about him to begin with.

Of course, I hadn't listened.

But I realized I didn't even know where my phone was. Where had I left it after getting that awful email from my agent? Probably the living room.

I grumbled under my breath as I stuffed a bunch of underwear into a small cube. I was fucked because no way in hell was I going back out there to make a fool of myself.

It was bad enough that Penn was *here*. Let alone that he had seen me naked and watched me humiliate myself. I didn't have to make it worse.

Plus, what the hell did I have in common with those people? I threw the cube into the suitcase. They all looked famous with their fabulous clothes and perfect hair and manicures and stylish makeup and easy confidence. They'd had their life given to them on a silver spoon. And I had grown up with nothing. Amy had money, but even she wasn't rich like this.

There was rich, and then there was wealthy.

And I didn't even follow the lives of the rich and famous, but I knew the name Kensington carried its weight in gold.

I was an idiot. I'd known in Paris that he had money. He'd opened doors that I couldn't fathom even now. But it had never occurred to me that he was the heir to the Kensington fortune. That he was *that* wealthy.

A knock on the bedroom door broke me from my silent rant.

"Natalie?" Penn called from the other side.

What the hell? What was he doing, trying to talk to me?

I'd basically run away from him and his friends on his

suggestion. It hadn't been long enough for him to consider his offer of privacy expired.

"Yes?" I took a half-step toward the door and then stopped.

"May I come in?"

Come in? What the fuck? No!

I checked my clothes. Still in shorts and an oversized Grimke University T-shirt. It was one of the best damn private schools in the South and had the added benefit of being in Charleston. But still...it wasn't much better than my dress.

Shit, why did I even care?

Oh, of course I cared. He was hot as fucking sin. The man made *delectable* a proper noun. It was ridiculous.

I finally settled on. "Uh...why?"

"I wanted to speak with you."

Very specific.

I rolled my eyes.

"I guess so."

The door handle turned, and I tried to look natural. As natural as a deer caught in headlights. A gazelle staring down a lion.

Sometimes, I really wished my writer brain would turn off.

Like right now.

Penn stepped through the open door, and my breath caught. He'd removed his suit coat and his black tie. The white button-up underneath was undone on the first two buttons, and it fit him as if it had been made for him. Broad shoulders that narrowed down to his trim waist and those incredible legs.

I admonished myself with an imaginary smack in the face and met his cool blue gaze. "Can I help you?"

He leaned against the open doorframe and slid a hand into his pocket. Habit maybe. "I came to check on you."

"Why?"

"I wanted to make sure that you were all right." His eyes moved to the open suitcase on the bed and the mess of clothes between it and the drawer. He straightened. The only sign that my packing had taken him by surprise. "Are you leaving?"

"Yeah. I'm just packing now, and I'll be out of your hair by the morning."

"That was not what I meant."

"Well, why don't you say what you mean?" *For once*, was the implied addition. "I'm kind of busy."

"You don't have to leave."

"Of course I do. This is your house. I was hired to watch and maintain an empty house for the season before some big party in November. Not only is the house not empty, but I also assume I'll be fired by Monday. So, I might as well get started." I stuffed another shirt into the suitcase to make a point.

"Why on earth would you get fired?"

I released an exasperated breath. "Lark hired me. After that performance, I can't imagine her reporting back kindly."

"Lark…isn't going to report back to my mother."

Now, I turned to him fully. My own surprise clear. "Why ever not?"

"This is actually her first real vacation in three years. She got the weekend off from the office, and I dragged her here with the others after her last event." He gestured to his suit as if to say, *Hence the outfit*. "The fact that it slipped her mind that you were here is a testament to how much she needs it. So, you can imagine work is the last thing on her mind."

I couldn't imagine. Her life sounded horrible. Who didn't

take any time off for three years? What kind of slave driver *was* Mayor Kensington?

"But," he continued when I didn't respond immediately, "we can get out of your hair. Head back to the city or something. So see, you should stay. And we'll go."

"No, that's absurd. This is *your* house. I'm the interloper here. Even if Lark doesn't report me, which I'm still doubting, I would get in the way. There's no reason for me to be here if you're here."

"But it's your job. None of us"—he paused on the word us, as if contemplating whether what he was about to say was true—"wants to take that from you. So, you should stay."

"I'm already halfway packed."

"Natalie," he said softly.

He stepped forward into the room and placed his hand on one of the posters of the bed. His gaze softened and bore into mine. I was transfixed once more. The way he said my name. The way he stared at me. Oh god, he was such a menace.

"Don't," I snapped.

His eyebrows rose in response.

"Don't say my name like you know me or even care whether I stay or go. We don't know each other. And I'm certain I don't want to know you."

It was harsh but honest. And I didn't feel bad, saying it.

"Fine," he finally muttered on a sigh. "We'll figure it out in the morning once you've cooled off."

"I don't need to cool off," I bit out. "I'm perfectly levelheaded."

"Just stay," he barked.

"No, I think I should go."

He walked back to the door. "Do whatever you want, I guess. I came to check to make sure that you weren't humiliated after what happened. But it seems that your pride is too great to even continue staying under the same roof as us. You don't have to stay," he said, glancing back at me. "But, if you do, try to stay out of the way."

He snapped the door closed behind him, and I threw the closest thing I had at the door. The pair of socks thudded uselessly against the door.

Here was the real Penn Kensington.

He wasn't trying to make everything better. He was trying to keep from having to leave tonight while I was around. I was a nuisance and needed to stay out of his way. He made me want to scream. And not even in the fun way!

I didn't even know how to respond to him. Pack or stay, it seemed I was playing into his hands. I flopped back onto the bed, sinking deep into the down comforter. When would I catch a break?

No. I wouldn't succumb to this shit.

That was the old Natalie. The idealist who had let herself get taken advantage of. The new Natalie wasn't going to play that game anymore.

I was the one who was supposed to be here. I was the one getting paid to watch the house. I wouldn't stay in my room and cower. Not from Penn Kensington or his beautiful friends.

NATALIE

4

I needed to get my phone.

Or at least that was my excuse.

I had my notebook and computer, but after those rejection letters, I didn't feel like writing. My scant few paperbacks held no sway tonight. I just wanted my phone, so I could kill a few hours scrolling through Crew, the latest social media app the entire world was raving over. Maybe, if I had the nerve, I'd call Amy and tell her how much of a disaster this new job already was.

But I wouldn't let that disaster hold me back from going out there to retrieve my phone. I needed to persevere and manage to escape this encounter unscathed.

Bolstered by the lingering side effects of all the bourbon I'd imbibed, I left my bedroom. The confidence I'd had while blow-drying my hair the last twenty minutes—thank god Amy had gotten me a Dyson for my birthday—was quickly evaporating like water on blacktop during a hot Texas summer. Trust me; I'd know. We'd spent two years in San Antonio when I was in elementary school.

I creeped down the hallway and stopped when I heard voices coming from the living room.

"We're actually going to leave because of this girl?" I heard a female voice ask with annoyance in her voice.

Probably Katherine. Lark had seemed kind of cool at least. Understanding for sure.

"It's my fault," the other female voice said. Definitely Lark. "I should have known."

"Stop saying that," Katherine said. "We don't have to apologize to anyone for showing up to a house one of us owns."

"We could just go to your place," a voice said. Sickeningly sweet. A taunt.

I peered into the living room and saw that it was Lewis who was grinning like a fool at Katherine.

"You *know* why we can't go to *my* place," she ground out.

"Yeah, stop goading her," Lark said.

"Have you met me?" Lewis asked.

Rowe gruffly laughed once. He was staring down at the tablet in his lap. His laugh was the only indication that he was paying attention to the conversation.

"That's enough from you," Katherine said, gently smacking him on the arm.

He looked up once, quirked an eyebrow, and then looked back down.

"Well, we're here tonight. It's too late, and I'm not leaving," Penn said, his voice the commanding presence of his friend circle. They all looked up at him standing with his hands in his pockets. "Not after that party."

From a bird's-eye view, I felt like I could watch them interact all day. The writer in me—my writer's curse, as my father had always called it—made me pick out all the various details about them. The feel of their connection. The depth of their affection for each other. The little smiles and quirks and tics that made them function as a unit...practically a family. Not *my* family, of course. One even stronger than our dysfunction. Family where you found it. It was magic in its own way.

I'd hardly even observed them, and I could tell that something had drawn them together. Something strong, deep, and unyielding. Tying string around each of them and knotting it into place. Speaking words of a spell around the string to let the magic bind them.

Something about it was mesmerizing. Knowing that life had chosen these five people and cast them together. Not nature, not because they had been forced into a unit. But because they had *chosen* this familial bond.

A brief memory fluttered back to me of Penn saying that he'd taken his best friend to her debutant ball. That his friends had all gone together and had such a good time. If I closed my eyes, I could almost see them all there in ball gowns and tuxedos. Paired off but together. Apart but one.

Then Katherine's eyes shifted to my hiding place, still standing in the hallway, peeking out. And her eyes lit up with something like excitement.

Shit. I'd been caught.

"Natalie, come on out," Katherine said.

I straightened even further and stepped from my hidey-hole. "Sorry to disturb you. I realized I'd left my phone out here."

"By all means." Katherine gestured with her hand to come in.

I didn't glance at Penn, but I could feel his cold eyes track me through the enormous space. I tiptoed through the Kensington cottage, trying to keep my feet from squeaking on the hardwood floor. I'd failed miserably at ballet when I was younger and had the grace of an elephant unless you threw me in the water. Years of competitive swimming in high school and later at Grimke had made me a Little Mermaid in reverse; I'd practically grown a fin.

I'd thought that would be another perk of staying at this incredible home. Besides the fact that it was a square two-story home with bay windows, the most comfortable bed in existence, and a freaking library, it had a massive refitted Olympic-sized pool. The place had been on the island since the 1800s and continually brought up to modern standards while keeping its old-timey charm. And the pool was one of the best parts.

Too bad I'd never get a chance to step foot in it.

And there was my phone. Lying on the side table where I'd left it. I picked it up and held it aloft for them to see. "Got it. Thanks."

"Why don't you stay and have a drink with us?" Katherine suggested.

"I..." I had no words for that.

I hadn't expected them to want to include me. As much as a unit they looked from the outside, it had never occurred to me that they would allow outsiders into that dynamic.

"Come on. It's one drink. Anyone who can annoy Penn as much as you have in the short time since you've been here is someone we want to toast to," she said with a tinkling giggle.

Penn grumbled something under his breath that I didn't catch, but Katherine just grinned like a Cheshire cat at him.

"Really. Come sit." She patted the seat next to her on the couch. "I insist."

"Yeah," Lark said, joining in. "It'd be nice to get to know you since I wasn't able to meet you when you came into the city."

My eyes flitted to Penn's and back reflexively. Should I do this? He clearly did *not* want me to be around his friends. I could tell in the change of his stance. The way he crossed his arms and looked away in frustration. Was it *me* he was embarrassed by, or was I just intruding on his perfect little life?

He'd told me to stay out of the way. But no, I didn't have to listen to that. And I didn't have to care whether or not he wanted me to hang out with his friends.

"Sure," I said. "Maybe we should polish off the rest of my bourbon."

Lewis laughed from his corner chair. "I like her already."

I wandered back into the dining room where I'd left the bourbon and lifted it into my hand. I'd had more than I thought, even counting the amount I'd poured on the letters. No wonder I'd yelled at Penn. I probably would have done it anyway, but the alcohol had sure helped.

My eyes wandered to my phone. No new text messages or emails. My agent and her assistant must have gone home after sending me the bad news. I huffed and switched to Crew to see if I had any notifications. Mostly nothing, except for a guy from Grimke who I'd swam with. I closed it out and hefted the bottle up as I walked back in. I took the seat Katherine had offered and I set the bottle down on the coffee table.

Lark bit her lip. "Glasses?"

Rowe snorted. Katherine smacked him.

Lewis stepped up and reached for the bottle. "Like the good ole days." He opened the bourbon and took a long swig. "Phew! That's the good stuff." He admired the bottle with a nod. "Jefferson's Ocean. Girl has taste."

I wasn't about to admit that I'd had no clue. I'd just liked the name of it. Not that I'd thought there would be a bottle in their wet bar that wasn't high quality.

Rowe held his hand out and nodded his head at Lewis. Lewis seemed to understand Rowe's silent request because he handed him the bourbon.

Katherine reached out and twirled a strand of my silvery-white hair between her fingers. "I love this. So original. You don't see this...sort of thing where we're from."

I shrugged. "Thanks. I started doing it in college, and it's kind of my signature now."

"It suits you," Katherine said, releasing my hair. "How exactly did you meet our Penn?"

I pursed my lips, and my eyes met his in the distance. He arched an eyebrow. A question or a command?

"We met in Paris. We were at the same party."

"Anyone I know?" she asked Penn.

He sighed as if this was a great hardship. "Harmony Cunningham."

Lark chuckled. "Oh, that's too good."

"Was her mother there?" Katherine asked with a sigh of almost lust.

"Who...is Harmony Cunningham?" I asked softly.

Katherine's eyebrows rose. "Only the heir apparent to Cunningham Couture."

"Oh," I said softly. "That Cunningham."

I didn't follow fashion, especially expensive designers. I had no need for their clothes, and I couldn't afford them even if I wanted to. The most I knew were the fancy shoe designers that Amy was obsessed with. She called them the trifecta—Manolo Blahnik, Jimmy Choo, and Christian Louboutin.

"She's almost as famous as Lark's mother," Katherine said with a wink.

My head snapped to Lark. Who was her mother?

Lark sighed through her nose and looked like she wanted to throw her shoe at Katherine. "My mother is Hope St. Vincent, and she runs St. Vincent handbags and cosmetics."

Now, that one I did know.

"My best friend carries St. Vincent bags."

Lark smiled shyly. "I love what my parents do, but that's

not me. So, ignore Katherine. I have no interest in working with my mother. You all *know* that I prefer campaigns."

"Yes, yes," Katherine said. "We tolerate you doing your charity work."

Lark rolled her eyes.

"It's like Penn working as a philosophy professor," Lewis said with a smirk of his own. "Totally impractical, but we think he'll come around one day."

I tried not to look too interested at that tidbit.

When I'd met Penn, he'd been a budding philosopher. Always writing down his own philosophical musings in his leather-bound journal. He'd wanted to be a professor despite his family.

Hmm…maybe it hadn't *all* been a lie. Just…most of it.

"And what do you do?" I asked Lewis.

"I work with money."

"Like…a financial planner?"

A burst of laughter erupted out of Rowe. "Lewis. A financial planner. What a riot."

"No, I manage hedge funds and try to get hotels on Boardwalk," he said casually.

"As you do," I muttered.

"It's for the best. We keep things going, like Broadway and museums and publishing."

My ears perked up at that. But it was Penn who beat me to it.

"Natalie is an aspiring author."

I wanted to hit him even though it was true. Every time he pulled a fact about me out of thin air, it felt false. Like a joke to him. That he could remember anything from that night and not immediately want to apologize to me for being an asshole made me viscerally angry.

"Stop acting like you know me," I snapped at him. "You don't know me. That was six years ago."

"You no longer wish to pursue your passion?"

"I do, but..."

Penn's lips just quirked up in a smile that said he'd won that round.

"Lewis is a Warren," Lark safely interjected.

My brain caught up with the rest of me, and I turned to Lewis, gaping slightly. *"That* Warren?" I asked. Like the Warren who had *just* sent me a nasty rejection letter today. Though I didn't say it. The words were on the tip of my tongue.

"Indeed," Lewis said.

"Jesus," I whispered. I turned to Katherine and Rowe. "And what do you two do?"

"Katherine here is a socialite," Penn said. "She looks pretty, so she doesn't have to work."

Katherine shrugged. "Whatever. I'm good at it. And who wants to work if they don't have to? Being pretty is way underrated." She nudged me with her shoulder, as if we were old girlfriends.

What the hell was this life?

"And Rowe?" I asked, uncertain if I even wanted to know.

"Tech," he said.

It was his friends' turn to laugh at him in that short, abrupt way of his.

"You working in tech is like saying that Lewis is a financial planner," Lark said with an eye roll.

I looked between them all as if I was missing something. Who did I know by the name of Rowe in tech? I was sure that I'd heard it before. It was on the tip of my tongue. Shit.

"Rowe designed Crew," Penn said.

My jaw dropped. "Like...the social media platform?"

"Yep," he said with a shrug.

"Wait, wait, wait, you're *Archibald* Rowe?"

Rowe groaned. "Please. Don't ever use that name."

The rest of the room tittered at the name that apparently was never used, except in press briefings and public appearances.

"So, like, Facebook tried to buy you out, and you wouldn't sell?"

He nodded. "Didn't need the money."

"And Crew…" I looked between Penn and all of his friends. Wasn't that what Penn had said earlier. That I shouldn't have to meet the crew like this. "That's…you guys."

Penn nodded. "Welcome to the crew, Natalie."

NATALIE

5

Oh god.

I couldn't believe this. I needed a minute to process.

I was so overwhelmed with the money and influence in the room. A billionaire professor, a publisher, a socialite, an heiress, and the most influential tech designer since Mark Zuckerberg.

These were Penn's friends? His crew? How had he found me interesting at all? Had I been a total joke to him that day?

He had to have known that I didn't have connections or wealth like him. Yes, I'd been at the right party that day when we met, but he wasn't stupid. Surely, he'd thought it would just be funny. I couldn't fathom another reason.

"How…how did you all meet?" I stammered out.

"We grew up together," Lewis said. "Prep school, all the way up."

"Crew is what they called us in high school," Katherine filled me in.

Rowe laughed. "Sure they did."

"Fine. They called us the Cruel Crew," Katherine said

with an eye roll. "We stole the name and made it ours. It's what prompted Rowe to design Crew for us, so we had a place for us to meet online. It branched out to our all-girl and all-boy private schools and then, as you know…worldwide."

I was too stunned to respond. I had only one thing to say to that. "Pass the bourbon."

Lewis grabbed it and walked it over to me. His eyes glittered with interest and humor. "That's a good answer."

"So, what about you, Natalie?" Katherine asked.

"Me?" I asked, trying not to squirm.

"Yeah. Where are you from?"

I laughed. "Nowhere. Everywhere. Depends on the day." When everyone stared back at me in confusion, I confessed, "My father was in the Air Force. He retired in Charleston. But I was born in California. My sister, Melanie, was born in Texas. And my parents are from Iowa. So…nowhere."

"Military," Lark said with a smile of understanding. "That must be why you like this vacation-home-watching thing. I couldn't figure out who would want to travel that much."

"I can't figure out why anyone *wouldn't* want to travel this much," I told them honestly. "Nowhere has ever really felt like home to me. Now, I get to see all these amazing locales and live there for a time while I write."

"Except Paris," Penn mumbled under his breath.

"Have something to share with the class?" I drawled, holding out the bourbon bottle and waving it around.

Penn's eyes darted to mine, and I narrowed my eyes. He removed his hands from his pockets and stepped carefully across the living room. All eyes were on him as he reached forward and plucked the bottle from my hand.

"You felt like Paris was home," he said casually before tilting the bottle to his perfect lips and drinking.

I watched the way his lips wrapped seductively around

the bottle. The amber liquid disappearing down his throat. His Adam's apple bobbing as he savored the liquor.

I swallowed. Why did he have to be so damn sexy, even when he was so fucking irritating?

"Right?"

"Someone ruined Paris for me."

I reached to take the bottle back, but he walked it back across the room with him.

"You're still a lightweight."

Cleansing breaths. Deep, cleansing breaths. Because whatever was about to come out of my mouth was going to unleash on him.

But it was Katherine who laughed and defused the tension. "Don't make her snap your head off, Penn. We're in a safe place. She can drink as much as she wants."

"That's right. I can," I told him.

"It's not like you've always been virtuous," Lewis said with a smirk.

"You all are enjoying this, aren't you?" Penn asked.

"Immensely," Katherine said at the same that Lewis said, "Oh god, yes."

Lark laughed, and Rowe just shrugged, as if to say, *Obviously*.

"My own crew. Traitors, one and all."

But a smile had returned to his face. One that seemed to be reserved for the people in this circle. And, for a second, that smile moved to me. And I felt like I was part of that secret place in his life.

It was absurd, of course. I had just shown up. If anything, I was an irritating nuisance rather than part of his crew that he'd known practically his whole life. They had something truly unique here. Something that I'd always craved and never found, except with Amy.

"You're lucky to have them," I told him.

He startled, as if surprised to hear me speak in his favor or to address him without mirth.

"I mean, I can tell that you're close."

"We are lucky, aren't we?" Katherine said. She threw her arm around Rowe and laughed as if having these close-knit friendships were as natural as breathing.

Rowe took one look at her and said, "Don't hug me."

That just made her laugh harder. She kissed his forehead and then stood. "I haven't been this giddy since…" She trailed off.

"The engagement?" Lewis asked with a devious smirk.

"You're engaged? Congratulations!" I said.

Katherine lost her pep and then glared at Lewis. "Look, you ruined it." She turned back to me and held out her hand to reveal the most massive diamond ring I had ever seen in my entire life. "Yes, I'm engaged. Camden Percy."

I took her hand in mine and admired the stone. "It's stunning. I'm sure you're going to tell me that he's the same Percy as the hotel chain or something equally ridiculous."

Katherine didn't blink. "He is."

"Oh!" I gasped. "Well, wow."

"I can't believe you brought it up, Lewis," Lark said. "None of us like to hear about that asshat."

I glanced between the crew and realized that my excitement might not have been warranted. Perhaps Katherine's engagement wasn't a good thing. I couldn't see why a woman like Katherine, who had the beauty of Audrey Hepburn and an exorbitant amount of wealth, would ever marry someone she wasn't in love with.

"Always here to bring the group back to reality."

I felt like there was something I was missing in this. But I didn't know what it was. And, quite honestly, I was too drunk to try to figure it out.

My eyes involuntarily skittered to Penn's, as if to find my

footing in this misstep. His eyes were focused on Katherine with a flash of concern. Then, it was quickly replaced with something neutral before finding me. Whatever that neutral was…it was intense. It was smoldering.

"Nothing like an arranged marriage to ruin the party," Rowe muttered under his breath. Then, he held his phone up victoriously. "Update complete." He tossed it to Lark. "Should have all the new settings now. Crew 3.0 activated."

"Thanks!" Lark beamed. "I promise not to go so long between seeing you next time."

"I thought Crew was only 2.0," I muttered.

"It is." Rowe smiled, and it was the first real one I'd seen from him.

It was that moment I realized he was nearly as handsome as Penn and Lewis. Dark blond hair with hazel eyes and a square jawline that gave him old-school Hollywood vibes. But then he quickly averted his eyes and reached for his tablet once more.

"Ugh!" Katherine groaned. She stood and stretched her long, lean limbs. "You've all ruined my fun. So, I think the get-to-know-you sesh is over. Let's go for a swim." She held her hand out to me. "Come with?"

"Sure," I said, standing unsteadily on my feet. Oh shit, how much had I had to drink? I really didn't have an answer to that question. I teetered. "Whoa!"

"I think we need to switch you from the hard stuff," Katherine said. "I happen to know where a bottle of bubbly is. Lark is an expert at opening them." She tilted her head to the side, and Lark laughed before following her out of the room.

Lewis looked at Rowe and coughed. "So, man…pool?"

"Huh?" Rowe asked.

"Now, dude."

Rowe looked up from his tablet and seemed to realize

that it was just the four of us. He glanced between me and Penn and then said, "Oh! Right. Social cues. By all means, we'll leave them alone."

Lewis tilted his head to the ceiling and sighed. "Tact, dude."

"What's that?" Rowe asked as Lewis shuffled him out of the room.

Penn shifted from one foot to the other and then stilled. His eyes were on me, and I knew that I should look up and meet them. Also that I should probably let this anger cool. He'd been kind tonight. He'd let me hang out with his friends even if unwillingly. He'd even remembered some of our night so long ago. I shouldn't blame him.

But I did.

And I couldn't push that away. Definitely not while I'd had this much to drink.

While I loved his friends and how good it felt to be included in their antics, I knew it was temporary. They'd had Penn for a long time. They liked annoying him, but if I had to guess, my first instinct was right. They didn't let strangers in their circle. The Crew was a solid group of five, and my presence was a fun one-time thing. Just like my presence had been with Penn in Paris.

A one-time thing.

That was it.

I realized then that I didn't have anything to say to him. He'd used and manipulated me into sleeping with him. Then, he'd disappeared without a thought for me. He'd shown me what men were really like. That those fantasies I'd had about romance were fiction. And men who agreed and dreamed about the same passions and who spoke of them so sincerely were probably just using it as an opportunity to get in my pants.

Par for the course.

I heard a cork pop in the other room and moved in that direction. Katherine must have found the champagne.

They giggled and then dashed through the back door, calling out to us as they slipped through, "Hurry up, you two!"

Penn stopped me with a hand on my elbow. "I don't think this is a good idea."

I finally looked up into those too-blue eyes. "And I don't think you get to make that decision for me."

"You should just go to bed."

"Why?" I sputtered.

"Natalie, please, you don't belong here."

I wrenched back out of his grasp. "Excuse me? I don't *belong* here? Because I'm not a socialite or a tech genius? Your friends don't seem to care."

"That's not what I meant."

"And we all know that you have trouble saying what you mean," I spat back.

He breathed out in frustration. "Stop twisting my words."

I arched an eyebrow. "You do that all on your own."

"Look, I remember that night. I remember us in Paris. Taking you around the city and showing you the real Paris and being so present with you. But this wasn't you."

I narrowed my eyes. "You're right. It wasn't."

I didn't say anything else. I didn't tell him about the end of my innocence. The realization that my dream of love had been just that—a dream. Reality was so much more of a slap in the face.

No matter that I'd felt that love-at-first-sight feeling with Penn, it had all been a lie. And it was still a lie. He was a lie wrapped in a pretty package. Like tearing into gorgeous Christmas wrapping paper on the morning of the twenty-fifth, only to find coal on the inside.

I pushed past him, and he turned to watch me go.

I heard him call out, "I'm warning you. This is a bad idea."

"What's a bad idea?" I asked, whipping around. "You? Trust me; I already know."

"Natalie…"

"What upsets you more, Penn? That your friends like me or that I'm not falling all over myself for you?" I gave him my best look of faux sympathy. "Doesn't seem like you handle either very well."

His jaw unhinged at my comment. As if he couldn't believe I'd just said that. To him. He'd probably never been spoken to like that.

And it was a glorious victory.

The most glorious victory that made me feel utterly hollow.

But I still forced myself to savor the last word.

PENN

6

With great effort, I remained where I stood, watching Natalie's ass disappear through the door. I had no idea how all of that had gone so terribly wrong.

The last time I'd seen her was six years ago. It had all been so easy. Like breathing. Honestly, I'd never thought that I'd see her again. And, now that she was here, in my summer home, it was hard not to remember why I'd wanted her in the first place.

And I hadn't been bullshitting her when I told her that I remembered our time together. I remembered it vividly. That whole weekend. She was the only highlight of the whole godforsaken thing.

She'd been this bright light. Unobscured by the drama of my world. Completely innocent to the glamour I had thrown over our interactions. The gentle exaggerations I'd fabricated into our encounter. But it hadn't been a lie. If anything, fuck, I'd been too honest with her.

She'd made it easy to be honest.

And, now…

Now, I had no fucking clue who this girl was.

Woman. Fuck, was she a woman now.

When she'd walked out of that water to me like the water goddess Melusina—a spirit in form, having just lost her tail for the night to find a husband—water had dripped down her form. Her silvery-white hair soaked and glowing in the moonlight. She'd looked…buoyant. Unguarded and radiant, even in the faint light from the embers and moon. Transcendent. It had felt like a dream.

A dream that had quickly run off the tracks.

A lot could happen in six years. That much was obvious. I'd obviously changed since then, not that she wanted to give me the benefit of the doubt. But she'd been so young and vibrant, and now, she was jaded and cynical. Somehow, both suited her.

Fuck! I was so fucked.

The smart thing would be to walk away from this. To let her be pissed at me for leaving that day. To let her have the one night of fun with my friends, the assholes they were, and then disappear again. Her life had moved on. It would do it again.

But, somehow, my feet didn't listen. I was intrigued. And I wasn't easily intrigued.

I found the outdoor stereo and flipped it on, connecting it to my phone before turning on Matt Maeson's "Cringe." Then, I walked out onto the back deck. The rest of my crew and Natalie were down to their underwear and enjoying the heated pool. Even though I'd just seen her completely naked, my eyes were still drawn to her figure only dimly hidden by the water.

"Come on, Penn," Lark called. "Don't make me splash you."

"Wait!" Katherine said. "I know you love your obscure

music, but can't you put on something a *little* more mainstream?"

"Some TSwift for Katherine," Lewis said with a laugh.

"Hey, she's nice!"

"Can we just agree you all have the worst taste in music?" I asked on a sigh.

"No," Katherine and Lewis said together.

"I do!" Lark said with a laugh. "I admit it."

I should have known they'd make me change the song. If it wasn't from an artist they recognized they always complained. "Here."

I switched it to Panic! at the Disco's song "Don't Threaten Me With A Good Time" and waited for them to roll their eyes at me, which they did, as if on cue.

A laugh escaped me. Typical. I kicked my shoes off and then slowly stripped off my button-up. I couldn't help but look up at Natalie as I removed my pants and tossed them to the side.

Normally, I read women so easily. The hunger in their eyes. The desire painted on their faces like makeup. But Natalie wasn't wearing makeup, and from the distance, she didn't even seem to be paying attention to me unclothing. Suffice it to say, that wasn't a normal occurrence. I was gifted with some pretty lucky genes, and the hours at the gym before I went in to lecture sure didn't hurt. It was one of the few times I could get my brain to shut off, so I went religiously.

I slipped into the pool as Katherine dived into a story about the upcoming gala event she would be attending. I was only half-listening. I hated gala events. If I never had to go to one again in my life, I'd be happy.

But I wasn't that lucky.

Not with a mother in politics and the last name Kensington.

I'd become a professor to escape it all, and it had only half-worked. At least I had an excuse now when I wanted to leave. Most people tended to zone out when I started discussing my research in ethical theory. Almost a guaranteed end to a conversation, which worked in my favor.

"Oh my god, Natalie, why didn't I think about this before?" Katherine asked, downing the rest of her flute of champagne and refilling it.

She offered some to Natalie, but it looked like the alcohol was finally catching up with her. She declined.

"Think about…what?" Natalie asked, her words slurring together.

"You should come to the event. Come see me in the city."

Lark and I shared a look. We both knew what that meant. Katherine had found her new project. She'd had a few since I'd known her. None had ended well.

"But Natalie is working here all fall," I reminded Katherine.

"She could still come into the city. It doesn't take that long, especially this time of the year."

"Yeah. That's a great idea," Lewis said.

He moved over to Natalie's side and slung an arm around her shoulders. I clenched the edge of the pool. My knuckles turned white.

"Is it?" Lark asked quietly.

Thank god someone was on my side. Lark, always the sensible one. We were the only two who had real jobs that weren't because of our parents. But I also saw her the least. Her real job, like mine, kept her away from us far too often. If I wanted to see her, I had to fit into her insane work schedule. Between the two of us workaholics, it didn't happen often.

"Of course it is," Katherine said.

"Sure, sounds fun," Natalie said.

She swayed on her feet, leaning into Lewis for support. He looked perfectly chummy about it.

"Great! It's a date."

Natalie nodded and then blinked. "That champagne kicked my ass. I think I need to..." She pointed at the door. "Before I black out."

"Oh dear, okay," Katherine said as if she hadn't been pumping her full of alcohol all night. "Get some sleep. We'll follow up tomorrow."

Natalie nodded and then waded to the stairs. She stumbled on one step and reached for the railing before righting herself. She laughed softly. "Where did that step come from?"

"Always been there," Rowe said seriously.

I couldn't help the laugh that escaped me. Classic Rowe.

But Natalie's eyes narrowed at me. As if I'd been laughing at her near fall. I arched an eyebrow in her direction and admired her body before she reached for a towel. She slipped it around her figure as if she were suddenly shy about it. Even though she'd been skinny-dipping and now nearly naked in front of the rest of my crew. It was cute. Like a glimpse into the Natalie I'd known for that brief time before.

Then, she was through the door. She didn't turn around even though my eyes tracked her the whole way.

"Oh, I like her," Katherine mused. She finished another glass of champagne and then swam to my side. "She has teeth."

"I'm not dense, Ren. I know that you were just being nice to her for my benefit."

"Me?" Katherine gasped. "I'm always nice."

The rest of the crew laughed.

"Are you though?" Lewis asked. "Don't get me wrong. We love you. But...you are Katherine Van Pelt."

"I'll remember this," she said, pointing at them. "I'm nice to people who deserve it."

"Who deserves it in your estimation?" Lark asked, fighting back a laugh.

"Fine," Katherine muttered. "But Natalie makes it easy to like her. Especially with the way she insults our Penn here."

She slid her arm around my waist, leaned into my side, and fluttered her eyelashes at me. The thing with Katherine was complicated. Always had been. And when she did things like this, all she did was blur the line.

I moved out of her embrace. "She's just hurt. Not the first girl I've hurt."

Rowe snorted. "Or the last."

"I think you have your work cut out for you," Katherine said smugly.

"It's not like that," I said automatically.

Even as I said it, I knew it was a lie.

I wanted Natalie. She confused me. She intrigued me. And despite all my training in ethics, I wanted to throw my morals out the window and go after her. Fuck that smart mouth. And have her crying my name out.

And if I didn't stop that train of thought…it would become pretty evident what I was thinking about.

"We all know that look, man," Lewis said. "She gets under your skin."

"You love girls who get under your skin," Lark said.

"She doesn't get under my skin."

"Yeah, okay," Rowe said.

"So, fine. Whatever. It's hardly a challenge if I've already slept with her."

"I really don't think so," Lark said.

"Nope. No way," Lewis said. "She seems to hate you."

"I'm sure, if I tried at all, she'd be eating out of the palm of my hand," I muttered like a fool, trying to hold on to a sliver of pride.

Katherine grinned slyly. "I'll take that bet."

"What? No. I don't have to bet on that, Ren."

"Afraid you'll lose?"

"No, I think it'll be too easy," I said confidently.

"Guys, please don't," Lark said. "Don't you remember what happened last time?"

"I remember winning that one, too," I said with a challenge leveled at Katherine.

"Still too soon," Rowe said.

"Feels like old times," Lewis said. "You two whipping out some ridiculous bet. Well, I'm with Penn on this one."

"See," I taunted Katherine.

"Well, man, it's because you need the most help. Natalie is going to eat you alive."

I shot him a frustrated look. "So much confidence in me."

"Well, I'm out," Lark said, crossing her arms. "This is my vacation, not another chance for you two to go at each other's throats."

"It's just for *fun*, Larkin, my love." Katherine wrapped an arm around her shoulders.

"Until it's not."

"What are the terms?" I asked.

Lark sputtered, "Seriously?"

Katherine leaned forward, dragging Lark into this, too. "You have her *eating out of the palm of your hand* by, say, your mom's annual party. You bring her to the party, and we'll get an impartial judge to weigh in. You have two months."

I shrugged casually. "Easy. I only needed a night last time."

"And, if I win," Katherine said, tapping her chin, "you're mine for a night."

The pool was silent. I should have anticipated her answer. Should have seen where this was all heading. This wasn't about Natalie. This wasn't because Katherine had liked Natalie and wanted to see her stand me up. Oh, it went much deeper than that.

That meant…I had to hit her where it hurt.

I smiled and saw her own smile waver. "Fine. And, *when* I win, you set a date for the wedding with Percy."

Katherine flinched.

"Harsh," Lewis muttered.

"You guys don't have to do this," Lark whispered once more, trying to be the voice of reason.

But she'd known us long enough. She knew we were two of the most competitive people in existence, and neither of us could back down from a challenge. Especially from each other.

"Fine." Katherine stuck out her hand. "*If* you win, I'll set the date."

I shook her hand. "Deal."

I didn't let her see that I was enjoying this. The bet was a pretense. Now, I could go after Natalie without any shit from my friends. I could get her back on my side. Figure out what lay under that guarded exterior. Discover all her new truths. Claim her. Touch, lick, kiss every inch of her beautiful body.

Under any other circumstances, we wouldn't have worked. We came from two different worlds.

I was Manhattan royalty. She was the help.

But I wanted her all the same.

PART II
LET THE GAMES BEGIN

NATALIE

7

I never wanted to drink again.
Ever.

The next time I thought about downing nearly an entire bottle of bourbon, I was going to just knock myself out instead. It would be faster. Maybe even less painful.

I shielded my eyes against the blinding sun, ignored my grumbling stomach, and then all but fell out of bed. What the hell had I been thinking last night? So much of it had this hazy film over it, as if I were seeing it through an out-of-focus lens. I remembered the ritual burning of my rejection letters and skinny-dipping. I remembered the bottle of liquor.

And Penn.

Penn fucking Kensington.

"Fuck," I groaned into the silence of my bedroom.

Had he really been there last night or had that been some kind of manic dream? Because…it couldn't be real. He couldn't be here. He certainly couldn't be a Kensington. That would be too horrible to consider.

I noticed my laptop was open and lurched toward it.

There, in an incoherent babble, was some sort of story I'd written while I was drunk last night. I skimmed through it and groaned some more. Apparently, I'd written out more or less what actually happened after drinking an obscene amount.

Great.

I swiped sleep out of my eyes and slammed the laptop closed. I didn't want anyone else to see what I'd written. That would be even more humiliating than what had happened the night before.

Snatching up my cell phone, I hastily changed, cleaned myself up, and then stumbled out of my bedroom. All of the doors were closed on the way to the living room. In fact, there was no sign at all that anyone had been there. The bottles had all been picked up. Nothing was on the tables. The pillows were all exactly how I had left them. No indents in the couch cushions.

I shook my head in confusion.

Had I been *that* drunk?

I had an active imagination. I made up stories in my free time. But I couldn't have made last night up. Could I?

The kitchen was similarly empty and pristine. But when I pulled out the drawer for the trash, the bottle of bourbon was there as well as an empty bottle of champagne. I had a vague recollection of having champagne. That would explain the headache.

Okay, I wasn't totally insane. People had been here. I'd actually seen Penn and his insanely incredible friends. So… where were they?

My phone told me it was already noon. They'd stayed up later than me. Were they all still asleep?

I had no interest in opening doors to find out if anyone was still around. It was easier to assume that they'd just vanished as quickly as they'd appeared the night before. Penn had said that they might just go somewhere else. Maybe they had.

Fuck, I didn't know.

Part of me hoped they were gone. I had clearly been drunk off my ass last night to be able to keep up with them at all. They were all on another plane of existence. I was here, watching Penn's mom's house for a living while I got unlimited rejections from my agent's assistant. Not even from my *agent*. They were all off, living these wonderful lives and making millions or whatever.

The other part of me wished that they'd stayed. Not for Penn. Though the man was sexy as hell, he was still on my shit list. But I really did like his friends. I liked the bond the crew had and how they'd survived all these years together. To feel a part of that for even a second had been exciting.

I'd only ever had one real friend. And I was certain that Amy would probably want to hear about this.

I grabbed a bottle of water out of the fridge and dialed her number.

"Hey," Amy drawled lazily. "How's the new place?"

I laughed. "It's…interesting."

"Why do I feel like that's sarcasm?"

"So…remember that guy from Paris?"

"The one you gave your V-card to?"

I nodded my head and plopped down on the couch. "Uh-huh. Penn, the douche who had sex with me and then ghosted."

"Right. The, like, sexiest man alive who gave you a dozen orgasms and who you still begrudgingly claim is the best you've ever had."

"Well…" I grumbled, hanging my head. Leave it to Amy to bring up that shit right now. "He's here."

"What?" Amy shrieked.

I wrenched the phone away from my ear. "Hangover. Take it down a notch."

"I'd say I'm sorry, but I'm not. What do you mean, he's there? How can he be there?"

"Turns out, Penn is actually Penn Kensington."

Amy chuckled, and then it turned into a full-body laugh. "Oh, this is too good. He's the mayor's son?"

"He is. And he showed up here last night with his friends."

"Did you fuck him?"

"What? No, of course not! He was an asshole. I have no interest in him."

"But you're in a dry spell!"

"No! Amy, focus. I am working for his mother. There's no way that is happening."

"Fine. So, what are you going to do?" Amy asked.

"I don't know. Avoid him?"

Amy laughed. "Girlfriend, a guy like that cannot be avoided."

"I was hoping that you'd have advice. You're the one who deals with guys and people."

"My advice is to sleep with him. But since you're not listening to me—" Another voice came through the speaker. "Hold on a second, Nat. There's someone at the gallery."

"No problem."

Amy ran an art gallery on King Street in downtown Charleston. It had started out with a bang. Since she had an in with the art community, she'd started it straight out of college with her shiny art history degree in hand. Grimke University had even featured her as an esteemed alumnus.

I finished the bottle of water while I waited for Amy to return to our call. Not that I was certain she was going to give me any real advice about what to do about Penn and his friends. I still thought the best answer would be to just never see them again.

I was there to watch the place. The mayor was doing some remodeling and upkeep before her annual party in November, and she needed someone to be here to deal with the repairmen and interior decorators who would be floating in and out. I had only a vague idea of what was actually going to be happening, but I wasn't doing any of the work, just orchestrating it. I had a list in my email somewhere of what was going to start on Monday. Otherwise, I was free to enjoy the Hamptons.

The door clicked open, drawing me away from my thoughts, and my eyes bulged when Penn walked into the living room. I hung up the phone and jumped to my feet. I'd call Amy back later.

"You're still here," I blurted out.

"I am," Penn said.

"I thought you might have left already."

He arched an eyebrow, and my gaze traveled down his fit body. I'd never seen him in anything other than a suit and naked. Today, he was dressed comfortably in a sky-blue polo and khaki pants with boat shoes. He'd always lived in a suit in my mind. It was strange to see him like this. Though...he still looked fucking hot. Damn him.

"We didn't leave. Just had brunch. I would have woken you, but I figured you needed the sleep after last night."

I ran an absentminded hand through my tangled hair. "I guess."

In that moment, Katherine bounded through the front door. "Morning, Natalie," she said with a smile. "We brought you a pastry from the restaurant. Eat up and then get changed. We have plans." Katherine shoved a white bag into my hand.

"Thanks," I said automatically. I was surprised they'd thought of me at all. Not that I was hungry. I still felt a little queasy from all the alcohol. I wanted plain toast and a Gatorade.

"Of course. Don't forget your suit. You'll need it."

Katherine traipsed off, as if she hadn't had any alcohol at all last night. Lark and Rowe followed behind her, nodding in my direction. Then, Lewis appeared in the doorway in a similar outfit to Penn's. He quirked a smile at me.

"Hey, Natalie. Are you feeling better?" Lewis asked, sidling up to me.

"Uh, not really."

Penn was glaring at Lewis, as if his presence next to me irritated him. It was almost humorous. If I didn't feel so out of my depth with them all.

"That's too bad. Maybe I can whip you up some breakfast."

"You cook?" I asked. That wasn't something I had expected.

"I do. Grew up cooking with my mom."

"Well, you don't have to do that. I can make my own food."

"Don't even worry about it." Lewis started for the kitchen. "Just let me know if you have any food allergies."

I shook my head in confusion. What was happening here? I'd thought last night was some kind of weird dream. Penn's friends had hung out with me just to annoy him, but now, they were making it seem like…I was almost one of them. Like I belonged.

And then there was Penn.

He didn't casually stand around with me like Lewis had. He stood with his hands in his pockets and blue eyes staring intently into my own.

"What?" I couldn't help but ask.

"I want to apologize," he got out quickly.

"You…want to apologize?"

"I think we got off on the wrong foot last night. I was surprised by your appearance and had no right talking to you the way that I did."

I eyed him suspiciously. This was a one-eighty from how he'd acted the night before, and *he* hadn't been drunk.

"Okay."

"Just okay?" he asked.

I shrugged. "I don't know what you want me to say. We didn't get off on the wrong foot because you were rude last night. It's because of what you did when we met in Paris."

"That was so long ago."

"And that means you've changed?"

"How would you even know if I had?" he asked, stepping closer to me.

There was fire in his eyes that turned me on as much as it infuriated me.

"I wouldn't. And I don't want to."

"I'm not the person that I was six years ago. But everything wasn't a lie."

"Fine," I said. "Everything wasn't a lie. Just enough of it to get in my pants."

"Natalie, I didn't need to lie to get in your pants," he said very calmly. I could tell that the charm he had used on me was coming back out. "I spent time with you because you were interesting. And I still think that you are. We're going to be hanging out this weekend, and I'd like us to at least be civil. For you to give me a second chance."

I blew out a harsh breath and rolled my eyes. "What happened to you overnight? Did you have a brain transplant?"

His eyes bulged in surprise. "What?"

"This," I said, pointing at all of him, "I don't need to deal with right now."

I shook my head and brushed past him.

"Where are you going?"

"Didn't you hear Katherine? We're going out."

"Natalie…"

"Penn, just save your breath. I don't need an apology or the *everything wasn't a lie* speech. You're here for the weekend. I'm here until November. We can be amicable, but don't push your luck."

NATALIE

8

"When you said *out*, I thought you meant the beach or something," I said with my jaw nearly on the ground. "Not a yacht."

Katherine laughed and linked arms with me. "Welcome to our world."

We walked off of the dock together and onto what had to be the largest boat I had ever stepped foot on. It had to be the size of most houses…or bigger. Certainly nothing like the dinghies my sister, Melanie, always went out in with her friends back home.

"This is incredible," I murmured. "Did you guys rent this for the day?"

Rowe laughed behind me. "No."

"This is Lewis's yacht," Lark answered for him.

"Why on earth would you stay at the house when this yacht is only a twenty-minute drive away?"

"His father needed it for most of the weekend, but this afternoon was free on the schedule. So, we're taking it out for a spin," Katherine said. "Now, stop worrying about everything and enjoy yourself."

I snapped my mouth shut to keep from asking the million other questions poised on the tip of my tongue. I wasn't here to investigate them. I was here to enjoy myself. But it was in my nature to be inquisitive. It was part of my writer's curse to ask questions and get all the details. It was what had made me remember Penn's face. I never forgot a face. But it also sometimes kept me apart from a group. It made me an observer instead of a participant. I didn't want to be that person right now. I wanted to live in this moment. When else would I have the opportunity to step foot on a mega yacht anyway?

We walked down a hallway and then into an elaborate foyer that was nothing like the *Titanic* but reminded me of it nonetheless. I piled into the elevator with Katherine and Lark, and they waved at the boys as we were whisked upstairs. It felt totally surreal to be in an elevator on a boat.

But it was even more surreal when I stepped out onto the deck and saw the Atlantic clear before me. A swimming pool glittered invitingly, and Katherine was already stripping down to her bikini to get in. I ditched my bag and removed the flowy blue dress I'd put on over my bathing suit.

"Come on. Get in. We don't have to wait for the boys," Katherine said, walking into the pool.

A butler appeared then from out of nowhere. "How can I help you?"

"Mimosas!"

My stomach lurched at the thought, but Katherine was twirling her finger in the air. "For the lot of us and keep them coming."

"Of course, miss."

My stomach roiled uncertainly as I moved toward the swimming pool. I was still hungover, and things that didn't make that better included swimming pools, boats, and alcohol. Maybe this wasn't such a good idea.

CRUEL MONEY

Then, the guys appeared.

I turned around to see Penn and Lewis laughing. That smile on Penn's face was electric. It completely lit him up from the inside out.

It felt like some strange parallel universe. The Penn I knew had smiled for me, but it had gotten twisted in my memories. I'd remembered him more somber. I'd envisioned him more insidious. All of our good times together had gotten tangled up with the bad aftermath. And it was hard to disentangle the Penn I knew and the Penn I'd imagined after the fact. It was even harder to reconcile him with the person standing in front of me, staring at me as if I were his next meal.

I blushed and turned away, walking confidently into the pool. I didn't need to look at him like that or think about him like that. I absolutely didn't need to think about what Amy had said earlier…because I was not going to have sex with him or think about having sex with him. Because I didn't trust him nor was I sure that I even liked him.

And still, my eyes ventured back to him as he stripped out of his polo to reveal the six-pack abs underneath. My eyes trailed lower to the perfect V that cut into his flesh and moved lower and then lower. His swim trunks were cut, and I could just make out an outline. And, holy shit, I was staring.

"Natalie?" Katherine said.

I whipped my head in her direction. "Hmm?"

"Mimosa," she said, passing me the drink.

"Thanks." I didn't even want the drink but anything to keep from looking at Penn. I wandered deeper into the pool toward the waterfall that flowed from the Jacuzzi and into the pool. The water beat on my shoulders and kept me focused as both Penn and Lewis stepped into the pool.

"Rowe, come on," Lewis called.

Rowe flipped open his laptop and promptly sat down. He flipped Lewis off.

"Get your ass in here," Katherine said.

"I don't want to burn."

Lark scoffed. "I'm the redhead."

"Yeah, well, I'm blond."

"I thought we promised, no work this weekend," Penn reminded him.

Rowe looked up at him with a sigh. "Honestly?"

"If he doesn't want to come in, he doesn't have to," I spoke up for him.

Rowe pointed two fingers at me and grinned. "Let's keep her."

The others laughed and went for more mimosas. It was in that second that the boat moved. I lurched forward, nearly losing my drink and my stomach. But Penn was there somehow. His reflexes were outstanding. I hadn't even seen him reach for me, and now, my wet, naked body was nearly pressed against his.

"Are you all right?" he asked.

My eyes flicked up to his. No wonder I'd lost control around him last time.

I jerked back. "Fine. Just...still recovering."

"Are you sure you want to drink?"

"God, Penn, leave her alone," Katherine said. "She's a big girl."

Penn held his hands up. "I was just trying to be helpful."

"It's fine," I said. I didn't want to argue with him all day. It was exhausting, and anyway, he had kept me from face-planting into the water.

"Uh," Rowe said, "someone's phone is going off over here." He pointed at my bag.

"That's me."

I made a hasty retreat from the pool and stumbled a step

before gaining my sea legs. Not that I could feel the boat moving that much, but it wasn't the same as walking on the ground. I dug through my bag and pulled out my phone. Amy had called twice, and now, she'd sent a text.

You hung up! I wanted to hear the rest about Penn. Call me back.

I bit my lip as I grinned. Then, I snapped a picture to show her exactly where I was. Her response was almost immediate.

You bitch!

How dare you!

I cannot believe you are on a yacht without me. Are we even friends?

I giggled. I loved her so much.

Okay, fine. Have a good time. But I need all the deets after! And just...please sleep with him, so I can live vicariously through you.

I'm not sleeping with him! But I'll call you later to dish. xo

After I put my phone on silent, I went back to the party on the boat. Penn had put some music on, and Katherine was already complaining about it. I didn't know the song, but I liked it. I liked his obscure choices. But he just rolled his eyes and turned on "End Game" by Taylor Swift to make Katherine happy.

"My reputation precedes me, I know," Katherine said with a laugh and then started dancing in the pool.

To my surprise, I fit right into their little group, and the afternoon passed like a dream. Mimosas and culinary masterpieces that they all clearly took for granted. We danced and sang and laughed, and I never wanted it to end. I could get used to this life. Even though I knew it wasn't my own.

I leaned against the railing and watched the sun sliding low on the horizon, bathing the coast in yellows, oranges, and pinks. It was stunning, and I wasn't ready for the day to come to a close.

"Hey you." Lewis sidled up next to me.

"Hey."

"You seem distant. What's going on under that intense gaze?"

I shrugged. "Nothing. Just not ready to go back. Today has been so much fun."

"I feel like that every time I come out here. Sometimes, I wish I could work from the yacht and not have to be in the city."

"Really?" I asked in surprise. "I thought you all loved the city so much."

"Don't get me wrong. New York is my home. But this feels like a great escape."

"Then, maybe you shouldn't bring your work here."

"Ah, but it's so equipped for it. Did I tell you that my father's suite has a built-in library and study with a private room attached for an assistant?" He grinned. "Or bodyguard, depending on who he's dealing with."

"Is your father in the mob?" I asked with a laugh.

He chuckled. "Sometimes, it feels like it."

"Well, I'd never be opposed to seeing a library."

I leaned my hip into the railing and smiled up at him. He really was incredibly handsome. And it was hard not to smile around him with his easy demeanor and charm. If I'd met him first, I might have even been interested. But that wouldn't be possible now. He and Penn were best friends. Not a good idea by any stretch of the imagination.

But especially not because I couldn't seem to stop comparing them in my head. Lewis's easygoing ways. Penn's intensity. Lewis's strong jaw and quick smiles. Penn's penetrating looks and magnetism.

Okay, I needed to stop. It wasn't like I was going to hook up with either of them. So, this compare and contrast was going nowhere.

"I'd be happy to show you," Lewis said.

He gestured back inside, and I followed him down two floors and into his father's private suite. It didn't occur to me until we were there that this probably looked really bad to everyone else. Why else would I go alone to the private cabin?

I doubted anyone would guess it was to see his father's library collection. Only a writer would go to see someone's library and not consider the enormous dark, wooden bed in the other room.

"I am thoroughly impressed," I told Lewis as I scanned the walls covered in books. I couldn't imagine what his house must look like if this was just on his yacht.

"Yeah. My dad is a bit of a collector. Comes with the publishing side of the business, I think."

"He has good taste. Dickens, Wilde, Austen...oh, and one of my personal favorites, Huxley."

"*Brave New World?*" he guessed. "Let me guess you love the symbolism?"

"I do." I slipped the book off of the shelf. I leafed through the pages, remembering all the joy this novel had brought me when I first read it in high school.

"That's one of Penn's favorites, too."

I snapped the book shut. "Of course it is."

"You know, he's not a bad guy."

"I'm sure he's not," I said as I replaced the book on the shelf.

"I hear the sarcasm in your voice," Lewis said. He plopped down into a chair and crossed his leg at the ankle. "You have to get to know him. I don't know what happened with you in the past, but he's not the same guy he was."

"Maybe he's not," I said carefully. "Why are you defending him?"

"He's my best friend. I've known him my whole life. He's had a lot of ups and downs. He's had it harder than you'd think."

"I don't need his sob story."

Lewis chuckled and reached for me as I moved to step past him and out of the room. He grasped my hand and tugged me closer to him. "Don't get all heated. I'm not saying you have to fuck him or anything. I'm saying you don't have to *glare* in his direction every time he says something."

"I don't glare," I said softly.

Lewis arched an eyebrow. "Don't you?"

"And here I thought you were coming on to me," I said. "But maybe you're coming on to me for Penn?" I couldn't keep the laugh from escaping my lips.

Lewis stood, and for a second, I thought he might kiss me. He had this look in his eye that I'd seen before on a dozen guys. But then it vanished, and he smiled. "I was just showing you the library. Come on. Let's catch up with everyone else."

He was the first out of the room, and I followed him in confusion. Lewis was a bit of an enigma. In fact, all of them were. I couldn't seem to put my finger on who any of them were beyond what was showing. On some level, I thought that they were really being themselves because they were together. But they never seemed to relax completely. As if secrets and lies were so ingrained in who they were, they could never escape them.

We were almost back to the swimming pool when we came upon Penn standing alone on the deck. His eyes landed on the pair of us, and something passed so swiftly across his face that I didn't even catch what it was. But Lewis nodded at him and then hastily moved past.

Penn held out his hand, as if to stop me.

"What?" I asked. Venom was in my voice, and Lewis's comments in the library came back to me. Maybe I did glare at Penn when we were together. I sighed and met his gaze, trying to keep the anger out of my tone. "Did you need something?"

"What were you two doing?"

"I wanted to see the library."

Penn's eyebrows jumped up his face. "Is that so?"

"Yes. Lewis was kind enough to show me."

"Mmm," he murmured.

Obviously, he didn't believe me. Whatever. I didn't have to answer to him.

"What are you doing over here?"

"I was thinking." He shifted his gaze back out to the sea and seemed to disappear for a moment. The look was so familiar from our brief time in Paris that I sucked in a breath in surprise.

"About what?" I whispered, entranced by that faraway look.

"Do you know what *eudaimonia* is?"

My eyes narrowed. "You-da-what?"

He shifted to the side and laughed at my comment. "I'll take that as a no."

"No," I agreed. I couldn't figure out why in the world he was even talking to me about this.

"It's a Greek term for happiness or well-being. It's more

accurately translated as human flourishing or prosperity. In ethics, we use it to describe Aristotle's idea about how ethics contributes to happiness and that the goal in life is to reach *eudaimonia*."

I stared blankly at him. "You lost me."

He nodded. "I've seen that look on my students' faces. There aren't a ton of us anymore for a reason."

"Is that what you teach? Aristotle?"

"Ethics mostly. That's where my research interest lies."

"Interesting."

I surprised myself by leaning against the rail next to Penn. I should have stepped back and ignored this conversation. I didn't need a philosophy lesson in the middle of an incredible day. I could just walk away from this. But, somehow, I couldn't. I wanted to know more. I wanted to hear him speak about his passions. It was what had enticed me in the first place. And even knowing how this had ended before didn't get me to back up.

"So…happiness?" I prompted.

"See, for some people, the past is a dark place. It's everything you knew you shouldn't be but were anyway. Until you find a way to achieve happiness and then abandon your past. To achieve a happier, more fulfilled life."

His eyes bored into mine when he said it, and I read him loud and clear. Who he'd been before in Paris wasn't who he was now. He was trying to be different, better than he had been. Of course, I had no proof of that fact. But he wasn't trying to force his opinion on me here. He was giving me a lesson.

"Are all of your classes like this?" I asked with a hesitant smile.

He laughed and shook his head. "No, my job is much more boring than being with you."

I opened my mouth to respond but then closed it. I didn't

know how to respond to that. I didn't even know how I felt about that...or Penn. This trip had been confusing.

Before I had to come up with something to say, Katherine appeared then. "Natalie! There you are. Come on. We're all in the hot tub."

"Sure," I said.

My eyes darted to Penn, who looked solemn and reserved. Charming one moment and blank the next. Which one was an act for my benefit, and which one wasn't?

"You coming, too, Penn?" Katherine asked with a quick, vicious smile.

"Yeah. I'll be there in a minute."

I looked back at him one last time before following a chattering Katherine to the hot tub and trying to forget about her talk with Penn. And how easily I had slipped into such deep conversation with him. And how irritated it made me that I'd fallen for it...again.

PENN

9

"Do you concede yet?" Katherine asked. She draped her lean body across my bed back at the cottage. She had changed out of her bathing suit but was only clothed in a red silk nightie. She was clearly trying to woo me to her side with all of this display, but I'd never liked things that weren't a bit of a challenge.

"Hardly," I said. I turned my back on her, snatched up my notebook, and then sank into a chair. "We've just begun."

"She disappeared with Lewis down below for, like, a half hour. What do *you* think happened?"

"I think she looked at his library."

"Oh, is that what they're calling it nowadays?" Katherine quipped.

I rolled my eyes. "She's a writer. She actually had an interest in the library, Ren."

"Whatever." Katherine twirled her left hand in the air. The diamond caught the light, and she frowned at it. "I think she's not going to let her little heart out on the line again."

"And is that why you have Percy's ring on your finger?"

She rolled over onto her stomach and smirked. "Jealous?"

I ignored her and turned to my latest entry. I scratched notes in the margin as the idea I'd had on Warren's yacht about Aristotle's *Nicomachean Ethics* finally came together.

"Are you writing about me?"

"Uh-huh," I murmured.

"What does it say? You never let me read your work."

"It says you're a bitch."

Katherine scoffed. "Liar."

I grinned up at her. "You haven't read it. How would you know?"

"Because I know you, Penn Kensington."

I added another note with a sentence reminder about the treatise I wanted to decipher. Then, I stuck the pen in the notebook and tossed it onto the table.

"Why are you so obsessed with my notebook?"

"Because you're always writing in that damn thing. Who wouldn't be interested in it? You never let us read it."

"You'll just have to die of curiosity, I suppose."

Katherine rolled her eyes and then slinked off of the bed. Her steps were predatory as she moved toward me. I just stared back, impassive. Katherine and I had been playing another sort of game for a very long time. One that didn't have a winner. It usually resulted in anger or sex or tears or screaming. Sometimes, all of the above. It never ended well. Fuck, it never started well.

We were great as friends. But we were terrible—utterly fucking terrible—as anything else. She knew it. I knew it.

And still, she straddled my lap in her tiny lingerie-clad body and brushed her fingers up into my hair.

"Let's play something else tonight," she purred.

I kept my face blank, neutral. "I'll pass."

"It'll be fun."

"You're not going to win this way," I told her evenly.

"Who said anything about winning? Maybe I just want you."

I scoffed and stood, dropping her onto her ass. "We're playing one game, Katherine." I wielded her full name like a weapon. "I'm not interested in any others."

She somehow made scrambling to her feet look graceful, but I could see the venom in that look. Here came the anger...and probably the screaming. Though I never knew which side of Katherine I'd get.

"I was just teasing," she finally said. "You can restrain yourself."

Restrain myself. Fuck. Restrain myself?

Sometimes, I swore she said things just to piss me off. There was a reason I'd stepped away from my family. That I'd stepped away from it all. I loved my crew fiercely. But it was so easy to backslide around them, around Katherine.

"Were you?"

"Was I what?" she asked, stopping halfway to the door.

"Teasing?"

"Obviously. Watching you make a fool out of yourself is a fun sport. I like to watch myself win without lifting a finger."

"As if you're not playing yet."

She grinned wickedly and then gingerly stepped back across the room. She ran one manicured nail down my cheek. "When I play, you'll never see my moves coming."

Then, she winked and sauntered out of my room.

I sank back into the chair. Good riddance.

As much as she irritated me, I couldn't help but worry about what moves she was already planning. The one thing I did know about Katherine was to never, *ever* underestimate her.

NATALIE

10

It was Monday morning, and the crew had been gone a whole twenty-four hours. They'd left the day before without fanfare. Now, I was back to my regularly scheduled programming.

My arms cut through the water as I swam laps to stay fit. I'd been on my high school swim team and even competed a few years in college. It calmed all the voices and let me concentrate. Or at least, it usually did.

I flipped at the next edge and pushed off the wall like it was a spring before darting to the other side. This was supposed to be relaxing and not filled with thoughts of a guy who had flitted in and out of my life as easily as he had six years ago.

At least I hadn't slept with him this time.

I came up for air. My heart was racing, and I took deep breaths, gulping in oxygen after my workout. I snagged my water bottle and guzzled half of it. Then, I leaned my elbows against the side of the pool and stared out to the ocean.

It was a beautiful day with the high still in the mid-80s. The first round of consults for the renovations would be here this afternoon. The job was getting real. That meant I needed to focus less on the events of this weekend and more on the manuscript sitting unfinished on my computer. I had two months to finish my draft. I could make this book the *one*.

Suddenly, I heard a strange jingling noise coming from the house. I turned toward the noise with a furrowed brow. What the hell was that?

And there it was again.

Had I left a door open or something? I hadn't turned the TV on since I got here. Even Netflix hadn't been switched on. Still, the noise persisted.

Then, to my utter shock, a tiny yet incredibly long-legged puppy bounded out of the back door and onto the deck.

"Oh my goodness," I crooned.

I pushed off and moved to the other side of the pool. The little puppy sprang right over to me in his cute, slightly uncoordinated way. I held my hand out to him, and he licked it and then my nose a couple of times in greeting.

"Where did you come from?"

I hauled myself out of the pool and sat on the edge. The puppy nudged its way into my lap and tried to find a way to get his awkward limbs all onto me. I petted his shiny gray coat and rubbed its cute too-big-for-its-head ears.

Then, footsteps followed, and I heard, "Aristotle!"

The puppy nuzzled down in my lap and nudged my hand to keep petting him. "We need to figure out who you belong to."

But the answer was there in the doorway before I even had a chance to stand.

"There you are!" Penn said with a sigh. "I knew that you were going to be trouble."

I stared up at him in shock. "What are you doing here?" I gasped.

"Just getting out of your way."

I scooped up the puppy and held him in my arms as I stood. This...made no sense. Penn had left yesterday with all of his friends and all of his problems. He wasn't supposed to show back on Monday morning. It made no sense.

"You were supposed to leave yesterday. Why are you back? Did you forget something? Do you need me to look for it, so you can be on your way?"

"Well, you've found what I was looking for." He pointed at the dog clutched in my arms. "Natalie, meet Aristotle."

"You named your dog Aristotle?" I asked in disbelief. "How mean are you?"

Penn laughed, and it was a light, musical thing. "At the time, it seemed like the perfect name. But, after his actions the past couple of weeks, I think he is far more belligerent and might have been a better Nietzsche."

"Why do you hate your puppy?"

"I don't hate him."

"Don't worry," I said, scratching Aristotle's ears. "I won't call you that ridiculous name. From now on, you'll be... Totle." Totle's ears perked up, and he licked me in the face. I giggled. "You like that, huh?"

"You are not calling my dog Totle."

"Well, I'm not calling him Aristotle. You must have lost your mind. And, anyway...you didn't answer my question. What are you doing here?"

He sighed and took another step outside. "Can I have the dog back first?"

"That remains to be seen."

He slid his hands into his pockets and shook his head at me. I could see the machinations working in his mind. Trying to figure out how to not make me mad at him while also somehow getting his dog back. I was pretty sure he was going to fail on both accounts.

"I'm on sabbatical this semester."

"Okay." I had a vague idea of what sabbatical was, but my blank stare must have been enough to trigger him to explain.

"A professor can take a semester off from teaching to accomplish a specific goal. Sometimes to finish a project or run a journal or travel for research. That sort of thing. Most assistant professors don't get a semester of sabbatical. It's given out after you get tenure."

"But you're getting it...pre-tenure?"

"Yes. I made a case for getting the semester off to finish my book project. I had enough riding on it that they awarded it to me. It's the book that I'm hoping will *get* me tenure at Columbia, but we'll see about that in another year or two."

"Okay," I said, trying to keep it all straight. "So, you're writing a book."

"Yes. I have been working on it since graduate school, but I wanted to have a deep dive into the material to get it all into place. I have an advanced contract with Cambridge for it. So, I can't procrastinate on it anymore."

My head swam with all the new information. Sabbatical. Tenure at Columbia. Advance contract at Cambridge. I found for a split second that I was insanely jealous of his life. Obviously, he'd put the work in, and I had no interest in academia, but a contract for a book was such a dream.

"That all sounds...amazing," I admitted. "But what does it have to do with why you're here?"

"I planned to stay here for the semester."

"What?" I asked with wide eyes.

"That was always the plan. I just had to go back and get Aristotle."

"You always planned to stay," I said hollowly.

"Well, yeah."

"Penn..."

"I'm going to stay out of your way."

I snorted. "As if you'll actually do that. You were here for a weekend and completely disrupted my life."

"Is that what you call hanging out with my friends all weekend?"

"Yes!" Totle whined in my arm, and I bent to kiss his head. "Sorry, buddy. Look, you're already scaring Totle."

"That nickname," he said with an eye roll. "I promise you won't even know that I'm here. We don't have to see each other unless we want to."

"We don't want to."

"Right," he said with his hands raised. He moved forward until he was standing before me and started petting Totle. "He's really just the cutest dog ever."

"What is he anyway? A whippet? He looks so small."

"Italian greyhound. He's only a couple months old. He'll get a little bigger, but he'll probably only be, like, fifteen pounds."

"Are you going to race him? Do they have baby greyhound racing?"

Penn scoffed. "Are *you* kidding this time? Do you know how hard those dogs are run into the ground? I want Aristotle to live a long, full life." A smile lit up his face when he looked at the puppy. It was something I'd never seen on him before. Apparently, puppies changed everyone. "No racing for him and lots of treats."

Totle's ears jumped up at that, and he pawed at Penn.

"Yes, yes, I know. I said the magic word. Come on. Let's get him something."

I set Totle down on the deck, and he loped awkwardly after Penn. I grabbed a dress to throw over my bathing suit and then followed them both inside to the kitchen. Totle lolled over to the only available piece of carpet and sat down. His tail wagged excitedly, and he then he dropped down with his legs out before him like he was trying to lie down, but with all his limbs, he looked ridiculous.

"Good boy," Penn said, handing him a treat from a bag.

Totle barked at the treat twice and then went to town, trying to figure out how to eat the thing between his long legs.

"He's adorable."

"I know." Penn grinned down at him. "Ridiculous and needy as hell, but I love him." He glanced back up at me. "Look, I really wanted to stay here before I knew you were here. I plan to be invisible. We will be roommates and nothing more."

"Don't you think your friends will show up all the time and, I don't know, ruin your solitude…and mine?"

"I didn't tell them that I was coming back."

"And they won't be suspicious that you're not in New York?"

"I don't get to see them much when I'm teaching. I'm usually too busy. We meet up for events, which I'll probably go back for anyway sometimes. No one will be the wiser. I don't want to be interrupted either."

"But…"

"Can we have a trial period? Maybe two weeks. And, if it doesn't work out, then you can kick me out."

"Of your own house?" I asked skeptically.

"You're the one getting paid to be here. This is your job. I assume you can kick me out of here if I'm getting in the way of you doing your job."

"Seriously?"

"Seriously."

I chewed on my bottom lip and looked from him to Aristotle. "And Totle is staying, too?"

"Yeah. Sorry, I can't leave him alone."

"He was the deal-breaker."

"Natalie…come on."

"No, I meant, if he wasn't staying, neither were you."

He laughed. "Well, Aristotle is staying."

"Okay. Well, I suppose we can try a trial period."

"Great. I'll just take Aristotle and get out of your hair."

"Whoa, whoa, whoa, Totle is no bother. It's only you I have an issue with."

He rolled his eyes and reached for the leash on the counter. Totle jumped up and down until Penn put him on the leash. "You're not like anyone else I know, Natalie."

"Maybe you should meet more people."

He walked toward the back door. "I don't want to meet anyone new." He glanced at me over his shoulder. "You're interesting enough all on your own."

NATALIE

11

*H*e had to be bluffing.

I didn't think it was possible for us to live in the same house and never see each other. Especially with Totle between us and the renovations on the house beginning that afternoon. But still, I'd agreed on two weeks to take this situation for a test drive. I was pretty certain that he'd do something irritating between now and then that would let me kick him out.

I was curious why he was really back. If it was because he had planned to write his book. Or if he had only come back because I was here. I was probably flattering myself with that last thought. It wasn't like he'd come on to me this weekend or anything. Past experiences still clouded how I viewed him. No rose-colored glasses for me.

But he managed to surprise me.

Time moved easily. Restfully. Peacefully even.

We wandered in and out of each other's space. The renovations began that afternoon, and I walked through the list I'd been given to handle everything. But for the most part, I let people inside and made sure nothing was stolen or unaccounted for.

Then on Tuesday morning, the aroma of coffee wafted invitingly from the kitchen. When I stepped out there in my gray polka-dot pajama bottoms and white tank, I found a pot of coffee already brewed. There was a note next to it in crisp, neat handwriting that said, *Help yourself.*

Wednesday, I let Totle swim with me when I was supposed to be doing laps. But no sign of his owner.

On Thursday, I caught my first glimpse of him running with Totle down the beach, shirtless. My cheeks turned the exact shade of a ripe tomato, and I quickly pulled myself away from the window. Later that day, I found a half-empty bowl of water and a set of sandy paw prints next to the outdoor shower.

I didn't see Penn again until Sunday. I'd been cooped up all weekend, working on my book. It hardly held my interest at this point. There was a new idea scratching at the back of my brain, and I kept going back to it when I knew I should be working on the book I'd promised my agent.

I desperately needed a break from the desk I had been utilizing in my room. Walks down the beach were nice for brainstorming. The deck was good for piecing it all together. But I was a creature of habit, and I liked a little structure for my work, which was how I ended up in the library.

With a yawn, I pushed open the door to the library and was immediately attacked by Totle.

"Sorry," I murmured when I saw Penn sitting at the bay window, scribbling furiously into his notebook. The pen scratching against the paper was music to my ears.

His hand yanked on his hair, as if it might help him fit his writing together into a masterpiece. "Do you need this space?" he asked.

I shook my head. "Nope. Didn't know you were in here."

"I can leave," he said quickly.

I scooped up Totle. "Just going to steal him."

Penn laughed. "By all means."

Monday night, he ordered pizza. It was the first time he'd actively sought me out in our first week as accidental roommates. And he only did it to make sure that I didn't have any allergies or if I had a pizza preference. When it showed up, he knocked on my door to let me know it was here.

I ate a piece in the kitchen as I jotted down notes on my newest character arc. I'd given up on the other book. This one was better. Much better.

Tuesday, we had cold pizza for breakfast in front of the kitchen. Totle stared up at us, begging for scraps. I found I liked Penn better in his unassuming clothes with stubble on his jaw and ink on his fingers.

Wednesday, I watched him write on the back deck. His intensity was unparalleled. I didn't know what he was writing. Philosophy, of course. But besides the fact that he taught ethics, I knew nothing about what had driven him into the study. I didn't know how much of what he'd once told me about his passions was true. It'd seemed true, and still, I was hesitant to believe that it was.

But this was what had interested me about him in the first place. That damn leather notebook and ballpoint pen. A far-off look that said he was discovering the secrets of the universe and that he had plenty of secrets of his own. As a writer, his love for the written word drew me in like a moth to a flame.

What was he writing?

Why did he have to look like that when he did it?

Thursday, I had to deal with the interior decorator who wanted me to walk her around the house all day. She seemed talented, which made me question why she wanted my input. I didn't get any writing done. I didn't see Penn either.

Friday, I played catch-up on my work and crashed into bed early. I was exhausted from all the words I'd written. It was finally flowing like water down a river. I had definitely made the right choice in switching books.

A weight landed on the bed.

My eyes cracked open, and I jolted backward in fear. What the hell was that?

I peered through the darkness. That was when I saw a small puppy-shaped blob walking across the bed. I relaxed with a sigh. I must have left the door cracked. Totle scratched at the covers, and I pulled them back, so he could crawl under them. He nuzzled into my stomach and then unceremoniously plopped down. I giggled while petting his head. Then, I promptly fell back asleep.

Saturday morning, I woke to frantic calls from outside my door.

"Aristotle!" Penn cried. "Totle! Totle, come out now. We're not playing a game. Totle!"

A second later, Penn pushed into my room without an invitation and rushed forward as if he were determined to search every inch of the house.

"Have you seen Aristotle?"

I pointed at my chest. "Safe and sound."

"Oh Jesus," Penn said. He sank down onto the bed. "Thank god. I didn't know where he was or if he'd gotten out last night. I was terrified that he'd gotten onto the beach or the pool."

"Well, don't worry. He's fine. He just found a new place to sleep."

"What a lucky guy," he deadpanned.

I cracked up. "Want to see him?"

"Is that an invitation?"

"And you were doing so well," I said with an eye roll. "Get out of my bedroom."

"I'm kidding. Yes, let me see Aristotle."

"I heard you call him Totle though."

Penn offered a smirk. "It's catching."

I peeled the covers back inch by inch to reveal the small dog curled up against me. He opened one eye in disdain, as if to say, *How dare you take the covers away*. Then, he saw his dad, and his tail started wagging.

"There you are, you little shit. You scared me," Penn said. "Who knew I could ever freak out this much over anything?"

"Well, just look at him."

"That's how he fools you," Penn insisted.

"He's not the only one," I muttered.

Penn frowned and then seemed to realize that he wasn't just in my room, but he was also lying on the bed. We were having a totally normal conversation.

"You're not going to kick me out for this, are you?" he asked with a sly grin.

I sighed. "I mean…you broke the rules."

But I couldn't hold back the smile from my face. He had done everything I'd asked. There had just been this…awareness of him at all times. The knowledge that he was there. So close yet so far away. Half-naked on the beach. Playing with the puppy. Writing, always writing. And it hadn't been *bad* per se. In fact, it had been a bit too inviting.

For that alone, I should walk away and never look back.

Because no matter how well behaved he'd been for almost two weeks, I knew who he was, where he had come from, and what he was really like. Even if he didn't want anything from me, I didn't trust myself enough around him for us to stay neutral in each other's territory.

I wasn't neutral when it came to him.

Not even close.

"Well, you broke the rules, too," he argued.

I had. I definitely had. Because I couldn't stop looking at him.

Even now in lounging shorts and a pink T-shirt, he was sexy as sin. Dark hair wild, as if he'd been running his fingers through it all night while writing. Those bright blue eyes that just did me in. He was a work of art. Even when he wasn't dressed like James Bond, he projected the same aura. The same intense vibe that said he was commanding the situation and dominating every endeavor.

I liked it. I shouldn't like it.

"I did," I conceded. "We both did."

"But…"

"But I think it was okay."

Lies. It wasn't okay. It was so, so far from okay.

"Me too," he said with that smile that said he was imagining all the things he could do to me in this bed. "Trial period over?"

I held up a finger. "We have one more day!"

He laughed and rolled off the bed. "One more day then."

I didn't need another day. I was going to let him stay.

And I was going to regret it.

NATALIE

12

Part of me really wanted to see Penn mess this up. It would be better for my sanity; that was for sure. But the other part of me, the stupid part of my psyche, said that having him around had been nice. Even as scarce as he had made himself.

Of course, there were always signs of him or short glimpses of him in other rooms. But he was staying in the master suite, which was about as far from my room as a person could get in a house the size of a small planet.

I shook my head in frustration at myself. Penn was doing the right thing here. He hadn't been a jerk once.

Still, it had been a bit like coming upon a lion in the wild. Seeing it in its natural element was beautiful and also…terrifying. You wanted to run for your life, but you were afraid to move, or the predator would pounce.

I made sure to spend my day away from him, but by evening, I'd given up on work. I barely had any words and knew it wasn't going to get any better. I stepped into the kitchen and thumbed through the mail. The house barely got anything, except spam. All the bills went to the city to be paid. I usually even forgot to check it. Penn must have gotten this yesterday.

I dumped the first couple of items in the trash and then stopped on a cream matte envelope with my name on it. What the hell? I hadn't gotten any mail here. I hadn't even given my parents this address. It made no sense.

With a bite of curiosity, I tore open the envelope and dug out what appeared to be a party invitation. My eyes bulged. Holy shit!

Without a second thought, I burst out of the kitchen and out to the back deck. I wasn't surprised to find Penn there. I'd heard the door close and Totle's distinctive jingle while I was working. I found him reclining on a chair with Totle curled up next to him, half under a blanket. He had a glass of bourbon in one hand and a pen in the other. His notebook was open on his lap, but he was staring off toward the ocean.

He glanced toward me as the door slammed behind me, and Totle's head popped up. "What's up?"

"Have you seen this?" I asked, thrusting the invitation in his face.

"Uh..." He glanced at it. "Oh, yeah, that's the gala that Katherine mentioned. I see she sent you an invite."

"I didn't think she really would."

"She follows through on her promises."

"Well, I can't go." I sank into a seat across from him and pulled my knees up to my chest.

"Why not?"

"Do you really have to ask that? I would never fit into something like that. I showed up here with two suitcases for my entire worldly possessions. I don't remember stuffing a ball gown in there."

Penn cracked a smile and took a sip of his drink. "I'm sure that Katherine would help with that."

"I don't need charity," I spat.

"Katherine would see it as fun, I assure you."

"I'd never be able to afford it. Or pay her back."

"I wouldn't worry about it."

"Well, I *do* worry about it! I wasn't raised like that."

"Money is not an object, Natalie," Penn said evenly.

"Maybe for you."

"Do you want to go?"

I stared down at the invitation. I *did* want to go. It sounded like a dream. Or a fairy tale. Something people did in the books I read religiously and in the movies I'd grown up on. But it sure didn't sound like me.

"Yes," I admitted.

"Then we'll go."

My head popped back up. "We?"

"Not together," he replied hastily when he saw my scrutiny. "But I can drive you into the city and drop you off with Ren. She'll handle it from there."

"And the money?"

He shrugged. "Money doesn't matter."

"Spoken like someone who has it."

"For someone who works for people with money, you sure seem to have a great disdain for it."

I pursed my lips. "It's not that. I just...I've never had money. You and your friends are the haves. I know how the have-nots live. Seeing the other side is magical and depressing. It's something I'll never have. No matter how hard I work."

"That's not the American Dream."

"Yeah, as if *pull yourself up by your bootstraps* works for people like me," I said sarcastically. "Most people are held down by the circumstances they were raised in. Few have real opportunity to jump classes, Penn. And, even when they do, they're not really accepted."

"That's an incredibly jaded perception of our world."

"Or an incredibly realistic one."

Penn reached over and scratched Totle's head. "Can I ask you a question?"

I shrugged. "You can stay."

He grinned. "Well, that's a relief. Though that wasn't my question. I kind of already guessed that one based on the fact that you're actually speaking to me right now."

"Fine. I must be transparent."

"Trust me. You're not."

I blushed at the look on his face that said he wanted to unravel my mystery. "What do you want to know?"

"What were you doing that first day on the beach?"

"You *saw* what I was doing," I said with a shy laugh.

"No, I mean, why were you out there in the first place? I could never piece it all together."

"Oh." I stared down at my hands. This wasn't really a story I wanted to tell. Not because I was embarrassed by what I'd done, but more about why I'd done it. How could I tell the person who had everything that I had nothing? How could he even relate to my rejection? It felt like opening myself up to vulnerability that I didn't know I could handle.

"Look, you don't have to tell me if you don't want to."

I sighed and met his gaze. Honestly, what would it hurt? I hadn't told anyone else about it. I'd even kept it from Amy. She was still learning the publishing process, and she had such faith in my abilities without any real knowledge of how it operated. It might actually be nice to talk to someone who knew about how it worked even if it was from academia and not fiction.

"The day that you and your crew showed up, I had just gotten several nasty rejection letters from my agent. Well, from my agent's assistant. They basically said that I couldn't write, my characters were flat, boring, and unlikable, and overall, I was a hack."

"Jesus."

"Yeah. Well, it turned out that I wasn't even supposed to get those emails, but my agent's assistant had mistakenly sent me the unedited versions of the letters. I got an apology email Monday morning, but by then, it was too late."

"Way too late. That assistant should be fired."

I dismissively waved my hand. I didn't want to get anyone fired, but yeah, it was a huge mistake. And I still felt the ripple effects of those comments in my current work.

"Anyway, I was so angry that night. I printed out every rejection letter I'd ever received and burned them in, like, ritual sacrifice. Then, for my cleansing, I…well, you know."

"Skinny-dipped. Yes, I recall that part."

I rolled my eyes at him. "That's right. And I felt so much better, like I'd let the weight fall off my shoulders. I was ready to take on the world. Anything thrown my way, I could handle."

"And then I appeared."

"And then *you* appeared," I parroted.

"Ah. No wonder you were so angry. And drunk."

I crossed my legs into a pretzel and tilted my head up to the stars. "You didn't make it any better, you know?"

"I know."

"What if I never write a book worth reading?" I whispered my greatest fear into the silence.

I didn't know why I'd said it at all. Let alone to Penn. What had he done to deserve this confession from me? Nothing. But, for some reason, it was so easy to talk to him. Maybe it was because I had been cooped up in this house for two weeks. Maybe it was because I was lonely. Or maybe it was just him.

It had been easy to talk to him in Paris. Though I had been a different person then. I didn't know why I had done it, but it was out there now. Too late for me to take it back.

"I don't think that could possibly be the case."

I snorted in disbelief. "You obviously didn't read the rejection letters."

"I have a number of peer-reviewed articles published. I had to send them out to a lot of different journals before they landed anywhere. And I constantly got feedback from other philosophy scholars about my work. Most of it was far from positive or constructive. It might surprise you, but I know all about rejection."

"It does surprise me," I said with an eye roll. I doubted many *women* had rejected him. That was for sure.

"Look, rejection doesn't mean that what you've written isn't worth reading. It means, it didn't work for that person or the next person or their marketing team or whatever it is. Harry Potter was rejected, like, a dozen times before it was picked up. I bet those other editors feel like idiots right about now. You'll find the right place for your work, and then those other editors will rue the day they rejected you."

"We can only hope," I murmured. Though I did feel slightly better. It helped hearing it from someone who had been there. Even if tangentially.

"You'll get there."

I chewed on my bottom lip and nodded. I hoped he was right. "What's your book about anyway?"

"My book?" he asked in surprise.

"Yeah. Penn Kensington's philosophy. What interests you?"

He closed his notebook on a chuckle and tossed it onto the table between us. "Sex."

I sat up straight. "Are you kidding me?"

"You asked."

"I was asking about your work," I insisted.

"Get your head out of the gutter, Natalie. I was talking about my work."

I furrowed my brows skeptically. "You write about sex…professionally?"

"I study ethics. One of my areas of focus, including the one that I'm writing my book on, is the philosophy of sex."

"Okay. What does that mean exactly? You're looking at whether having sex is ethical?" I asked, suddenly intrigued.

"It's complicated," he said softly. "I'll back up. Philosophy is the study of what really matters, such as knowledge, reality, and existence. It looks at how we know what we know, whether or not there's a god, if we have free will, what is right and wrong behavior, et cetera. Ethics is the latter."

"Who knew I'd be getting a philosophy lesson tonight?" I said with a laugh.

"I don't have to explain," he said with a shrug.

"No, keep going. I'm interested," I insisted, leaning forward. "We're talking about right or wrong."

"Yes. The ethical theory that I most agree with is from Aristotle."

"Hence the dog."

"Indeed. As I mentioned on Lewis's yacht, for Aristotle, you want to reach eudemonia, the ultimate state of happiness. And developing that happiness is done by creating good habits…essentially."

"This has something to do with sex, I presume." I tilted my head and smirked.

Penn arched his eyebrow. "Well, the general theory regarding sex is what we call the standard view. Sex is okay between two people in a committed relationship—preferably marriage—and the purpose is for procreation."

I couldn't roll my eyes hard enough. "Well, that's incredibly outdated."

"Is it?" he asked calmly. "I think most people will say that waiting to have sex is a smarter, safer choice."

"Yeah, and those same people are having sex before

marriage," I pointed out. "I doubt *anyone* only has sex to have kids."

"Right. I don't think people follow the standard view, but that's what is set up as the paradigm. It's the best way to mitigate the risks of having sex."

"I'm going to go out on a limb and say that you don't subscribe to this mentality," I said cheekily.

"I do not."

"Color me shocked."

"I enjoy sex," he said blatantly. "Most people enjoy sex. It's a pleasure unto itself and for much more than procreation. And the basis of my research is dismantling the standard view in an Aristotelian ethical fashion. It's proving to be challenging."

"I couldn't imagine doing what you're doing. Challenging sounds like an understatement. You're trying to disprove a cultural stigma."

"Well, in philosophy, we try to explain the existence of God and our reason for being. I would hope that I could explain why sex for pleasure brings us happiness."

I laughed and nodded. "Fair."

I sank back in my chair again and assessed him. I knew nothing about philosophy. But I could probably listen to him talk about it all night. His clear love for what he was doing drew me in. I found it interesting that, of all the things that he'd said and done with me in Paris, it was this that felt the most real. That he'd wanted to escape his family and become someone else. That he'd wanted to be a professor and study philosophy. I hadn't known how much of that was bullshit, but six years later, he was living it.

"You really were telling the truth in Paris," I said softly.

"About everything that mattered."

"Huh," I said, getting to my feet and moving to stand before him. I took the glass of bourbon out of his hand. He looked surprised when I drained it. "Would have never guessed."

"Disappointed?"

I shook my head. "If I could change in six years, maybe you could too."

"Maybe?"

"It's still up for debate."

"Seems fair."

I held up the empty glass. "Want another?"

"I can get it."

"Yeah, but I offered."

"Are you going to get your own or keep drinking mine?"

"That's up for debate too."

"Then, make it a double," he said with a flash of a smile.

"Be careful, Kensington. Leading an ethical life comes from creating good habits. Wouldn't want to see you slip up," I teased as I walked back toward the house.

"One philosophy lesson, and she's already teaching the teacher."

"I'm a quick study."

"Don't I know it?" he said, his eyes molten.

I knew that look. I knew exactly what he was thinking about—every minute we had spent together where he taught me just how much sex *wasn't* for procreation. Now, I was thinking about it, too. And I knew that we absolutely couldn't have a repeat. Ever.

Lord help me. This man. Fuuuckkk.

NATALIE

13

"Aristotle, you cannot drive," Penn said. He tilted his head to the side and narrowed his eyes at his puppy, who was currently standing in the driver's side of the Audi convertible with his paws on the steering wheel, as if to say, *Ready to go, Dad!*

"Aww, let him drive," I said. "What would it hurt?"

"Us!"

I laughed as he hoisted Totle out of the driver's seat.

We'd spent the last week slowly getting used to being in each other's presence. I'd been careful not to veer the conversation back to dangerous waters again. Being attracted to him was one thing. Inevitable. But acting on it…that would be blatant stupidity. I trusted him about as far as I could throw him.

The last thing I wanted was to fall back into his trap. So far…we seemed infinitely better as tentative friends. And I was okay with that.

"Give him to me." I held out my hands for Totle.

"By all means."

He passed him to me, and I let Totle nuzzle down into my

lap in the passenger seat. Penn threw our things in the trunk, and then we were off.

"I still can't believe that you only brought one tiny bag."

"We're just in the city tonight," I reminded him.

"Yeah, but every other woman I know would need a whole suitcase for that."

"You're exaggerating."

"Not by much," he said, fiddling with the stereo.

"Well, that's absurd. Katherine is the one who is going to doll me up. I literally only need pajamas, a change of clothes for tomorrow, and my toothbrush."

Penn shrugged. "I agree, but that's not the norm."

"I guess not."

Penn drove around the circular drive and out onto the main road toward the city. His phone connected to the stereo, and soon, music filled the speakers. To my surprise, I recognized the song.

"Is this 'Bad Habit' by Liz Longley?"

He raised his eyebrows. "Yes, it is. I didn't think you'd know this one."

"Oh my god, I love her music. I went with my little sister to see her perform with Delta Rae once, and she's so funny in person."

"I've never seen her before. Every time she's in town, I'm too busy."

"Well, next time, we can go," I said before I could stop myself.

Penn grinned.

"As friends," I quickly clarified. "Just friends."

"Of course," he said. "I didn't know that you had a sister either."

"Oh, yeah...Melanie," I said, turning to look off in the distance.

"You're not close?"

"Are you close with your brother?" I may or may not had Googled the Kensingtons since Penn moved in and found out he had an older brother, Court, who seemed like a troublemaker.

"No."

"Why not?"

He slid his gaze to mine and then back to the road. "You're avoiding my question."

"Melanie is wonderful. She's seven years younger than me. She dances and sings and has straight As. She's had the same boyfriend since we moved to Charleston when she was eight. Basically, she's perfect."

Penn snorted. "Possibly the opposite reason as to why I'm not close with Court."

"What does that mean?"

"My brother is…a professional fuckup. He's never actually held a job, he has no real passion, he's fucked nearly every eligible woman in the city, and he doesn't give a shit who sees."

"How does he even survive?"

"Charm and a trust fund."

"Well, I guess Melanie isn't looking so bad."

"I don't get why you don't get along with her," Penn said. "What did she do to you?"

"Nothing. It's more how she made me look to my parents. Hard to compete with perfection. I'm not your brother, but this isn't exactly what my parents thought I'd be doing with my life."

"Now, that I completely understand. I'm pretty sure no one in my life wants me to be a philosophy professor."

"But you're so passionate about it."

"Doesn't matter."

I couldn't imagine Penn doing anything else. Not when I'd heard him speak about what he was working on in his book. Maybe other people just saw what he was doing rather than how much he clearly loved it and made snap judgments. Obviously coming from money and the Kensington name, it had to be hard. Most families would be ecstatic if their son had such a prestigious job but not the Kensingtons.

I decided to let the subject drop. It was clearly a sore subject. He'd been studying philosophy for more than a decade, and his family still didn't accept it. Talking about it wasn't going to help.

We changed the subject and got on easier topics. The music changed multiple times with all sorts of songs I'd never heard before. I was considering stealing his playlists. But he shocked me even further when he turned on Journey's "Don't Stop Believin'." With the top down and the wind whipping my hair in my face, we sang at the top of our lungs and enjoyed every minute of it.

The drive seemed to take half as long as it had when I first came out to the cottage. Either it was because I had an idea of where I was going or if it was just Penn.

Between the three weeks we'd spent alone in that house.and the careful truce we'd drawn that night out on the deck, things had changed with us. Penn hadn't come on to me since he had that look in his eye. But I couldn't deny that I found him attractive, and he was easy to talk to. He was too good to be true, which probably meant he was.

And I needed to stop fooling myself.

There was a reason I had been angry with him.

For everything he'd done to me that night in Paris. For the person I'd become due to those actions. How cheap and used I'd felt.

I never wanted to feel like that again.

But sometimes, when we were alone like that, it would all disappear. And I'd forget entirely why I was mad at him in the first place.

It was dangerous. He was dangerous.

I needed to be very careful.

"All right. Here we are," Penn said as he finished navigating the New York traffic like a pro.

My eyes traveled up, up, up the building off of Central Park. Somewhere up there, Katherine was waiting for me. Nerves bit at me. I liked Katherine. She seemed nice enough, but I couldn't figure out why she wanted to do this for me. I didn't know enough about her to make a judgment about who she really was. And until then, I knew I needed to keep my guard up.

"What are you going to be doing?" I asked.

"I'll be at my apartment with Totle. I brought some work with me," he said, gesturing to the leather messenger bag in the backseat. "I'll take your stuff up to my place with me."

"Okay. Maybe I should just…hang with you and Totle. I have work, too."

"Go on. Get out. Have a good time."

I sighed heavily and slung my purse over my shoulder. "Fine. I'll see you tonight."

"Looking forward to it," he said with a brilliant smile.

Then, I was on the sidewalk, alone, in New York City, and he was taking that beautiful smile and his even more adorable puppy far away. I double-checked my phone for instructions to get to Katherine's apartment and took the elevator upstairs.

I stepped hesitantly inside. I'd never seen an elevator that took you into a person's actual house. That was a bit disorienting.

"Hello?" I called out as I turned the corner.

"Natalie!" Katherine squealed and rushed toward me. She hugged me tight. "I'm so glad that you made it. Come inside. Mimosa?"

"Uh...sure," I said, taking the champagne flute out of her hand.

"How was the drive?"

"Easy."

Since Penn's friends didn't know that he was staying in the Hamptons, we decided not to enlighten them. I didn't mind them coming out to visit, but it would disturb the peace we had out there. And all the time I'd spent writing on my new project, which I still hadn't figured out a title for. My agent had been asking about it because I'd finally confessed to putting the other book aside. But I just wasn't ready.

"Good. I'm glad. Okay, let's get started."

"Started?" I choked out.

She'd told me that we were going to have a full day of pampering, but I hadn't thought she actually meant a full day. What could possibly take all day?

"Yes! We have a full day ahead of us—massage, facial, waxing, tanning, hair, and makeup."

My jaw dropped. I'd had massages, sure. When I'd swam in college, the trainers and physical therapists would sometimes massage out knots from the pool. They were usually intense and made you cry. For some reason, I didn't think that was the kind of massage she meant. The rest I'd never had the money to splurge on.

"It's going to be great!" Katherine said, tugging me into a bedroom that had been transformed into a day spa.

Then I was quickly whisked away by Emmanuel, who was gorgeous enough to be a male model. He spoke the entire time about his boyfriend, who actually *was* a male model. Besides that, he had a constant stream about how much I clearly needed these treatments. About how my skin was *begging* for hydration and how my body had more knots than a sailor and how utterly transformed my face was with carefully sculpted eyebrows. When he trimmed my hair, I quaked in fear that he'd lop it all off. But he was right that it needed it...that I needed all of it.

"This color is so trendy," Emmanuel said as he blew my hair out.

"Thanks. I like the silver more than my natural blonde."

"Well, it's not something I see often around here. More likely in the Village than the Upper East Side," he said with a laugh.

I bit my lip and nodded. I loved my hair, but it didn't exactly blend in. I could have walked off of the set of *Game of Thrones* with my Targaryen-white locks. Likely, I would be more comfortable in the Village too, but somehow, I'd landed on the Upper East Side.

"Everyone will be raving about this," Emmanuel said.

I just didn't know if it was going to be in a good way.

But when I stared at my reflection in the bathroom after six hours of pampering and another half hour of trying on designer dresses, I hardly recognized myself, even with my signature silvery-white hair down in voluminous super-model waves.

"Look at you," Katherine said. She twirled her finger in a circle, and I spun for her. "Who knew those incredible cheekbones and amazing eyes were hidden? Just look at your hair! It's so glossy. So *silver*. And that dress. It's perfect!"

"I can't thank you enough. I've never done anything like this before."

"Well, you will have to do it more often because damn."

I laughed and covered my mouth.

"Don't touch your face," Emmanuel said in dismay. "Or your hair."

"Right," I said, dropping my hand with a laugh. "You're incredible. Thank you."

"Rock it tonight, ladies," he said with a wink.

"Okay, final touches!" Katherine cheered. "Come with me."

I obediently followed her out of the bathroom and across the apartment to her bedroom. We stepped into her gigantic closet. She entered a code into a punch pad attached to a dresser, and it clicked open. She pulled out one of the drawers and revealed row after row of glittering jewelry.

"Holy shit," I breathed.

She laughed. "Basically."

She pulled necklace after necklace out of its case and held it against my neck. She'd admire it for a few seconds and then veto the selection.

"So," she said, holding a sapphire-studded choker against my throat, "have you spoken to Penn since he left?"

"I…"

She giggled at my reflection. Seeing my uncertainty about how to respond as discomfort. "It's okay. You can tell me. Obviously, you two have history."

"Yeah, but…it was a long time ago."

"Seemed pretty relevant that night he found you on the beach."

"Well, yeah, I hadn't seen him in six years."

"You're going to see him tonight though."

"Right. He's going to be there." I was a terrible liar. It was definitely not my forte, and sparring with someone like Katherine, it seemed relatively impossible to keep it up.

"Oh, yeah. Of course. I would just be careful," Katherine said, holding up a new necklace with a teardrop ruby at the center.

"Careful?"

"You know how Penn is."

"I know how he was."

Katherine shrugged. "Can a tiger really change its stripes?"

That was the question, wasn't it? The one I'd been asking myself for three straight weeks. I wanted to say yes. I wanted to believe that people could change. But I didn't really know if they could.

"Oh, this is the one!" Katherine crooned. She strung the band of diamonds around my neck and nodded. "They're perfect."

And they were.

Who knew that adding thousands of dollars' worth of diamonds could completely transform but not overpower an ensemble? Not me.

"Let me step into my Manolos, and we can head out," Katherine said.

I tried not to think about what Katherine had insinuated about Penn as we left her apartment and took a bona fide limousine to the gala. I wasn't here for Penn. Nothing was going on with us. And Katherine had merely been curious because of our history. That was all.

Luckily, it was easy not to think about seeing him again since I'd never been in a limo before. Nor had I ever been to a gala. And I couldn't believe it when there was a real red carpet and photographers waiting for us. Katherine exited the limo like the socialite she was to a roar of approval and the flash of cameras. She reached back to get me to climb out of the backseat. To my surprise, the crowd cheered again.

I was a nobody. Why the hell were they cheering for me?

"Smile, Natalie. They think you're beautiful. Own it."

I laughed and pushed my shoulders back. If I was going to spend one night living my fairy tale, I might as well enjoy it.

We walked the red carpet like stars. Katherine, I supposed, legitimately was, but she included me so completely that no one guessed that I wasn't. I was just another socialite out with my friend. Katherine assured me that, by the end of the evening, I'd have party invitations with everyone in the city who mattered. If we made it onto Page Six, then I'd have designers asking me to their fashion shows and offering for me to wear their clothes. It was the most bizarre night but totally addicting at the same time. No wonder Katherine did this full-time.

I smiled at the final camera and then took my last step into the main room where I stopped dead in my tracks.

Penn stood at the bottom of the stairs in a sharp-cut tuxedo. He looked up at me as if I were a dream. His mouth hung open slightly. His eyes swept up my body from the blue silk gown that revealed a sliver of leg in a thigh-high slit and hugged my curves to the diamonds at my throat and finally landed on my face. Our eyes met and locked. A current of desire shot through me. Mirrored and matched.

I walked the final steps down to his level.

"You look stunning," he breathed like a prayer.

"Thank you," I said. My cheeks flamed at his attention. I hadn't been embarrassed by any of the photographers outside, but one look from Penn, and I was a goner.

He held his arm out like he was a prince. "Shall we?"

And lost in my own fairy tale, I nodded and let him whisk me inside.

NATALIE

14

"Katherine did a pretty good job, huh?" Penn's gaze swept over me again. "Truthfully, you look equally as beautiful, lounging around in pajamas with your hair in a bun on the top of your head."

I laughed and swatted at him. "Stop. You're joking."

"Am I?"

And suddenly, I wasn't sure if he was.

"Well, a tux suits you. And I was just getting used to you in regular clothes."

"Just getting used to me?" he asked as he walked me through the room. He grabbed champagne for us off of a passing waiter's tray and then continued toward his friends.

"For so many years, you were this guy in a suit in my head."

"Did you think about me often?" he asked with a smirk on his pretty lips and raised his glass to take a sip.

"Only when I wanted to murder the male population."

He sputtered on his drink and burst into laughter. "How often was that?"

"Men do a lot of stupid shit. You'd be surprised how regularly I am prone to murder."

"Duly noted."

The truth was that I'd thought about Penn way too often in the last six years. He'd been my first. And the best. I might have been young, naive, and stupid, but I knew a good orgasm when it hit me. Nothing had really come close.

It was probably because he was more experienced than anyone else I'd ever been with since. A lot of sex had the ability to make him a better lover. Except...it could also have the ability to make him utterly selfish, and he hadn't been. And many men after him certainly had been. I didn't want to think that it was anything else though. I still couldn't admit to our chemistry. Even as I felt it bubbling up between us now.

Penn directed us to a corner of the magnificently decorated ballroom to where Lark, Rowe, and Lewis stood.

Lark moved forward first and pulled me into a hug. "Natalie, it's so good to see you!"

"You too."

"This is my boyfriend, Thomas," Lark said by way of introduction.

Thomas shook my hand and smiled as his eyes swept my dress.

"Nice to meet you," I said, quickly pulling my hand back.

I hadn't known that Lark had a boyfriend, and I was surprised she was into this guy. He was handsome, but I could read sleazeball all over him.

"You too. How do you know the crew?" he asked.

Penn swept in smoothly and said, "We're old friends."

Because saying I was the help probably wasn't right for this company, which sent a twinge of discomfort through my body. Tonight, I was someone else, which was fun. But also, it meant that who I *really* was…wasn't good enough for the occasion. And that put me on edge.

"That's right," Lewis spoke up. He stepped forward to hug me. "Good to see you again, gorgeous."

"You too," I said. Though I didn't know why I was going along with it. I wasn't ashamed of my job.

"How has the alone time at the beach been?"

"Rejuvenating. I started a new book."

"So, you're an author?" Thomas asked. "Have I read anything by you?"

Lewis slung an arm around my shoulders. "We're keeping her under tight wraps right now."

"Ah, so she's with Warren then?"

"Obviously."

I chewed on my bottom lip and said nothing. I remembered the horrible rejection letter that I had recently gotten from Warren. And now, I was standing around with the owner's son.

"What do you do?" I asked to get the heat off of me.

"I'm a senior executive for St. Vincent's Enterprises," he said smoothly with a wide grin at Lark.

"Wow."

The boyfriend working for her parents. Not exactly original. But it seemed like so much of this Upper East Side world was incestuous. Not that I had any room to judge. I'd only gotten into vacation home watching because I started with Amy's parents' place. At least I'd worked my way up on my own.

Penn cleared his throat. I turned to face him, and he was staring very pointedly at Lewis's arm still around my shoulders. I hadn't even noticed really. I wasn't sure if I was reading his look right because it couldn't possibly be that he was…jealous. Lewis was his best friend. He wouldn't do that to Penn. And we were just friends. Me and Penn and Lewis. Friends.

Still, I shrugged Lewis's arm off of my shoulders and glanced down at my empty champagne flute. "How did that happen?"

Penn held his hand out. "Why don't we dance?"

"Uh," I muttered.

Déjà vu hit me like a two-by-four. I remembered the time we had ballroom danced in Paris. The feel of his body against mine. The almost kiss that had left so much to the imagination. Dancing with him, even thinking about dancing with him, was putting me in uncomfortable territory. It was making me think not-so-friend-zoned thoughts.

We stood there for a second with his hand held out and mine half to him and half away. And then Katherine appeared, easily breaking the ice as she slid between us.

"There you are, love," she said to me, playfully linking our elbows. "I lost you in the crowd."

"I found her," Penn said.

"Ah, thank you for keeping her safe for me," Katherine said with a toothy smile. He didn't return it.

"We were just about to dance."

"Sorry to disappoint, but she's my date, not yours. And we have things to do, people to see."

Rowe snorted from where he had silently stood this whole time with his face buried in his phone. "Typical."

"Can't we just have *one* good night?" Lark asked on a sigh. "The mayor is here, and I can't have us fighting. Not when the First Lady is coming into the city next week."

"We're not fighting," Katherine said cheerfully. "And why ever would the First Lady come to the city? President Woodhouse has New York locked down. Shouldn't they be spending more time in swing states for his reelection bid?"

Lark grinned. "It's like you've actually been listening to me."

"Don't hold your breath," Rowe muttered.

"His challenger is from the Northeast, and he just wants to shore up his bets. Give a show of good faith."

"Plus, Elena Woodhouse loves my mother," Penn said. "They went to Harvard Law together."

My head was spinning with all the important talk. I had never felt more like a nobody from nowhere.

"You…know the First Lady?" I asked.

Penn shrugged. "I suppose."

Katherine rolled her eyes. "Enough with this. Come on, Natalie. I have some other people I want to introduce to you."

"I…okay," I barely managed to get out before Katherine dragged me away from the rest of the crew.

"So, the first person I want you to meet is a model friend of mine, Tara. And then there's this designer. You would so love her work. I also think Elizabeth is here. She designed the dress that you're wearing, of course."

I half-listened to her ramble on about a world of people I would meet and probably forget their names in a heartbeat. And I had no idea why it was even happening. Did she think, somehow, I was going to become her? Because I could wear her clothes, but this could never be my life.

Still, I followed in Katherine's vivacious wake. She knew *everyone*. In a room full of people, she wasn't just a magnet. She was a tornado. People didn't just gravitate to her. They were sucked into her vortex. I had never seen anything like it. It was both incredible and terrifying.

And exhausting.

Really exhausting.

Though she seemed totally energized by the experience. I

had clearly spent way too much time alone the last year to feel this excited about so many strangers.

"Oh my god, we just need to pop over and say hi to—"

Before she could even finish the statement, I jumped in, "Go ahead. I'm going to wait here for a minute. I need a breather."

Katherine frowned. "Are you sure?"

"Yeah. I'll be over in a minute."

She shrugged. "All right. I'll send champagne over. Yours is empty again."

I glanced down into my glass and frowned. Honestly, how *had* that happened? I had no idea how much I'd had to drink at this thing. My glass was constantly full. I never even had to think about it, and suddenly, there was more alcohol in my hand.

"Hey there," a strong voice said to me.

My eyes lifted to find a rather attractive man standing before me. He was clean-cut and in a sharp tuxedo with a square jaw and perfectly groomed hair. His eyes danced with mirth, as if he were enjoying a private joke, and his smile said something else altogether. He reminded me of every sleazeball frat boy who had tried to have sex with me in college. He was pretty but dirty underneath the two-thousand-dollar suit. It was as if he had a sign painted on his forehead that read, *Run away*.

"Uh, hi," I said carefully.

"Katherine sent me over here. She said you needed another drink."

"Oh, thanks."

I took the proffered drink in my hand, but I had no intention of imbibing any further. I was already tipsy, bordering on drunk. But something in my gut said not to trust this guy. He could have slipped something in the drink. I had no idea.

"Katherine says that you're one of the new Cunningham models."

"I...what?"

"Your dress is obviously the work of Elizabeth Cunningham, right?"

"Yes," I said quickly. Katherine had mentioned that was the designer. "Yes, this is from Cunningham Couture."

"And you look so"—he took a step closer—"delectable in it."

"Thank you," I said, edging a step backward.

He brushed my silver hair off of my shoulder. "Did you just get in from Hollywood?"

"Hollywood? Um...no."

"Huh," he said, eyeing my hair. "The hair is different. Not exactly New York fashion, is it?"

I shrugged. I really had no idea.

"I don't know if you know, but I have a special connection with a number of the Cunningham models."

"I didn't know that."

"We could get out of here, and I could show you."

"Who-who are you exactly?" I stammered.

I wanted out. Out, out, out. He gave me creep vibes. And I felt suddenly cornered.

"Katherine didn't tell you?"

"Why would she?"

He smirked and opened his mouth to reply, and then Penn was standing at the guy's elbow, jerking him backward. He whipped around as if he were going to punch Penn in the face and then stopped.

"What are you doing, Percy?" Penn growled.

"What I'm doing is none of your business, Kensington."

Percy?

Oh, for fuck's sake.

This was Katherine's fiancé, Camden Percy. The owner of

one of the largest chains of hotels in the world. No wonder everyone had seemed down about the pending nuptials.

"If you didn't notice, Natalie here seemed uncomfortable with your attention." He placed himself between me and Camden. "So you should back off."

Camden smirked devilishly. "I think we were getting along just fine."

"I know how you get along with women. She is not going to be one of them."

"That almost sounds like a challenge."

"Yeah, it is," Penn said calmly, his eyes seething.

Camden said with an eye roll, "I know you're all bark and no bite."

"Try me."

"Boys, boys, boys," Katherine trilled as she drifted over to where we were all clustered together. "Play nice."

Neither of the guys said anything. They just stared at each other in mutual hatred.

"I swear, you two are children." Katherine stepped over to me. "So, what do you think of my new project, Camden?"

Project? What did *that* mean exactly? I hadn't thought I was a project. I'd thought I was a...friend.

Camden slowly dragged his eyes from his staring death match with Penn to really look at me. "You said she was a Cunningham model."

Katherine waved a hand, and a wicked grin painted her face. "And you believed me."

"She's incredibly convincing," Camden said dryly. "In appearance at least. She doesn't seem to have a personality."

"Just because I have no interest in the way you approached me doesn't mean that I don't have a personality."

Katherine giggled. "See, she's perfect."

Camden narrowed his eyes. "Congratulations, Katherine," he said in a way that did not *at all* sound congratulatory.

Katherine frowned in disapproval as if she was waiting for the slap in the face to follow.

"You managed to make her beautiful. Money can buy almost anything it seems. Except class."

I winced, but he had eyes only for Katherine.

"But I guess class can buy you money if arranged properly."

"Percy," Penn said warningly.

Camden just smiled at him. "What? Can't you just wait until the day that I own your little Katherine?"

Katherine said nothing. Just stood there as stiff as a board.

"I'll be sure to rent her out to you," Camden said and then strode away as if his work there was done.

"Ren," Penn said softly.

"I'm fine," she said sharply.

"I'll just leave you two…" I said, backing away. I'd gotten the gist of that conversation. And there was enough to unravel that I felt like I needed a moment alone.

"No, Natalie," Penn said.

"You two look like you need a minute. I'll, uh, be in the powder room."

"I'll come with you," Katherine offered.

"No. No, that's okay. I can find it on my own."

Then I hurried away from their watchful gazes. From the man I'd thought I was getting to know. And the friend I'd thought I was gaining. And their shared history, a deep well that Camden had pushed us all into.

NATALIE

15

I stared at my own unreadable expression in the bathroom mirror. Well, tonight was a failure.

Penn and Katherine.

I didn't know how I hadn't seen it before. Now that I knew, it was so obvious. They were close friends. They'd known each other their entire lives. It wasn't unthinkable that they had been together or something...at some point.

I didn't know why I cared.

Because I did care.

Whenever I thought about it, I got this sick feeling in the pit of my stomach. Penn and I had just formed some kind of truce. We were living together, roommates, but that was it. I found him attractive. Very attractive. But I had no intention on acting on that. Or I hadn't until this moment—when jealousy hit me green in the face.

"Are you using this sink?" a short blonde woman asked me.

I hadn't even realized anyone else was in the restroom.

"Oh, no. Sorry." I stepped aside for her and tried to get myself back under control.

She washed and dried her hands methodically before turning to face me. "You're Natalie, right?"

"Yes," I said cautiously.

"I'm Addison, but my friends call me Addie."

She held her hand out, and I automatically shook it.

"Um…hi."

I got a good look at her. The honey-blonde hair, the very straight nose, and easy smile. She looked…familiar. But I couldn't place her. I didn't think I'd ever seen her before.

"I'm Rowe's twin sister." Her smile brightened. "I'm older by two minutes."

"Oh, wow!" I gasped. That was the resemblance. Now that I knew, it was uncanny. "I didn't know that Rowe was a twin."

"Yeah, we don't exactly dress alike anymore."

"Funny. And you call him Rowe?"

"Old habits. It's only weird when I stop to think about it." She shrugged. "We both hate our names, but he really got the short end of the stick. Archibald was never sticking, and Addison became Addie so easily."

"Makes sense," I said with a smile.

"I don't like to be the one to do this, but you can't trust them."

"What are you talking about? Trust…who?"

"The crew."

"Oh. We're just friends."

"They're not your friends. They lie and manipulate. It's like breathing to them. They can't stop it, and they don't care about who gets hurt in the crossfire."

"Where is this all coming from?"

"Look, I feel strange even saying this, but I thought I should warn you. I was part of the crew for years. But I got out. And as someone who has been there, I am telling you that they are not what they seem."

"Then how do I know that *you* are what you seem?"

She stuck her hand on her hip. "You don't have to believe me. But you are being used. Whatever they've said or offered, however they make you feel, they are using you for their own purpose. And you would be an idiot to let them."

I took a step back at the blunt way Addie had phrased that. I didn't want to believe what she'd said was true. I didn't know Addie at all. This was coming completely out of left field about people I hardly knew.

"I don't know you, and you don't know me or anything about my relationship with them."

"You're right," Addie said with a shrug. "But don't say I didn't warn you."

"Thanks. I guess."

Addie pushed open the restroom door ahead of me, as if her work here was done. But then she stopped and glanced back at me. "Just…do your own digging. Do you even know who Katherine's father is?" My blank expression must have said as much. "Ask around. Their closets are lined with skeletons."

She breezed out of the restroom in a swirl of yellow chiffon.

Well, I hadn't expected that. I felt strangely uneasy about Addie's revelations. I didn't know if she was telling the truth or if she had some ulterior motive. Nor did I know how much of it was true. If any of it was true.

I'd wanted a breezy fall, stuck on a beach in the Hamptons to finish my book. No distractions. No boys. Nothing but me, my computer, and lots and lots of words.

Suddenly, that seemed like such a distant illusion. And this felt like a dream I needed to wake up from.

My night hadn't been like *Cinderella*. I hadn't kissed my prince at midnight. I wasn't about to lose one of these shoes. I couldn't even imagine the price tag on the red-bottomed heels. But I was still going to turn into a pumpkin when all of this fake grandeur fell away and left me as the help once more.

I needed to leave.

That much was certain. I was out of place here. This wasn't *me*. It had never been me. Amy had forced me into a tight dress for that party in Paris six years ago. I was bohemian by nature. I liked my hair down in disarray from the sea salt or up in a messy bun on the top of my head. I liked flowy, oversized dresses in crazy prints with bell sleeves and lace. I wore wide-brimmed hats and no makeup. And in my world, there were no galas or diamond necklaces or sexy men in tuxedos, but there also wasn't any backstabbing or arranged marriages or skeletons in the closet.

So, it was time to go.

As much as I hated to admit it, I needed to tell someone. Someone who wasn't going to try to talk me out of it or argue with me. Someone like…

"Lewis!" I called, hurrying as fast as I could in these heels over to where he stood with another guy.

He said something to said guy and then met me halfway.

"What's wrong?" he asked immediately.

"Nothing. I'm just going to…head out. Could you tell Penn for me?"

"Wait, wait, wait, what?" His dark brown eyes widened with concern.

"I'm leaving."

"I got that much, but where are you going to go?"

I shrugged. I hadn't gotten that far. I just thought I would figure it out as I went. "I don't know. Back to the beach house?"

"In the middle of the night? How are you even going to get there? Any way you look at it, it's dangerous."

"Okay, fine. You're right. I know. I'll get a hotel or something. But I don't think I want to be here any longer."

It would be smarter to stay and figure out what I was doing with the rest of the night. But Katherine was probably planning to stay, and I hadn't exactly made plans for a slumber party. Penn, I didn't even know if I wanted to face him right now. I didn't know if I could keep all the questions running through my mind from bursting forth from my lips. It was better to stay on my own and take the bus back to the beach house in the morning.

"What is this about? Camden?" Lewis asked intuitively. "He's a dick. I wouldn't let anything he said upset you."

"I'm not upset by him. I could tell he was a dick."

"Then, why are you upset?"

"I just…don't belong here," I finally finished.

"Says who?"

"Well, Penn did that first night. And maybe he's right."

"The Upper East Side, admittedly, isn't an easy crowd. But leaving now will prove that they can walk all over you."

"It's not going to prove anything," I said, raising my chin, "because I'm not part of this crowd, and I never will be."

I turned to leave, but Lewis reached out and grasped my arm.

"Don't go running off into the night. You can stay at my place if you need to."

"I couldn't…"

"I'm offering."

"What are you offering exactly?" Penn asked, appearing before us.

Lewis hastily dropped my arm. "I was just convincing Natalie not to run out of here alone."

"You were going to leave?" Penn asked.

"Well, yeah. I am." I defiantly tilted my chin up.

"You don't have to do that. Camden left."

"This has nothing to do with Camden."

He narrowed his eyes. "If not Camden, then what?"

"I really don't want to talk about it with you. Or anyone." I turned back to Lewis. "I accept your offer. Can you take me back to your place?"

Penn's head turned to look at Lewis with shock written across his face. "What?"

Lewis held his hands up. "Hey, man, I didn't want her to run off into the night. I tried to convince her to stay."

"After the last couple of weeks," he said, looking back in my direction, "you were going to leave without saying anything?"

"Technically, I told Lewis to tell you," I said with a shrug.

"Wait, weeks?" Lewis asked.

"Yes, I've been staying at the beach house with Natalie this whole time," Penn said with as much defiance as me.

"Hey!" I chided.

We'd said we wouldn't tell his friends that he was there, so they wouldn't come bug us. He was about to ruin all of that.

"Okay, okay. I officially rescind my offer for you to stay at my place. I see that I stepped into the middle of this," Lewis said.

"You didn't step into the middle of anything," I told them both vehemently.

"I think I did." He nodded at us both and then left us alone.

"So, what really happened?" Penn asked, his voice lowering in concern.

"I said, I don't want to talk about it. You know what? I'm just leaving."

"Fine. I'll take you back to my place."

"Don't you need to stay?"

Penn arched his eyebrow. "What part of this party made you think I wanted to be here for anything other than you?"

I snapped my mouth closed, speechless. That was not what I'd thought he would say.

"Me?"

He nodded. "I hate galas, but I came to this one to spend time with you. And then Katherine stole you the entire time. So, I would be happy to get out of here with you."

I didn't have anything to say to that. It was…romantic. I'd sworn I wouldn't go down that road with him again. And still, my insides squirmed at the attention. I loved that he was ready to leave the party with me. And the look of concern on his face. And all the things that I shouldn't care about. Including the uncontrollable jealousy I'd felt when I realized that he and Katherine had been…or maybe currently were an item. Going home with him would be against everything we'd worked toward.

But I found myself nodding anyway.

Then we were out of the building and into a waiting cab, headed toward his place.

Silence stretched between us. A silence that was tense. I'd never experienced this from him before. In Paris, we had conversed so effortlessly that it had been my undoing. The last couple of weeks of silence had been noticeable but easy. As if he had always been meant to be there. The conversations we'd had since we started talking again were like Paris all over again.

Now, we were huddled together in the back of a cab without a word to say to the other. And dozens trapped just under the surface. Pride and years of pent-up anger holding them in place.

I tried to ignore whatever was coursing between us as I slid out of the cab and took the elevator up to the top floor of his building. The elevator ride was a silent battle of wills to see who would crack first.

What I'd heard tonight from Camden and Addie warred with what Penn had said at the end of the night. Perhaps I was overreacting about it all, but mostly, I was confused. I didn't know what was true or if I should even care. Let alone what I felt for Penn. The person he had been versus the person he was now versus the picture others had painted. Somewhere in it all was the truth.

"Are you going to tell me why you're so upset?" Penn asked once the elevator closed behind us and he'd gotten Totle from the bedroom.

"I'm not upset." Totle ran around my feet, and I hoisted him into my arms until he calmed down.

Penn just raised an eyebrow.

"I'm confused. I don't know…who you are. I don't know who any of you are or what you want with me."

"What we *want* with you? Why would we want something from you?"

I shook my head and turned away. "I'm either a charity case or *project* or something. Either way, I just want to know where I stand. I don't want to be forced into another situation where you guys have to lie about who I am or what I do." I whipped back around. "I'm not ashamed about what I do for a living."

"You shouldn't be ashamed."

"Then why lie?"

"It had nothing to do with your job and everything to do with Thomas and Camden. We hate Camden, and Lewis and I aren't particularly fond of Thomas. They both look down on everyone they consider beneath them."

"So, I'm beneath them?" I set Totle on the floor and strode away from Penn. His apartment was incredible, but I could hardly enjoy it as my anger intensified.

"I didn't say *I* thought so," he said carefully, following me.

"Well, what is it then? Am I a charity case? Katherine's project? Where do we stand?"

Penn slid his hands into his pockets and observed me evenly. "You are none of those things to me. I enjoy your company. I would like to continue to enjoy it."

"Who is Katherine's father?"

Penn's eyes widened and then quickly recovered. "Why?"

"I want to know."

"That's a very specific question. Why do you ask?"

I didn't know. I hadn't planned to ask. I didn't know if Addie had been manipulating me as much as she claimed everyone else was. But I couldn't stop wondering.

"Just tell me, Penn."

"Fine. Katherine's father is in jail. His name is Broderick Van Pelt."

"Wait…what?"

"He's in jail for fraud. They lost everything when he went under. The only thing the government couldn't touch was her trust fund and her apartment."

"Wow."

"And that's why she's with Camden. None of us really like him, but he has the money, and she has her name. Together, they look good on paper. But he's horrible."

"Jesus. I couldn't imagine marrying someone I didn't love. Being forced into something for a name or money. It seems archaic."

"It is," he confirmed. "Now…who told you about Katherine?"

"I met this woman in the restroom. Addie."

"Oh god," Penn groaned. "Addie was there?"

"Yeah. She said that you all were using and manipulating me."

Penn sighed heavily. "That sounds like Addie."

"Why?"

"We had a falling-out during high school. She was one of us, and then we had a friend leave school. She blamed us and left our group. We've been cordial, but she still blames us."

"Is it warranted?"

Penn shrugged. "She thought it was. But strangely, it coincided with Addie and Lewis's enormous breakup after dating on and off their entire life."

"Oh," I whispered.

"You think so little of us, so easily."

"Past experience tends to blend with the present. And anyway, what was that shit about you and Katherine?"

"Why?" he asked, taking a step closer. He was standing so near that our breaths mingled in the space between us. "Are you jealous?"

"No," I growled.

Yes. Definitely.

"Would it make you feel better if I said that there is nothing between me and Katherine?"

"I don't feel anything," I lied.

His hand slid up my arm to my shoulder and then into the perfect supermodel hair. "Liar."

"You don't know anything about me, Penn Kensington."

"I know that, right now, you want me to kiss you."

"And what would Katherine think?"

"I don't care. I feel nothing for Katherine. Nothing." His blue gaze held mine firm. "I've known her my entire life. If I had wanted to be with her before now, I could have been. But I don't want her. I want you."

"You do?"

He nodded.

His thumb trailed across my bottom lip, evaporating all the objections I'd had. My eyes closed, and my breathing hitched. Warmth spread through my lower half. I wanted him, too. Fuck, that was so much easier to admit than I'd thought it would be. The last three weeks had been some kind of slow torture of wanting him so desperately and knowing I shouldn't.

"Penn..."

"Natalie..."

"We shouldn't."

"Why not?"

"It's...a bad idea," I whispered.

"It's not."

"We end in flame."

"Burn with me."

I groaned at the words and then did what I never thought I would do again—I kissed him.

And it was everything. His lips were even better than I'd remembered. His hands were in my hair. I grabbed his tux. Our lips melded together in a frenzy that spoke of endless passion.

I couldn't get enough. There would never be enough. It was like falling, falling, falling with no end in sight. Just spiraling through this abyss and never coming up for air. No hope of landing. At least, not successfully. Because it wasn't really a landing if all you did was crash and burn.

"Penn," I pleaded against his lips.

"Don't."

And then he was kissing me again. Making me forget all about how unlikely we were to come out of this unscathed. Instead, there was just the way his lips moved, the swirl of his tongue against my own, the need to touch him everywhere. Up his chest, over his shoulders, his hair, his cheeks, that jaw. Dear god, this man!

I couldn't deny how good he felt. How my brain, my overactive writer's brain, screeched to a halt under his careful ministrations. The way he coaxed life out of me and made me feel as if I was finally living again. Forget my recent dry spell, everything felt dull and gray next to his vibrant Technicolor.

"My room," he suggested, walking us a step backward.

I opened my eyes and met his blue with my own. Saw the desire laced in his expression. The need to have me again. Claim me as he once had.

It was powerful. Heady. Potent.

And a reminder of what had happened last time.

The girl I'd been.

The girl he'd ruined.

I jerked backward. My hand flew to my mouth. Those traitorous lips.

He saw it. He knew what it meant. "Natalie, please."

"I…I can't," I gasped. "I don't want this. I don't want you."

He reached out as if he could change my mind. And I was sure those hands could. I knew the power they held and the things they could do to my body.

But I didn't have any other words for him. I couldn't be that person again.

PENN

16

*W*hat the fuck had just happened?

Natalie had just fled.

This had never happened to me before. Not that every girl wanted to fuck me, but the ones who came back to my apartment and made out with me did. And here Natalie was, in my apartment, in that incredible fucking dress with bedroom eyes…and she'd claimed she didn't want me.

It was a bald-faced lie. And yet she'd looked terrified when she uttered it.

Terrified. Like I would hurt her again. Like I had the last time. Here it was. The moment of truth. My past coming back to bite me in the ass. Again. Just like it always did. No matter what I did to come out on the other side, it was always there, taunting me. And I saw it there on her face as clear as day. But I didn't want it there. I wanted to make it right.

I raced after her and got there in time to see her slam the bedroom door.

To *my* bedroom.

I sighed. Well, this was going to be…great. I knew she

wasn't going to like that. Not after her latest moment of fleeing from my presence.

"Natalie…"

"I don't want to talk about it."

"Trust me, I'm well aware. But that's my bedroom."

She was silent on the other side of the door for long enough that I wasn't sure if she'd heard me. She had clearly just gone into the first room that she found. And I didn't care if she wanted to stay in there. But I'd figured she'd want to know at least.

The door finally cracked open. She had her arms crossed over her chest. "Where should I sleep?"

"The guest room down the hall, second door on the right. I put your things in there this afternoon."

"Fine." She shouldered past me and went down the hallway.

I couldn't just let it lie. "I think we should talk," I said as I trailed her.

"No," she said flatly. "I said what I had to say."

"Your lips said something entirely different."

She wrenched open the guest bedroom door. "Just forget it ever happened."

I grabbed the door before she could slam it in my face. Our eyes met. Fury meeting desire. And then she softened for just a second, and she was back.

"And what if I can't do that?" I asked.

She dropped her gaze and sighed. "That's your problem. Not mine."

She tugged on the door, and I let it go, watching as it closed behind her.

Fuck.

Forget that kiss?

That kiss? Was she out of her mind?

No one was going to forget what had just happened. This

wasn't how I'd thought this night would end up. Not even fucking close.

We'd spent the last three weeks together, alone at the beach house. Bet or no bet, I wanted Natalie. I'd wanted her the first time I saw her in Paris. I'd wanted her that first night in the Hamptons. And every moment I spent with her intrigued me more and more. Her passion for writing, the hours she spent focused on her work, the way she read into my own passion with interest, and not to mention, her love for my ridiculous dog.

I knew that she had hated me after Paris, but I'd thought that we'd gotten past that. It appeared I was wrong. Really fucking wrong.

I couldn't put my past behind me. Why did I expect her to do the same? No, I needed to face it, it was always going to haunt me. The beast within clawing at my skin to get out and unleash once more. To break free from the cage I'd locked him in so long ago.

I wanted Natalie.

The beast didn't care how I got her. I did.

One step forward and two giant steps back. Natalie so close and yet so far.

I quieted the part of me that would lie, scheme, and manipulate to get to her. I didn't have to be that person. I could win her another way.

So, I retreated to the kitchen and poured myself a rather large glass of scotch. I plopped down on the couch and took a good, long sip. Maybe booze would help.

I'd spent the last six years of my life trying to find balance, to attain the good life. The one I'd read about from the greats. The one that I'd studied methodically. I'd fought my own nature and distanced myself from my past life. I'd been on the right path. Then one look at her, one touch from her, and I was throwing it all out the window.

What were ethics and happiness and attaining the highest level of philosophical reasoning when Natalie stood before me, a larger puzzle than them all?

THE DRIVE back to the Hamptons had none of the ease or comfort of our drive into the city. Natalie stared down at her phone the entire way, texting away. Totle was passed out in her lap. I tried to carry on a conversation once or twice, but I got sick of one-syllable answers real quick.

I had just turned up the music, drowning out my own thoughts with Mae's killer lyrics, when her phone rang.

She silenced the volume with a sigh and answered, "Hey, Katherine."

My ears perked up. Oh, this was going to be good.

"Yeah, I can't do brunch. I already left."

We had already left. *We*, I corrected for her.

"Oh, Lewis told you that Penn was at the beach house, too?" she said softly.

Fuck. Just peachy. I really wanted to hear the other side of this conversation.

"Yeah, he's here. But we're both working, so you probably shouldn't visit."

Thank god.

"Look, I know I'm some kind of project for you, but I can't hang out all the time. I have work to do and a book to finish. Maybe another time, okay?"

Katherine must have been backpedaling hard with whatever she said next. Natalie looked skeptical by it all, but she seemed to soften a tad by the end.

"All right. I get it. Maybe let's talk later."

She hung up the phone, and uncertain, I peeked over at her.

"What did Katherine have to say?"

Natalie shrugged and looked back out the window. It was several minutes before she said anything at all. "She said she hadn't meant project how it sounded and that she was sorry for hurting me."

I kept my face neutral. That was such a *line* from Katherine. She was never really sorry for how she treated people, but it wasn't as if I could say anything at this point. I was the other side of this bet even if my intentions were pure. Hers weren't, and Katherine had a tendency to dive in too deep.

"It was really Camden who was the dick anyway. Katherine was just reacting to him," Natalie murmured and then turned the volume back up, so she didn't have to talk to me anymore.

It felt like a lifetime before we got back to the house. As soon as I stopped, Natalie had Totle on his leash and was hurrying inside with her bag slung over her shoulder. I gritted my teeth. This was a mess.

I grabbed my own bag out of the trunk and followed her inside. To my surprise, she was standing in the living room, waiting for me.

"Hey," she murmured.

"She speaks."

She shook her head. "You know what? Never mind."

"Wait," I said, reaching for her. "What were you going to say?"

She sighed and dropped her shoulders. "I want us to go back to the way things were before…"

"Before what?"

"Before we kissed."

"Do you really think that's possible?"

She bit her lip, and all I could think about was sucking it into my mouth. The taste of her. The feel of her. Going back wasn't an option.

"It has to be. And if you can't do that, then…maybe you should go."

"I'm not going to leave, Natalie." I knew that I should back down, but I couldn't believe how much she was lying to herself. "There's something here. I know that you can feel it."

"I do," she admitted softly. "I really do. But even if I did, I am only here for another month or so unless my contract is extended. What would even happen? Nothing. I'd take another job and leave. It would be pointless."

"Or you could stay," I found myself staying. "And we could find out."

"You don't believe what you're saying." Her voice shook as she got the words out.

I arched an eyebrow. "Don't I?"

She opened her mouth and then closed it, as if she couldn't believe what I'd just said. I saw her resolve cracking. The tentative rope she had been balancing on tipping out from under her feet. She took a step forward. I took one closer. Then she stilled and straightened her spine.

"I'm not stupid. I am not the first or the last in the long line of women Penn Kensington has seduced. I don't want to be an idiot here and jeopardize my job or my sanity," she said very calmly. "I would rather if we remained friends. I thought we were good as friends."

Friends.

Fuck. I was being friend-zoned.

I knew that she wanted me. She'd admitted as much. Yet here we were. Our past getting in the way of our present. My past…once again. Fucking great.

"Okay," I finally muttered.

"Okay?" she asked with wide eyes.

"We can be friends."

"Oh," she breathed uncertainly. "What's the catch?"

"No catch. You said that's what you wanted, and I can respect your wishes."

"I…appreciate that."

"You don't have to appreciate when someone respects you. It should be expected."

She smiled tentatively. "Well, thanks anyway." She wavered in place for a minute, as if she couldn't decide whether or not I was really telling the truth. Then, she nodded. "Just so you know, my best friend, Amy, is coming into town next weekend."

"Oh, you can have friends over but not me?"

Natalie wrinkled her nose. "I think I had enough of your friends last night. And anyway, you already told Lewis that you were here and he told Katherine. So, cat is out of the bag."

"Well, maybe I'll invite Lewis next weekend too."

She shrugged. "Do whatever you want."

She went to the back door to let Totle inside, and I watched the sway of her hips with hunger. She said we were just friends. But damn that kiss. No one could deny that kiss.

Still, if she wanted us to just be friends, I could do that…for now.

PART III
ALL'S FAIR IN LOVE AND WAR

NATALIE

17

Kissing Penn had been such a dumb move. Now, we were in this strange in-between state. Not straddling the line between hate and friendship anymore, but between friendship and…more.

That left us teetering precariously in each other's presence.

And he was a mystery. I didn't know what he actually wanted from me, and I didn't want to find out either. I felt like I was just some conquest. A box to check off—seduced my one-night stand and made her like me again.

I would rather keep my heart and body safe. I'd said no distractions while I was here, and Penn was distraction number one. I needed to get past this and forget about him.

It amazed me how easily we had fallen back into the routine we'd adopted. The fact that he actually kept to his word. He hadn't made another pass at me. We hadn't even been close to each other. We'd just passed each other's existence with Totle as the ping-pong ball.

A few days later, I was out on the back deck, trying to figure out where I was in my story and absentmindedly throwing a small tennis ball for Totle, when my phone rang. The interior decorator had left earlier that morning, so I wasn't expecting to hear from anyone.

Definitely not my sister.

"Melanie?" I asked in surprise as I picked up the phone.

"Nat," she blubbered. "Thank god you answered."

Then she immediately broke down into a hysterical fit.

"Mel, are you okay? What happened? Is it Mom and Dad?"

"No, no, everyone...is...fine," she stammered through her tears.

"Tell me what's going on."

"Michael...broke...up...with me."

"Oh, honey," I whispered.

Michael and Melanie had been inseparable since, basically, the day that they met on the playground in third grade. They'd dated all through middle school and high school. I'd figured they would graduate together, get married, and have the requisite two-and-a-half kids.

"I can't believe...he did...this," she said.

"Me either. What happened?" I stood from my seat and walked to the edge of the deck.

Melanie and I had never really been close. We liked different things, and with the age gap, we'd never bonded. But I loved her fiercely and I was glad that she'd called me about this.

"He said that he just didn't...love me like that...anymore. That...that we'd always be friends. And oh, I don't know," she gasped. "I don't know what he was going on about. But, now, he's taking Kennedy Mathers to homecoming this weekend."

"Wait, isn't that your best friend?"

"Yeah." She broke down into sobs again. "Ex-best friend."

"Ugh, Mel, I'm so sorry. What an asshole. I can't believe he would do that to you after all the years you'd been together. And then to take your best friend to homecoming. What are you going to do?"

"What…do you…mean?" She hiccuped. "What can I do?"

Sometimes, I forgot how young Melanie really was. She'd only ever had one boyfriend, and she'd never been broken up with before. I, on the other hand, knew all about breaking up and being broken up with.

"Well, first of all, you can't text or call him from now on."

"What? How can I do that?"

"Second," I continued on, "you have to hide him on all social media. I'd tell you to block him if I thought you could handle it."

"I can't block him!"

"Third, you should come up to New York City this weekend with Amy and visit me. Then you won't be there during homecoming to bear witness to the bullshit he's about to unleash on you."

Melanie hiccuped one more time. "You want me to come visit?"

"Yeah, I do." And I found that I really did. She was my sister. She was family. "I don't want you to have to deal with Michael and Kennedy alone. I'd rather you be here."

"I don't know if I can get out of dance."

"Claim a family emergency or something."

"Okay," she said, already sounding stronger. "Okay, I'll come. I think…that'd be a good idea. But I'll have to convince Mom and Dad."

"Let me handle them. I've got this."

"Thanks, Nat. I'm glad I called."

"Me too."

I chatted with her for the next hour until she cried herself hoarse but didn't sound like she was going to keel over. I hated that some douche could bring her down so much.

Michael should be glad that I wasn't in town. I'd go to his stupid mansion and give him a piece of my mind.

After a quick call with my parents, I got the details confirmed for Melanie to come up to the city this weekend. Though it cost a small fortune, which I pitched in for. It was only Amy who groaned in dismay that Melanie was coming along for the ride. But Amy was like that about everything, so I didn't take it to heart.

The real question, the one I'd been putting off, dealt with a certain blue-eyed devil. I took a deep breath and then wandered back inside to find Penn. He was standing in the kitchen, prepping steaks for the grill tonight.

"Medium or medium rare?" he asked me when I entered.

"Uh, medium."

"Wrong answer. Medium rare is the correct choice for good-quality beef."

"Then why ask?"

He glanced up at me and smiled. My heart fluttered. I carefully reined it in.

"It was a test, not an opinion."

"You're ridiculous."

"Guilty."

"So, I have a question for you. My little sister just went through a terrible breakup."

"That sucks."

"Yeah," I said, sinking into the seat at the breakfast nook. "They'd dated forever, and he just broke up with her to take her best friend to homecoming."

"Low blow."

"Tell me about it." I wanted to chop off his balls and feed them to him, I was so mad at him. "Anyway, I told her to come into town with Amy. I kind of want to pick them up when they get in on Friday. So…can I borrow your car?"

Penn finished prepping the steaks and then turned to face me, leaning back against the counter. "That would be a no."

"Ugh, really? I don't want to take the bus, but I don't have a car here. It'd be so much easier."

"I could drive you though."

"That would not be necessary."

"Come on. That's what friends do for each other, Natalie."

I gritted my teeth as he threw my own words back in my face. "It would just be there and back. It'd be boring. You wouldn't want to come."

"No way. You can't do that to your sister. You know what the best thing for a breakup is, right?"

"Icing?" I guessed.

Penn laughed. "Icing? What the hell?"

"Amy's mother has this thing that, whenever something goes bad, she cracks open a tub of icing and eats it straight from the jar. It's a tradition now."

He shook his head in disbelief. "I was going to go with getting wasted in the city and having sex with a stranger."

"Oh my god, we are not going to take my seventeen-year-old sister out in the city, so she can hook up with someone."

"And here I thought you wanted her to get this guy."

"I want her not to think about him, not make the same mistakes I did," I said, standing.

"Haven't you ever heard the phrase, *The best way to get over someone is to get under someone else?*"

"Of course, but she's my little sister. And it's not like you would know anything about getting over a breakup!"

He shrugged one shoulder. "You'd be surprised."

Well, now, I was surprised…and intrigued.

"I don't think it's a good idea."

He shrugged. "If you say so."

"I do."

"All right. I'll drive you on Friday then. It's a date."

"It's not," I grumbled with the shake of my head.

"See you for dinner."

"That's not a date either," I warned him.

"Didn't say it was," he said with a wink.

"OH, OH!" I cried, pointing my finger toward the two brunettes standing on the sidewalk at JFK International Airport. "That's them."

Penn veered the Audi through the traffic toward where Melanie and Amy were waiting. Totle stood up on my lap with his head halfway out the window and barked at them. I laughed, holding on to him so that he wouldn't jump out of my lap as Penn pulled up to the curb.

I handed Totle off to Penn and then hurried out of the car. I threw my arms around Melanie first, and then Amy crashed into us. "Oh my god, I missed you so much."

"I missed you, too," Melanie said, already sniffling.

Amy shook her head and released us. "I mean, you're all right."

"Shut up. You missed me."

"Obviously. But I do love the perks of your job." Amy's head swiveled to find Penn stepping out of the car and walking toward us. Her eyes rounded. "All of the perks."

Melanie furrowed her brows at Amy's statement, and then she glanced over at Penn. The furrow disappeared, and her jaw dropped. "Is that...the guy you're living with?"

"Yes," I said tightly. "Melanie, this is Penn. Penn, my little sister."

He held his hand out with a bright smile on his stupid pretty face. "Pleasure to meet you."

"Uh, yeah, definitely," Melanie said.

"And you must be Amy," he said, moving to my best friend.

"That's me. The BFF. The one who knows all her secrets," she said evenly. She might find him hot, but she was still my bestie. The one person who knew how heartbroken I really had been after Paris. And the person I'd called after our kiss last weekend.

"Ah, so you're the person I bribe to get her to open up?" Penn asked as he reached for her bag.

"Good luck with that," Amy said.

"I can be quite persuasive."

"I bet you can," Amy drawled.

Penn just laughed, clearly entertained by Amy's antics. He popped the trunk and deposited the suitcases in the back.

"Don't mind Totle," I told them as I opened the back door.

Totle stood on all fours and stared out at them with big puppy-dog eyes. Both Melanie and Amy melted into a puddle of goo in one look. Forget Penn Kensington. Totle was the real chick magnet.

Melanie scooted in first, scooping Totle into her lap and cooing over him like he was a newborn baby. Amy followed behind her, reaching for the puppy and forgetting me entirely.

"Attention hog," I muttered.

Penn looked over at me and grinned. "All set."

"Great. Let's get back."

We dropped into the front seats. I turned down the radio and swiveled to look at my sister and best friend. Sometimes, I thought that they looked more like sisters than Mel and I did. I had white-blonde hair down to my waist and blue eyes. Melanie had shoulder-length brown hair and hazel eyes that looked green against her green dress. I preferred comfortable, bohemian styles, and she liked short, skintight attire that showed off her dancer body. She was as dark as I was light. Two sides of the same coin.

"You're going to love the beach house," I told them. "It's massive."

"Michael had a massive beach house," Melanie muttered.

"And we're not thinking about Michael this weekend."

"I know. I know. You're right."

"The other option," Penn said, cutting in as her veered us back into traffic, "is that we spend tonight in the city."

"Penn," I warned.

"I've never been!" Melanie crowed.

"I'm from here. So, I could show you around."

"We agreed we were going to go back because I have work."

"You don't have work," Penn responded.

"Oh, come on, Nat, please," Melanie begged. "I want to see New York."

"Yeah, Nat," Amy said with a Cheshire grin on her face. "We want to see the city."

"You've been before," I accused. But I saw the light in Melanie's eyes that hadn't been there a second before. And I couldn't deny her this if she wanted it. "Fine. We'll go to the city."

"Yes!" Melanie said. "I'm so excited!"

I sank back into my seat and glanced over at Penn. "Happy?"

"I am actually," he said. "I wanted to show you around last weekend and didn't get to. Now, I get to."

"Serendipitous," I drawled.

It wasn't that I didn't want to go into the city. I did. I wanted to show Melanie around the big city for the first time. Sip lattes with Amy at tiny craft coffee shops and shop at boutiques in Soho. Get Melanie into her first real club and dance the night away.

But...I didn't want to do all that with Penn. With that looming complication over my head. Now that he had weaseled his way into our fun, I had to figure out how to navigate his presence.

Of course, he'd done everything that I'd asked of him. He hadn't pressured me for more or even asked about the kiss again. He'd hardly mentioned it, except to repeat that we were friends. But the way he said the word *friends*...it spoke volumes about what he thought of it.

That we were absolutely not just friends.

And his lips had every intention of reminding me of that fact.

NATALIE

18

I shouldn't have worried. We'd had the perfect day in New York City.

We had dropped Totle off in Penn's apartment and then wandered the city. Penn took us to all of his favorite haunts—a coffee shop that was to die for, a sushi restaurant that I would have dreams about, and even an art exhibit that he and Amy swooned over for a full hour. We'd listened to a musician in Washington Square Park and watched an impromptu flash mob on the subway, and now, we were walking Totle around Central Park as the sun set on the perfect day.

Melanie was eating an ice cream cone as we walked down the stairs toward Bethesda Fountain. In our hours of walking, she hadn't complained once all day about the high heels on her feet. I wanted to complain, and I was in flats.

"I wish I could eat like this at home," Melanie said, groaning over the ice cream.

"You can," I told her.

"Ha! With dance and crop tops? No way."

Her life was sometimes so distant from mine.

CRUEL MONEY

"You work out so much; you can eat whatever you want."

Melanie shrugged. "I don't think so. We weigh in with the coach every week."

"Barbaric," Amy said with a laugh.

"Competition season is coming up. It's important to look our best." Melanie bit her lip. "Sometimes, it's really dumb though. I think it makes people eat too few calories. I just try to stay in a range, but I'm not going to starve myself or anything."

"Good. Mom would probably kill you anyway."

"She'd divine it," Melanie said, giggling.

"Tea leaves?" I guessed.

"Oh no, she's all about horoscopes and divining futures from the stars right now."

"Your mother might as well be a centaur," Amy said.

"Ten points for Gryffindor," Melanie cheered.

Amy scoffed. "Hufflepuff."

I shook my head at their antics. "She has her eccentricities."

"Don't we all?" Amy muttered.

"Oh, oh," Melanie said, finishing her cone. "Take pictures for me. My followers need to know about my family emergency."

Amy cackled and took her phone. "Let the artist go to work."

Penn watched our impromptu photo session with a pensive smile on his face. And for a few minutes, as we all jumped in and out of pictures, posing with Totle and each other, I forgot that Penn was a Kensington. That his mother was the mayor. That he had billions. That we had a history.

We were just a young couple enjoying the city with friends.

Harmless. Easy. Normal even.

He even took us to the Cherry Hill Fountain from *Friends*

and proceeded to take his shoes off, roll his pants up, and get *in* the fountain with Melanie. She screeched with laughter as they pretended to be the characters from the show, which was Mel's absolute favorite. I swore, she wanted to be Rachel when she grew up.

Amy was busy snapping pictures of them on Melanie's camera. I held Totle's leash.

"So, why aren't you fucking this guy?" Amy asked.

"Amy!" I groaned.

"Seriously, Nat. I don't get it. Look at him!"

And I did. I really, really did. Because dear fucking god, it wasn't even just that he was gorgeous—because he was. It was that he had given up a day of writing to make my sister feel better. He was in the fountain in the beginning of October, probably freezing his ass off in the water. He was doing all of this…for what? For me? I didn't have an explanation. At least not one that made sense to me.

"I know," I finally said.

"I mean, you're here for another month, right?"

"Pretty much."

"I think a month of really hot, casual sex sounds incredible."

"Amy, I can't."

"Why not?" she hissed at me, turning the camera to video and calling at them, "You need umbrellas!"

"Ahh! We need umbrellas!" Melanie said through her laughter.

"You know why not," I hissed back at her. "Our history."

"Just think about it, Nat. You'd get *that* for a month."

And oh, now, I was thinking about it.

I thought about it when they got out of the fountain and when we went back up to his apartment and as we got dressed to go out clubbing that night. Thank god Amy had something I could wear and Melanie and I had the same size feet.

Penn Kensington had gotten under my skin.

He'd crawled beneath the surface, and there was nothing I could do about it.

I thought he was hot. I clearly remembered how good he had been in bed. I even realized that everything that had happened that night so long ago wasn't a lie. But I never really gave him the benefit of the doubt that he could have actually changed. That he wasn't just some affluent manwhore looking to get his dick wet.

Up until this point, I'd had no reason to believe that he wanted me for anything more than sex. But today seemed... different. In his element, in his city, he was the king, lord, master, ruler of all. And still...funny, kind, and down to earth. It was a conundrum.

One I didn't know how to face.

"Ready?" Penn asked, appearing in the doorway to the guest bedroom.

"Yep." I pulled my hair over one shoulder. "Where are you taking us again?"

"Club 360. It's a rooftop bar on top of a Percy hotel."

I wrinkled my nose. "Camden Percy is hardly my favorite person."

"Join the club. But 360 is the best that money can buy. So, that's where we're going."

"Oh my god," Melanie said, veering out of the bedroom in a skintight blood-red dress. "Did you say Club 360?"

Penn nodded.

"Celebrities go there. It's on Page Six all the time."

"You do know that Penn is kind of a celebrity, right? His mom is the mayor."

Melanie waved her hand at him. "Yeah. But, like, fashion icons. I can't wait!"

She ran back down the hallway and called out Amy's name. As if Amy cared about fashion icons. The woman who liked poor, starving artists.

"You'll be able to get her in?" I asked hesitantly.

He just smirked. "I'm Penn Kensington."

"Right. Ye who opens doors."

"Shall we?" he asked, dramatically bowing at the waist.

"Who are you?" I couldn't help but ask. It was part-joking and part-serious.

My eyes bored into him, trying to discover the secrets buried down deep. Who exactly *was* Penn Kensington?

He straightened and opened the door. "Why don't you stick around and find out?"

I arched an eyebrow but didn't respond as Amy and Melanie filed out. We took a cab to Percy Towers, and good to his word, Penn whisked us straight to the top of the building and into Club 360. Everyone already apparently knew who he was and didn't care how old the three beautiful women he was escorting inside were. Melanie, to her credit, sauntered inside like she owned the place. All long legs, dancer's grace, and confidence.

Amy shook her head. "She is going to be a hellion when she goes to college without a boyfriend."

"Tell me about it. I don't know how my parents keep up."

"I'm pretty sure they've resigned themselves to Melanie's over-the-top personality and expensive tastes."

"Tastes they can't afford."

Amy shrugged. "Doesn't seem to stop her."

"No, it doesn't." I pulled Amy into a hug. "Thanks for coming. I know this isn't your scene."

"Well, I thought that I'd be lying on a beach all weekend with my bestie, but, eh, I'm with you. That's all that matters." Amy glanced around the glitzy locale. "I do wish there were at least a *few* artsy types here. In Paris, you get them at these sorts of places."

"Ah, Paris, where a girl can have a different deadbeat artist every night."

Amy sighed. "Living the life."

"I love you. Let's do some shots."

Penn touched my elbow and leaned into me. The music was already loud enough that Amy and I had to raise our voices, but Penn just put his lips against the shell of my ear. I shivered all over at the touch.

"I have a booth in the back. Follow me."

"When did you get a booth?" I asked.

"This afternoon."

"They weren't all booked?"

"This is my city, remember?" Penn said by way of explanation.

Amy watched me with keen eyes. I knew exactly what she was thinking. I held up a finger to keep her from saying anything. Or for my brain to go back to where his lips had just been.

The three of us followed Penn to a circular booth with bottle service. A bartender was already popping the cork on a bottle of champagne, and I laughed as I saw Lewis seated.

"Lewis!" I cried.

I was happier to see him than I'd thought I would be. Of all of Penn's friends, he had been the friendliest and most welcoming. Well, aside from Katherine, but I wasn't entirely sure that she didn't have ulterior motives. And it didn't sit well with me that she had called me her project. I'd enjoyed our time together, but I wanted to be friends, not someone she had to doll up all the time.

"Hello, gorgeous." Lewis dragged me into a hug and then pushed a glass of champagne into my hand. "Drink up and tell me who these lovely ladies are."

I introduced him to Melanie and Amy. He zeroed in on Melanie's scandalous outfit and grinned.

"My seventeen-year-old sister," I added quickly to the introduction.

Lewis's eyes snapped up, and Melanie huffed. "You don't have to tell everyone, Nat."

No, I didn't. But she was still my little sister, and I would protect her as much as I could.

Lewis turned to Amy instead. "What's your drink of choice?"

"Tall, dark, and broke," Amy said with a wink. "Sorry, handsome."

Lewis howled with laughter. "I must admit, that is one I have never heard before."

"Well, I'm Amy Montgomery. It's a pleasure. Know any broke artists who like to draw nudes?"

"I think we're going to be good friends," Lewis said. "Dance?"

Amy laughed in surprise. Usually, her brush-off worked on most guys. "Definitely. You're too cute to say no to."

"Cute," Lewis said, as if wounded. "Kiss of death."

"Ah, you've heard my nickname then," she said and then dragged him out to the dance floor by his tie.

Melanie downed a glass of champagne and then pointed in their direction. "I'm just going to go…"

"Stay close to Amy. We don't want to lose you."

"Thanks, *Mom*," Melanie said with an eye roll.

"Just be safe, okay?"

Melanie grinned at me as she disappeared into the crowd.

"She's not going to be safe, is she?"

"I have the bouncers watching for her already, so she can't leave without me knowing. And they'll stop her at the door. She's perfectly safe here."

I stared up at him in shock. "You already thought of all of that?"

He shrugged. "Yeah. We've had to do it before with Lewis's younger sisters, Charlotte and Etta. They hated us for it, but it kept them from doing anything really stupid."

"That's actually...kind of sweet."

"Yeah?"

"In an overprotective way," I said, raising the champagne glass to my lips.

His hand brushed my waist. "Come dance with me, Natalie."

I surprised both of us by putting my hand in his without complaint and letting him guide me out onto the dance floor. I didn't know what had compelled me to do it. Maybe it was Amy's comments. Maybe that kiss was still stuck in my head. Or maybe it was just how much fun we'd had all day, but I didn't want to argue with him. I just wanted to enjoy myself.

We moved into the center of the dance floor where Lewis and Amy were dancing mere feet away. My eyes were locked on his chest as his hands moved to my waist. I didn't know what to do with my own for a second, as if I'd lost all capability to process being this close to him. Then, my hands were on his chest, guiding up the firm pecs and to his shoulders. I tilted my chin up to look into that handsome face, and he smiled as if we were the only two in the room.

Our bodies swayed in that moment with a remembered fluidity. Hips rocked side to side. Movements synchronized to the music. Heat coming off of our bodies despite the evening chill.

His lips looked so inviting. And I needed to stop staring. Because I was the one who had said that I didn't want him. I was the one who had walked away from this.

I tried to turn in his arms so that I wouldn't have to face those intense eyes. But he held me in place.

"Don't," he said.

"Don't what?" I breathed.

"I like to be able to look at you."

"You're a real charmer. You know that?"

He grinned and tugged me even closer so that we were chest-to-chest. He shifted one of my legs between his and moved his hips in a way I distinctly remembered. My pulse quickened in tempo with the music, and I forgot all about us being in public or anyone else around us. I had no concept of time. Only that we were still dancing. My feet ached, and I needed another drink. But neither of us pulled away.

Until Melanie literally ran into us.

"Nat...Nat," she slurred. "Some guys bought me drinks."

I yanked away from Penn and reached for my teetering little sister. "How many drinks? Are you okay?"

"We did a couple rounds of shots. I've done worse," she said and then snorted.

"Did you watch them make the drinks? You didn't look away?"

"Yes, of course! Who do you think I am?" She swayed precariously on her heels. "I finally feel so loose. Who cares about Michael Baldwin and that bitch Kennedy anyway? Let's do shots, Natalie!"

"I'm not sure that's such a great idea."

Melanie dramatically rolled her eyes and then turned to Penn. She grinned drunkenly. "What about you?" She rested her hand on his arm. "You're pretty."

Penn chuckled and then removed her hand from him. "How about some water instead?"

"No! Shots!" she insisted.

"What's going on?" Amy asked, appearing at my side with Lewis.

"Melanie made some friends who got her wasted."

Melanie teetered again. "I think we should all drink more.

The night is young!" She leaned forward into Amy's face. "I'm young and hot. My boyfriend just dumped me, and I want to get laid."

Amy cackled. "Oh Mel, you are never living this moment down."

Melanie turned to Lewis. "Can I make out with you?"

Lewis opened his mouth and then closed it. He shook his head. "Sorry, jailbait."

Melanie turned in a meandering circle before facing me once more.

"I think maybe Penn is right, and you need some water," I told her.

"Oh, come on, Natalie. Don't you remember what it was like when you were seventeen?" Amy asked.

"Well, yeah," I grumbled. "I don't want her to make the same mistakes that I did."

"I think we all have to make our own mistakes," Penn mused.

"Okay, philosopher. *You* were my mistake. So, maybe we shouldn't let Melanie do what *we* did."

Penn raised his eyebrows. "Wait, at *seventeen*?"

Oh shit.

I hadn't meant to say that.

I'd never told him my age. Not then and not now.

"Well…I was eighteen," I added softly.

"Shit. That's better than seventeen, but, fuck, Natalie, I didn't know you were that young. Why didn't you tell me?"

"What was I supposed to say? There was no way to interject that into the conversation."

"No wonder you were so mad at me," he mused.

"Tell me about it," I grumbled. Not to mention the little fact that he'd taken my virginity—which I was *not* bringing up right now! I glanced over at Lewis and Amy, who were intently watching us. "Can we just talk about this later?"

"Oh, don't mind us," Amy said.

"Yeah, we're enjoying this," Lewis said with a laugh.

"Well, I'm not," Melanie said, her voice cracking.

One second, she was holding it all together, and the next, a fissure cut through her cool facade. A sniffle came first and then real tears streamed down her face. "Oh god, what am I doing? Michael dumped me. I'm alone. And I still love him. I don't know what to do, Natalie!"

I pulled her into a hug and held her as she sobbed on the dance floor. My little sister always tried to be so strong, as if nothing in the world bothered her. But she couldn't hold it together forever. And the alcohol only made it worse.

"Let's get you in a cab," I said, nodding toward the entrance.

"Why did he do this to me?" Melanie blubbered.

"I don't know. Guys are assholes."

Penn shrugged. "You're not wrong."

"No…I'm not," I said as I ushered my sister out of the club.

NATALIE

19

Melanie threw up as soon as we got out of the cab in front of Penn's building. It wasn't pretty.

We hurried her up the elevator and into the bathroom where she was probably going to stay most of the night.

"What a nightmare," Amy muttered. "I didn't think she'd be this sick."

"I think it's the alcohol and her grief about the relationship."

"Yeah. I don't think I was ever this sick about a guy."

"No, you weren't," I said with a laugh. "But you also never dated someone for ten years before he dumped you for your best friend."

"Yeah, fuck that guy."

"Pretty much."

The elevator dinged again, and I heard Totle's distinctive clicks as he raced out into the living room.

"Well, that's my cue," Amy said.

"Wait…what?"

"I saw you two out on the dance floor. Go for it, Nat."

"Ugh! I feel like there's too much between us from before."

"That was six *years* ago. You've changed. He doesn't seem like the douche you made him out to be. Maybe you should give him the benefit of the doubt."

"Maybe," I conceded. "But I don't know if I can give in to this. It would complicate things."

Amy rolled her eyes. "Only if you let it. Casual, Natalie. Casual."

"Do you know me at all?"

"Yes, yes, I do. That is why I'm saying that you should do this. I know that you've never really been a casual dater."

"I'm a serial-relationship person!"

"But you're not in one now," Amy hissed. "So, you should have some fun for the next month. You don't know what you're doing after this job. What's the worst that can happen?"

"I'll catch feelings that he doesn't reciprocate, and I'll have to drag my ass back to Charleston, brokenhearted."

"So dramatic. All that is going to happen is, you will have a month of incredible sex with a fucking hot billionaire and come home to Charleston, out of your dry spell. Then you can have a serious relationship like you always do."

"None of that is going to happen."

Amy held her finger up. "Actually, I was talking to Daron and Zachary the other day, and Zach asked about you."

My eyes rounded. Zachary Tipton and Daron Hartage had been the hottest guys in all of Charleston when we were in high school. I hadn't even known that they knew who I was.

"What?"

"Oh, yeah. He said he saw us on the beach one day and thought you were hot. He also didn't realize that you were the same Natalie from high school, but whatever."

"Sometimes, I love and hate you. The point is that I shouldn't have a casual fling with Penn. And before you go on with your master plan, I don't want a relationship with someone like Zachary Tipton, who has no clue who I am!"

"Just go get fucked and stop complaining," Amy said, shoving me down the hallway.

"Bitch," I hissed at her.

"Slut!" she shouted right back.

I ducked as if I could save Penn from hearing Amy scream that word at me. But she just laughed and hurried into the guest bedroom.

With a deep breath, I continued my steps. Totle found me first, jumping up and down with excitement. I hoisted him into my arms and carried him into the living room with me. He was a good barrier between us.

"Hey," I said.

"I got Melanie a water bottle and some crackers. I also picked up a Gatorade when I walked Totle. I figure she'll need that and some Tylenol when she's finished being sick."

"That's…really nice of you."

"Least I can do."

I watched him in the kitchen, arranging everything he'd gotten for my sister. He'd removed his suit jacket, and his sleeves were rolled up to his elbows. He'd clearly been running his hands through his hair again, as the ends were sticking up all out of place. He looked…handsome and wild.

Could I be casual with a man like Penn?

Did I want to find out?

"Can I talk to you for a minute?" I asked tentatively. My stomach was in knots at all the ways this conversation could go.

"You don't have to say *I told you so*," he said quickly.

I blinked, taken off guard. "About what?"

"Your sister." He glanced up at me in apology. "You were

right that we shouldn't have taken her out to get drunk. Now, she's just miserable. It would have been better if we had gone to the beach house."

"Oh, well, yeah. But we all had such a good day. I wouldn't want to trade that. We probably shouldn't have let her drink with strangers." I shook my head and soldiered on. "But that isn't why I came out here to talk to you."

"What do you want to talk about?"

"I want to have a month of casual sex," I blurted out.

He arched an eyebrow and just stared at me with that cool blue gaze. "Excuse me?"

"We're not just friends. Not after what happened in Paris. Not after that kiss. I'm here for another month. We might as well make the most of it."

"And to you…that means a month of casual sex?"

"Uh, yes," I said hesitantly. I'd never done anything like this before in my life. I couldn't imagine what he was thinking right now. "Unless you don't want to…and I'm making this awkward. And I should just stop talking…"

"Okay."

"Okay?"

"Yeah. Let's do it."

"Wait, just like that?"

"What guy is going to say no to that?" he asked with a smirk.

I opened my mouth to respond and found I had no answer. Obviously, nearly every guy in existence would be interested in sex with no strings attached. It was just something I had never really thought about other than when I was in Paris. Apparently, Penn brought it out in me.

"Well, I think that we should set up some rules about…"

One second, Penn was standing in the kitchen, listening to me talk, and the next, he strode to where I was standing, grasped my jaw in his hands, and kissed the breath out of me.

Having his lips on mine was like sweet relief. As if the past week together had just been the buildup to this moment. The questions I had about entering into this dissolved with the touch of his tongue.

I'd wanted this last week and stopped myself. It had felt so right, and I had forced myself to believe it was wrong. Maybe it was wrong. Maybe we should stop all of this. But I didn't want to.

It was crazy that one day out with my sister and best friend had completely changed my mind. But it had. There was no reticence in his demeanor. None of the carefully crafted bullshit from Paris. None of the Upper East Side bad boy. I'd seen him for him without all his many versions layered on top of that persona. And I liked what I'd seen.

Amy was right. I was here for another month. Why not try this?

"No rules," he murmured against my lips.

"But…"

His hands skimmed down my body and then hoisted my legs around his waist. I gasped as I held on to him. He effortlessly carried me down the hallway and into his bedroom, kicking the door closed behind him before Totle could follow us.

I'd been inside his bedroom that one embarrassing time when I stormed away from him and into the first available room. I'd admired the controlled chaos of the space, the stacks upon stacks of books, and his cherry wood French writing desk. Now, the only thing I could see was the king-size bed against the window overlooking Central Park.

Penn set me on my feet at the foot of the bed. He kissed my lips one more time and then waited until my eyes fluttered open. My breath caught at that look. That all-encompassing feeling like I was diving deep into that gaze. Lost to him.

And I wondered if I was doing this right. Casual sex. Because one look from him turned my insides to goo and pitched my breathing low and heated my body. It didn't feel casual. It felt like the culmination of weeks spent in that house, alone together without release. Watching him run and cook and drink and write...god, his furious indulgent writing in that notebook. It felt right.

This felt more like a reason to finally be with him. Whatever excuse I could grasp at. And I was going to take it because I wanted him even if I knew I couldn't keep him.

Then he slid the zipper down the back of my dress, and I forgot to care.

His hands were careful and methodical. Easing the zipper down slow and steady while maintaining my gaze. It was utterly sensual. I shivered at the touch, at the trail of his finger down the length of my spine. Until he reached the apex of my ass where he hesitated for just a second with an indulgent smirk on his face, and then he continued between my cheeks and over the lace of my thong, bringing the zipper to the base.

He left me in place and walked leisurely around my body until his chest was nearly pressed against my back. His hands moved up my exposed back to my shoulders and gently brushed the sleeves off.

"As I recall," he said, lowering his mouth to the spot where my shoulder met my neck, "you enjoyed this."

He pressed his lips to the spot, and my entire body erupted into goose bumps.

"Oh god," I breathed.

His tongue swept across the spot. Then he sucked in until my core throbbed with desire.

Fuck, he'd actually remembered that. How...how had he remembered that?

He deftly unclasped my bra and tossed it on the floor. My

breasts hung heavy with my nipples erect with desire. He pulled me back against his chest, cupping my breasts in his hands. My ass pressed up against his cock, hard and firm through his suit pants. My mouth watered to taste him again.

I swirled my hips invitingly as he continued to teasingly kiss me while kneading my nipples between his fingers. He pinched one roughly, and I cried out as pleasure hit me anew. He nipped my shoulder and then walked me forward to the bed.

My knees hit the mattress, and then he tapped my legs further apart. I groaned when his hands skimmed my inner thighs.

I wanted him. Fuck, I fucking wanted him. I didn't need the foreplay. I didn't need anything but his cock inside me right now.

But he had other ideas.

He pushed me forward, bending me at the waist to lie across his bed. My pussy soaked my panties. He could slip inside me right now with no resistance. And I wanted him to.

"Fuck, I have wanted you since the day I saw you walk up that beach."

He ran his hands down my back and to my ass, hooking a finger under my thong and dragging it down my legs. I stepped out of the material, leaving me exposed to him. And I didn't care one bit.

He returned to my ass, gently squeezing my cheeks before moving to the apex of my thighs. I bucked against the bed at the first touch against my core. He slicked a finger through my wet center. I swore, I knew his satisfied smirk was there without even looking at him.

I thought he was just going to undo his pants and take me right then and there. Honestly, I kind of hoped so. But the Penn from six years ago had believed in multiple orgasms, and it seemed *that* hadn't changed. And well...thank fuck for that.

His knees hit the hardwood floor. I glanced back in surprise, and then he buried his face in my pussy. I cried out, dropping my head, as all at once, I was overcome with sensation. His tongue was inside me. His thumb pressed to my clit.

This had...never happened to me before. I'd had oral, obviously, but from behind? And oh my god! Oh my fucking god! It was incredible.

I couldn't see him. I had no idea what he was going to do next. And it heightened every sensation.

I tried to turn around to look at him again, but he pushed my chest back down into the mattress.

"Oh fuck," I groaned as he brought me to the edge.

"Come for me, Natalie," he commanded.

And I was so close. Only a few more strokes of my clit as he lavished me, and I was there. Seeing stars. Utterly gone. Moaning into the duvet and clenching it for dear life.

His hand tangled in my hair, wrenching me backward. It wasn't entirely violent, but it wasn't exactly gentle either. Somehow, my body got more turned on.

"Mmm," I moaned as I arched my back to look at him.

Then his lips were on mine, rough and all demanding. I could taste my own arousal on him. I wanted more.

He wrapped an arm around my middle to help me back to my feet. I turned in place and saw that, in the midst of my orgasm, he had somehow gotten his shirt unbuttoned. All I could see was the six-pack abs beneath a sky-blue button-up. I ripped his shirt off of him and then ran my nails down that toned physique.

As much as I wanted to admire every single abdominal muscle, I moved past his sexy V to get to the main event.

I couldn't unbutton his pants fast enough, and then I hastily reached inside his boxer briefs to hold his long cock in my hand. It was firm and thick and mine for the night. I'd been young and innocent and had no clue what I was doing the last time we were together. That was no longer the case. And my body wanted another round.

"Get on the bed," he said.

"My turn." I stroked him up and down.

"I want inside you." He eased me backward onto the bed. His cock jutted out between us, and I licked my lips. "Next time, you can suck me off all you want. Right now, I want to own your body."

I slowly crawled backward, baring myself before him, aching and ready. "I don't know if you know," I muttered with a feral smile on my face, "but we are breaking the standard view of sex."

He stilled halfway to the side table and turned back to look at me. "Is that so?"

"Uh-huh." I opened my legs wider. "Philosophically speaking, we're going against the ethically appropriate way to behave."

"You have never been sexier." He snatched up a condom and rolled it on with practiced ease.

"You don't think this is…wrong?" I teased.

He crawled onto the bed toward me. "With you? Never."

"Are you sure?"

"The amount of pleasure we're about to have can't possibly be wrong."

"You know, we could almost call this research for you."

His eyes bored deep into mine. A deep, animalistic desire ran through that look as he tangled his hand back into my hair. His other pressed my hip down into the mattress. His cock was poised at my opening. He was in complete control, and I just wanted more, more, more.

"I think we're going to need to do *a lot* of research," he growled before pushing deep inside me.

I cried out as he filled me to the brim. Then he pulled out and slammed back in. Over and over again.

"A lot of research," he repeated. "Maybe all night."

"Oh god," I cried as he exposed my throat, kissing his way down my shoulder, never relenting on his pace.

"What do you think, Natalie? Up for an all-nighter?"

"Harder," I gasped.

He chuckled against the shell of my ear. "I'll take that as a yes."

Then he obliged me. Our bodies melded together. Him owning me and taking every single ounce of pleasure I offered him. I could hardly breathe. My heart galloped. My legs shook uncontrollably. And still, it wasn't enough.

Then he tugged both of my legs up onto his shoulders and drilled deep down into me, hitting a spot I hadn't even known existed. I screamed at the top of my lungs as my orgasm hit me so hard I felt like I might black out.

Penn came with me, as unrelenting as the sex had been. Then, we both collapsed, covered in a sheen of sweat and throbbing almost painfully. It was the most pleasurable pain I'd ever experienced. And I wanted it again.

He gently kissed my shoulder once. "I think you should talk dirty philosophy to me every time."

"Every. Time," I agreed.

"And you…you like hair pulling."

My lower half pulsed in agreement, and he chuckled.

"I can't wait to learn every single thing that turns you on."

"Mmm," I purred happily.

"This silver hair turns me on." He trailed his fingers through the long silvery-white strands that were my signature look.

"Oh yeah? Not too different for Mr. Upper East Side?"

"It's you. It's perfect."

I stilled under those words, but he was already getting up

and heading to the bathroom to clean up. Hardly casual sex words. But he'd done this before. He was the man who was writing a book on how sex in noncommitted relationships could be part of ethical living. I was probably just overthinking it.

Anyway, I liked that he liked my hair. I liked every single thing about what had happened. I just needed to figure out how to keep this all casual.

Because, when he walked back into the room, fully nude with a smile only for me, I knew it would be too damn easy to fall for him.

NATALIE

20

The sun streaming in through the window woke me the next morning. I blinked open my eyes, and the previous night rushed back to me. Penn. His bedroom. Sex. Lots of sex. So much sex that my body hurt when I shifted. And not just between my legs.

But the strange part was...the heater seemingly attached to my leg.

I lifted the covers and found Totle passed out between me and Penn. His unusually long legs were stretched out until he had shifted us about as far apart as we could be and still both be on the bed. It didn't even make sense that a ten-pound dog could take up so much space. But then he nuzzled against my leg and sighed happily, and I forgot any frustration. He was seriously the cutest puppy in the world.

"You're too cute. You know that?" I said as I scratched Totle's head.

"Why thank you," Penn murmured from the other side of the bed.

He rolled over, and those blue eyes cracked open. And for a second, I froze in place. He was still there. Still right where

I'd left him. I knew it was irrational to think that he might have left, even while I was in his place with his dog, but he'd done it once before, and I couldn't stop the fear from seizing me. But it had been unwarranted. He was here. And he was looking at me as if I was the most beautiful thing he'd ever seen.

"Good morning." I couldn't keep the smile from my face.

"Morning." He leaned across the bed and pressed his lips against mine. My heart fluttered.

"Well, hello to you too."

He grinned and kissed me again. "Up for round...what number were we on?"

I swatted at him. "I think I should check on Mel and Amy. And you should make some coffee."

"Coffee I can do."

He wrapped an arm around my waist and slid me across the bed. Totle grumbled and shifted to the end of the bed. I just laughed as Penn pinned me beneath him, dropping his face into my shoulder. His five o'clock shadow scratched against my skin, and his lips kissed the sensitive skin that he knew I was a sucker for.

"Penn, oh my god, if you keep doing that..."

"We'll stay in bed all day?" he asked hopefully.

"Possibly," I said on a laugh.

He slipped under the covers as he kissed and scratched his way down my stomach. I squirmed under his touch, enjoying every second.

He grabbed my panties in both hands. "How much do you like these?"

"I don't have any more with me!" I cried.

He grinned devilishly and then shredded the underwear between his hands. I gasped in shock as my thong disappeared over the side of the bed.

"I cannot believe you just did that!"

"I'll buy you more," he said as he dragged his lips down my inner thigh. "And now, you have to go commando."

"You're the devil. Pure evil, Penn Kensington."

He winked at me. "Now you're getting it."

He dropped his head between my thighs and squashed any further protest from my lips. His tongue swept across my clit, relentlessly teasing me. One finger and then another. In and out. My whimpers and pleading were just as passionate. The man was good with his hands.

Dear fucking god. How did he do that thing?

Fuck.

"Close?" he asked even though I was sure he knew.

"Yes," I practically screamed at him.

"Good."

He kissed my pussy one more time and lightly smacked my clit with the flat of his hand. I yelped at the shocking touch.

"That hurt!"

"Did it?" He arched an eyebrow. He slapped me one more time, and my whole body shuddered in pleasure. "That's what I thought."

He slid back up my body and kissed me. "Now you'll be feeling me all day." He hopped off the bed, leaving me completely exposed and a millimeter from orgasm.

"What the hell are you doing?" I asked as he pulled boxers and jeans on over his erection.

"Making coffee," he said innocently.

"If you do not finish the job, I'm going to."

He left the jeans hanging on his hips and then moved back over to me. He slipped two fingers back inside me, and I moaned.

"Finish the job then."

"What?" I gasped.

But his eyes were clear and intense. "You know how you like to get off. Show me how."

Was he serious? I'd never masturbated for anyone before. I'd never even *considered* doing something like that.

He pumped in and out of me once. I was so dangerously close and teetering precariously, but he never let me fall off the edge.

"I want to watch, Natalie."

I released the embarrassment I was sure I would have felt with anyone else. This was Penn. He was *asking* for this. It turned him on too. And god, did I want to get off right now. I liked everything else he'd done to me. Why shouldn't I do this?

With a deep breath, I trailed my hand down my front until I reached my core. I wet my own finger, pressing against his still buried inside me. The touch alone made me shiver with need. Then I brought my wet finger to my clit and swirled it around and around. My breath came out in hot pants as everything in my body tightened. Then Penn began to move his fingers again.

"Oh, yes," I groaned.

"That's right. Get yourself off."

And then my entire body contracted. My pussy pulsed greedily around his fingers, and a throb shuddered through me before I lay still, breathless.

"Sexiest thing I've ever seen," he told me as he kissed me one more time. "I'll get you that coffee now."

With an uncontrollable smile, I watched him and Totle leave. I'd never met anyone like Penn. I'd never felt like this with anyone else. Not that I'd had bad sex with other partners, but nothing compared to this. I hadn't been entirely adventurous in my past. Who knew what a big difference it was to have a guy who didn't just accept the bare minimum?

With a sigh of contentment, I rolled off the bed, took a

quick shower, and then headed out to the kitchen. I knotted my long silvery hair onto the top of my head and followed the scent of coffee brewing.

"Well," Amy said from her seat at the breakfast bar. Her eyes were wide, and she rested her chin on the top of her hands. "How was *your* night?"

"Oh, shut up," I said, pouring myself a cup of coffee.

"Or morning, for that matter," she added with a chuckle.

I glanced around to look for Penn but didn't see him anywhere.

"He's walking Totle," Amy told me.

"It was great. I took your advice."

"Aha! So, the casual-sex line worked?"

"Wait, what? It wasn't a line!"

Amy's eyes rounded, and she nodded in mock understanding. "Yeah, sure."

"I am going to just have casual sex with him. You're the one who said to do this."

"I know, but it's totally a line."

"Wait," Melanie said, walking into the kitchen. "You and Penn?"

"Oh, yeah. I convinced her to use the casual-sex line."

Melanie blinked. "That's a *line?*"

Amy laughed and patted her head. "Have you been with anyone other than Michael?"

Melanie shifted. "Well, no."

"Yeah, it's a line. And it worked." She turned back to look at me and winked. "You had some amazing sex."

"But Penn is a great guy," Melanie said. "He's hot and charming with a great place and job. He knows all the good places to go in the city. And he even has a puppy. I mean, why would you want something casual with him? He's, like, marriage material."

My jaw dropped at Melanie's profound statement. Of

course, she didn't have all the facts. She didn't know about our history. Or how difficult this all would be if I caught feelings.

Amy snorted. "You are so cute and innocent, Mel."

"We're just casual. No strings. All that," I insisted. "I didn't use it as a line, and I'm certainly not *marrying* him. Why don't we change the subject? How are you feeling, Mel?"

Melanie shrugged and stole my coffee. "Well, I woke up to Michael and Kennedy's pictures from homecoming last night. And about a dozen texts from him about how much of a mistake it was. That it should have been us there, like it always was. He's sorry and all that."

"What a douche!" Amy cried.

"For real," I seconded.

"But...what if he's telling the truth?"

"He left you for your best friend. There's no reason to believe a word he says. A dozen texts doesn't make up for what he did."

"Yeah," Melanie said unconvincingly, "you're right."

The elevator dinged, and Totle rushed out of it. Penn appeared a minute later, and my stomach flipped.

"You ladies want some brunch? I can get us into Norma's on short notice," he offered.

"Norma's," Melanie cried. "Oh my god, hell yes!"

"I guess that's a yes," Amy said. "What's Norma's?"

"Only the best brunch in the city," Melanie informed her. Her worries about Michael were gone as she dashed down the hallway to change.

I laughed and followed her. Thankfully, I could fit into Mel's and Amy's clothes. Even if they weren't my normal tastes. But it was good enough for New York in October.

Brunch was divine. As was the rest of the weekend as Penn and I entertained them back at the beach house. It was so nice, having them there that I almost forgot that I was there to work. But it was worth taking the weekend off to be with them. And I wasn't ready for them to go when it was time.

Amy kept giving me looks, as if she knew me better than I knew myself. She tried to give me advice on how to keep things casual. Apparently, even though she was the one to suggest it, she had never thought it was possible. Typical Amy.

I tasked her with looking out for Melanie. Because the way she had been talking and moping, I was worried she and Michael were going to get back together. High school drama and all that. Even though Melanie had insisted that wasn't going to happen. She was going to be strong. Blah, blah, blah. I had a feeling she'd be back with him by the end of the week after he continued spewing whatever bullshit he had been saying to her all weekend.

"She's going to be okay," Penn told me later. "She's stronger than you think."

"I know she is. I just still see her as my baby sister. Hard to get over that."

"I don't have a younger sibling, but it's how I feel about Lewis's sisters. They're like family to me. More so than my own family most of the time."

I was surprised he was even talking about his family. I knew that they weren't on good terms. That he didn't talk to his mother and hated his train-wreck brother. I didn't know anything about his father. He'd said in Paris that he wanted a different family, a different life. Clearly, he'd worked toward that the last six years, getting away with at least a bit by being a professor. But the Upper East Side almost seemed like a gang. Once you were in, you were in, and they never let you out.

"Do you talk to them much?"

His face went from open to utterly blank in a second. "My family? No."

"I see." I knew when to push and when to retreat. "Me either. Though I think I had Melanie wrong before. Maybe I just pushed my own frustrations about not being perfect on her."

"She seems great. You're lucky to have a sister like that. Someone who loves you."

"She is great," I admitted. I'd never thought that Melanie and I would be close. I was kind of glad to be proven wrong. "And I do feel lucky."

"I have so much work to catch up on," he said, reaching for his beaten-up leather notebook. He sank into a chair at the breakfast nook.

"Me too. My agent asked for the first fifty pages of my new book. I feel like throwing up, sending it to her."

"I could read it for you, if you want."

My stomach knotted. "Oh god, no. I think I'd actually vomit if you read it."

He laughed as he flipped open his notebook to a blank page. "I know the feeling."

"Though…I do think we should talk about us."

The laughter died on his lips. "No take-backs, Natalie."

"Take-backs?" I asked with my own smile. "What makes you think I want to take back what happened?"

"I heard you talking to Amy earlier. It sounded like you didn't want to do this," he admitted.

"That was…not the conversation we were having," I said, biting my lip.

It had been more about how to keep things casual. How to keep him at a distance. How not to get my feelings involved. How to let the sex lead and the rest just rest. Because I only had a month, and I didn't need the complication of a relationship that would go nowhere. Not with a guy like Penn. He didn't exactly seem like Mr. Relationship even if Melanie did think he was marriage material.

"I see. Is this about your rules again? Because I'm pretty sure sex is self-explanatory."

"No. I think I get it. Sounds like you're the one worrying about it."

"Not worry exactly, but I do want to make sure that you're comfortable. For some reason, this doesn't seem like something you would normally do. I want us to be open with each other."

"Okay," I said easily.

"Okay?" he asked with a smirk. "That easy?"

I stepped up to where he was sitting and straddled his lap. "What I was going to say was that I think, next time...I should be on top."

His eyes turned devilish. "That can be arranged."

"Like...right now?" I asked.

"Right fucking now."

NATALIE

21

"Natalie, can I speak to you?" Kristen, the interior designer, called from the living room.

I stared at the email I'd drafted to my agent on my phone. It had the first fifty pages of my new book, which was currently untitled, and an outline of the rest of the book as I had it set up now. I wasn't ready to go out with this one yet. Not while TOLD YOU SO was still out on its miserable run. But Caroline wanted to read it. Before I could think better of it, I clicked Send and rushed out into the living room.

"How can I help you, Kristen?" I asked.

The main room was still a work in progress from the renovations, but it was starting to look fully put together again.

"I wanted to let you know that we're moving on to that side of the house," she said, pointing at the rooms that I'd just vacated.

"Oh. I didn't know that you were doing the bedrooms."

"It's on the list. I have a plan for it. Shouldn't take as long as the living room."

"Okay. I'm just sleeping in there. All my stuff is in there," I told her.

Also, I liked that room. It was cozy and warm. The bay window was gorgeous, and I loved being able to see out to the ocean in the mornings.

"Just move to the master," Kristen said with a shrug.

Penn was in the master bedroom though. We'd had two days of great sex, but we still kept separate bedrooms. It was kind of nice to come back to my own space when I needed it. Now, I wouldn't have that.

There was another bedroom upstairs, but I hadn't really ventured up there since the first day I arrived. I'd have to see what Penn wanted to do.

"All right. I'll move my stuff out," I told her and then went in search of Penn.

I found him in front of a MacBook in the library. It was one of the first times I'd seen him at a computer. He did most of his best thinking in his notebook.

"This is new," I observed from the doorway.

"Ah, yes. Have to get it in a digital format at some point," he said. "Plus, I think I wrangled the main theory out of the notebook this morning. We'll see if it strings together on a computer."

"So…Kristen told me that they're renovating my wing of the house."

His head popped up. "Just move in with me."

My heart skipped a beat, and I swallowed back the bright smile that threatened to cross my face. There was nothing casual about my reaction to those words.

"Unless that's too much?" he ventured. "I can grab one of the upstairs rooms."

"No…it's not too much," I said, trying to keep my voice casual. That damn word. "Just wanted to make sure you were cool with it."

"You in my bed every night?" he asked. "Why wouldn't I want that, Nat?"

My breath hitched at that. My friends called me Nat. My family called me Nat. Penn had only ever called me Natalie. I loved the intimacy of it.

"Well, issue resolved then," I said, walking further inside and sitting on the desk. "I'll move everything over later."

"Need help?"

"Nah, military brat, remember? Expert packer."

"Right," he said with a smile before turning back to his computer. Then he looked back up. "Oh yeah, did Katherine email you about the concert next week?"

"I didn't have anything. What concert?"

I pulled my email back up, and lo and behold, there was an email from Katherine. She said she missed me and wanted to make up for the last time we'd hung out. Apparently, making up meant first row tickets to Chloe Avana, the biggest pop star in the country, with backstage passes and a meet-and-greet.

"Holy shit! Is she serious?"

Penn groaned. "So, you want to go?"

"Are you kidding? I grew up on Chloe Avana! Her on-again/off-again thing with Gates Hartman is the stuff of legends, and I'm not even as obsessed as my sister, who follows that stuff."

"She's so…mainstream."

"You sound so hipster for someone born on the Upper East Side," I said on a laugh. "And come on, you have to like that song that she does with Damon Stone. That's pure gold."

He grumbled under his breath.

"What? Didn't hear you."

"I said…that one is pretty good."

I laughed. "Great. Then…I guess we're going."

"Yeah, yeah. We're going."

I stretched across the desk and kissed him hard on the mouth. "I'm so excited."

"I have other plans for us for this afternoon though."

"Oh, yeah?" I asked huskily.

"After I finish this theory section."

"You're going to make me wait?" I pouted.

His eyes glinted with desire. "It'll be worth it. Wear white."

"White?" I asked with my head tilted.

He nodded. "Give me a couple of hours, and then we'll go."

"All right," I said, hopping off of the desk. "If you want to turn this down."

He slapped my ass at full force, and I shrieked.

"That ass tempts me all damn day. Maybe that'll be my surprise later."

My eyes widened, and he just grinned. He wasn't kidding. A thrill ran through me.

"We'll see," I teased back.

"Yes, we will."

I'D GUESSED wrong when he suggested white and worn a dress. Penn made me change into something warmer and tennis shoes before ushering me out of the house.

"I must say…this isn't what I was expecting," I told him.

"You don't even know what we're doing."

"Well, we're not having sex. So…it's definitely unexpected."

He laughed and moved his hand to my leg. "There's always time to turn around."

"I'm way too intrigued now."

"Good. Because I think you'll enjoy this."

We only drove a short distance before Penn pulled over

and then marched us onto a dock. My eyes widened in surprise. This wasn't the dock where Lewis had kept his enormous yacht that felt more like a cruise ship than the boats I was used to in Charleston. This dock felt much more familiar. Still wealthier than back home, but at least in a similar league.

"Have you ever sailed before?" Penn asked as he stopped us before a beautiful sailboat.

I shook my head. "Nope. But I've always wanted to try."

"Today is that day." He hopped onto the boat and offered me his hands. "Come on board."

I reached for him as I stepped down into the sailboat. "Wow, this thing is gorgeous."

"Thanks." He tossed me a life jacket. "Put that on."

"Super sexy."

He glanced up at me from the front of the boat where he was checking the sails and grinned. "Orange is your color."

"I feel ridiculous," I told him.

"Better safe than sorry," he said as he hopped back down and began to move us out of the dock.

He'd been right. It was a beautiful, windy day with a perfect, clear sky that I could only imagine made for good sailing weather. And Penn had obviously done this before... many, many times. He walked back and forth on the deck like an expert, pulling lines and hoisting sails and steering. It was hot as fuck to watch him.

I'd never cared much for boats or anything like that. It was Melanie who loved boats. She went out nearly every weekend with her friend Marina, whose family owned a boating company. I'd gone a few times, but I preferred the beach with a good book.

I thought, if I'd gone sailing with a guy as hot as Penn Kensington, I might have a different appreciation for boats.

"So...you sail," I noted the obvious.

"Little bit," he agreed, sinking back down to steer us.

"Did your dad teach you?"

His mouth tightened, and he glanced down. "Yeah, he did."

I could tell that was a sore subject. I didn't know why I kept bringing up his family. He clearly didn't want to talk about it. And we were casual. We weren't dating or anything. He didn't need to talk to me about his parents. I just wanted to know, and I couldn't help wanting to know.

I'd say it was the writer in me, trying to find out all his secrets and figure out how to piece him all together. But it was just something about the pain and anger that crossed his face when the parents were brought up that made me want to help put him back together. But...not today.

I changed tack. "So, how long have you been doing this?"

"Basically, my whole life."

"That's incredible." I leaned back, tilting my head into the sun and smiling. "This is almost as good as the beach. I can see why you like it."

"It's relaxing. It usually keeps my mind off of things."

"Like what?"

"Life. Everything. I don't know," he said. "It quiets everything that I have going on and that I have to deal with. So, it's just this moment."

"I get that."

"Hey, come over here," he said, gesturing to where he sat as he steered.

"Are you going to teach me?" I walked over to him.

"Do you want to learn?"

I shook my head. "Maybe another time. Right now, I like you in charge."

He pulled me down onto his lap. "Just right now?"

"Are you fishing for compliments?"

"Do I need to fish for them?"

"Oh my god, are you going to answer every question with a question?"

"Is there a reason I shouldn't?"

I pushed at his shoulder, but he just laughed and pulled my lips down to his.

"Tell me more about yourself," he instructed.

"Like what?"

"What's your favorite food?"

I slid off of his lap and quirked my eyebrow at him. "That's so generic. We went from your deepest, darkest secret in Paris to favorite food."

He kissed my shoulder. "I know so many intimate things about you. I want to know the rest. The mundane things."

"Why?" I couldn't keep the word from leaving my mouth. I wanted to tell him the mundane things. But it was hardly casual-sex material. It was more…first-date fodder.

"Is it so hard to believe that I enjoy your company and want to know more about you?"

"No," I said softly, "but…"

"Just answer the question and stop overanalyzing everything with your writer's brain."

I stuck my tongue out at him. "I can't help it."

"Trust me. I know."

"Fine. Pizza."

"I should have guessed. You practically drooled when I told you I was ordering some a couple of weeks ago. Guess I know what we're having for dinner. I know this place in East Hampton that's sinful."

That sounded like…a date.

No, it wasn't a date. It was just…friends hanging out. Friends with some pretty incredible benefits eating food. Normal. Chill.

"What about you?"

"Spaghetti."

"Yum. More importantly...favorite dessert?"

"You have a sweet tooth?"

I grinned. "I wouldn't say no to a doughnut."

"My favorite is probably the German chocolate cake my longtime cook, Tiffany, used to make for me. Nothing tastes like hers."

"Of course you grew up with a cook."

He stood to adjust something. "She taught me how to cook too. Told me it was the only way I was going to survive college. She was right."

"Your parents didn't send a cook to you for college?" I joked.

"They tried, but I wanted to get away, so I tried to distance myself from that lifestyle."

"Jesus," I muttered.

He sank back down next to me. "Favorite book?"

"Easy," I said, reaching for his hand on instinct. *"Pride and Prejudice."*

"Ah, and the romantic finally comes out."

"Oh, shush. What about you?"

"The Great Gatsby."

I rolled my eyes. "Tragedies. Right. I almost forgot."

"Gatsby is classic."

"You're right. It's genius but still so fitting." I stood and turned my face into the wind. "My turn...favorite road-trip destination?"

"Never been on one."

I gasped and whirled on him. "You're joking!"

"No," he said with a laugh at my reaction.

"Never?"

"I've driven to places before, but usually, it's like between the Hamptons and the city."

"That's insane. I started road trips young. My parents loved them even though I could never figure out why they wanted to be in the car for that long. But part of it was just the journey rather than the destination. Then, Amy and I road-tripped to Los Angeles one summer."

"Fuck! LA? Seriously? How long did that take you?"

"Two weeks. It's about three days of actual driving, but we stopped along the way. Her cousin was going to UCLA and didn't want to make the drive. Her parents offered to ship the car there, but Amy and I decided to drive it out."

"That's insane. Who would want to be in a car for three weeks?"

"It's the basis for my book actually."

"The one you won't let me read?"

"I won't let you read any of them," I told him playfully. "But no, not the one that I just sent to Caroline. This was the one I was working on when I first got here. I'm going to go back to it when I finish the new one."

"What's the new one about?"

I looked at him with wide, innocent eyes. "A woman's journey and love and finding the place she belongs."

"Isn't that like...half of all books?"

"Exactly."

"All right. You're not ready to tell," he conceded. "How about Christmas plans? What are you doing for the holidays?"

"Oh," I said in surprise. "It really depends on this job, I suppose. I'll probably go back to Charleston for the holidays with my parents and Mel. But, otherwise, I haven't thought about it. What about you?"

"Christmas is the best time to be in the city. But usually, I have an uncomfortable brunch with my family. Then I get together with the crew and exchange presents. Open a really expensive bottle of scotch and finish it."

"Besides the uncomfortable brunch, it sounds nice. You've found family with your friends, and that's important."

"That's a good way to think about it." He nodded at me. "Your question."

I chewed on my lip and tried to think of what to ask. I had a question I knew that I probably shouldn't ask. But I was extremely curious.

"Any exes?" I asked to the wind.

Penn froze where he was seated, which answered my question well enough.

"Never mind. That's awkward. You don't have to answer that. We're not dating or anything."

"No one important enough to mention," he said and then stood to grab me closer. "And I don't want you to answer."

"Really?"

He threaded his fingers up into my silver hair and brought our lips together in a sensual, intimate kiss that made my toes curl.

"I don't want to think about you with anyone else."

I melted into putty in his hands. Then I nodded. Not that I had anything to really say. Serial relationships or not...none of them had ever really mattered. It was hard to wonder what I'd seen in any of them when I was staring up into Penn's clear blue eyes.

"Come on now," he said. "I'm going to teach you how to sail."

"Oh god, really?"

"Yeah, get your sweet ass over here, and I'll show you how to handle a big stick."

I rolled my eyes. "Pretty sure I'm already a pro at that."

"Touché," he said and then went into a lecture on terminology.

Thank god he was pretty.

NATALIE

22

"If you ask me one more time which way is starboard or port, I will take my heel off and stab you with it," I warned him.

Penn chuckled. He was leaning against the doorframe in his Upper East Side penthouse bathroom. Totle was curled up on the bed unhappy that we weren't paying attention to him since we were getting ready for the Chloe Avana concert instead.

"You're going to get it eventually."

"I already have it! I just don't test well," I complained. Story of my life, honestly. Thank god Grimke University cared more for high school grades than standardized test scores.

"I'm going to make you sail next time, you know."

"I have done it once! That's not how it works."

"That's how I was taught," he reasoned.

"Not happening." I glared at him in the mirror as I pulled the straightener through my long hair one last time. It fell like a shiny sheet down nearly to my ass. "What do you think?"

"I'm thinking we're going to be late." He stepped forward and scooped me up into his arms.

"Oh my god!" I cried as he carried me into the bedroom and tossed me onto the bed next to Totle, who excitedly hopped up and licked my face.

"Aristotle, you're ruining the moment, little man," Penn said with a smile as he petted Totle's head.

"We don't have time anyway. We're already running behind." I pulled my hair over one shoulder.

"There's always time," he reasoned.

"The only thing we have time for is for you to tell me pink or red lipstick."

"Trick question?" he asked. "Red obviously."

"Why is that obvious?"

"Because later, when you're sucking me off, you'll leave a red ring behind, and I can think about that all night."

I blushed unexpectedly. "You have a filthy mind."

He gave me a hard kiss. "You've just hit the tip of the iceberg, Nat."

If this was just the beginning of how his mind worked, I was both terrified and excited to see what else there was to come.

I quickly applied a layer of cherry-red lipstick, and then we left for the concert. As easy as it was to be with Penn, I didn't know how I was supposed to act tonight. I wasn't part of his crew, but we weren't together either. We were somewhere in this in-between place. Casual…yet not. Friends with benefits…yet not. Not exactly at least.

Were we just supposed to be friends at this concert? Were we supposed to be nothing? Should I not be worrying about this at all? He was honest with his friends. Maybe they already knew what was going on between us, and I was second-guessing our arrangement for no reason. I didn't know how to bring it up either. So, I decided I would just follow his lead. If it was clear that they knew we were sleeping together, then it'd be no big deal. But if he hid it, then I could do that, too. Maybe...

We met Katherine and Lewis outside of Madison Square Garden. She looked stunning with her dark hair in her signature supermodel waves. I was sure that Emmanuel had spent hours on her appearance to make her looks natural and flawless. Lewis was more casual in jeans and a button-up. He still had a bit of stubble on his cheeks, and it looked good on him. His face lit up when he saw me and Penn walking toward them.

"Hey, gorgeous," he said, wrapping his arms around me and lifting me off of my feet.

I laughed and hugged him back. "It's good to see you."

"Lewis, please," Katherine said.

He set me on my feet and shook hands with Penn. "Bro."

Penn smiled back in that easy way he always did around his friends. I didn't always understand their dynamic or the way they all seemed to not be entirely themselves. But I could tell that there was love there. Born of long years spent together, going through the same chaotic times of their lives.

Katherine reached for my hand and veered me away from the boys. "Here's your pass."

In awe, I took the lanyard VIP pass from her hand. I'd hardly been to any concerts, growing up. And in college, Amy had dated the bouncer at one of the venues, so we usually just snuck into crappy shows. First row tickets to Chloe Avana at Madison Square Garden had to have cost a fortune.

"I don't know how I'll be able to pay you back," I told her.

"Oh, don't be gauche. It's a gift. No repayment needed. It's the least I can do, considering how bad I felt after the gala."

I was still not certain about Katherine. I liked her. I liked being around her and being in her circle of friends. But she seemed like the kind of person whose bad side you never, *ever* wanted to be on. That having her as a friend was a sincere privilege, and if you ever lost her favor, you would be better left to the dogs.

Her kindness made me uncomfortable. Especially because I knew there was no way that I could repay her. And I thought she liked that.

"I really didn't mean *project* like that," Katherine said carefully as we scanned our passes. The guys filed in after us. "I was just dealing with Camden. You can understand."

"He's awful."

"The worst," she agreed.

"Why are you marrying him?"

Katherine shrugged her petite shoulders and waved at a girl who was staring at her with round eyes. "It's a society thing."

"I couldn't imagine not marrying for love."

"Happens all the time," she said, fluttering her fingers at a group of girls in a corner. "And anyway, it's not like love matches have a perfect success rate. Love equals divorce a lot."

"True," I conceded. "My parents are still together."

"What a miracle. I suppose you could say that mine are too." She shrugged her shoulders. "Right through here."

We moved into the arena and to our seats, which were nearly dead center in the very first row. I could practically reach out and touch the stage, which was lit up before me.

"These seats are amazing," I groaned in amazement.

"Totally. And I have six of them. But Lark had to work, and Rowe backed out last minute."

"Why?"

"He said—and I quote—'Because I don't want to go.'"

"Classic Rowe."

"Tell me about it."

I pulled my phone out. "I'm going to need to take a video and put this up on Crew. My sister is going to kill me."

"Oh yeah, I heard that your sister came into town, and you all went out without me."

I hadn't even thought to invite Katherine that night. I'd been too busy with Amy and Melanie. I was sure that Katherine and Amy would clash. They were a match made in hell.

"Yeah. Sorry about that."

"No matter. I would have loved to meet your friends. Maybe next time."

"For sure," I said because I knew it wouldn't happen again.

"God, I need a drink," Katherine said. "Penn, darling, let's go get drinks."

"You want to go get drinks?" he asked in a perplexed voice.

My eyes shot to his, and I realized that I could read his discomfort in a way I certainly hadn't been able to before. And it wasn't just because he had no interest in being at a Chloe Avana concert.

"Go on ahead," Lewis said. "I'll chill here with Natalie."

"Be right back," Katherine said, latching on to Penn's arm and walking back out the way we'd just come.

"I can't believe she got us these tickets," I observed.

"Chloe gave them to her," he said, stretching out in his seat. "It wasn't a big deal."

"Wait, what? She knows Chloe Avana?"

"Katherine is a socialite. It's part of her job to know people who matter. And to be seen at events like this."

"Still trying to adjust to that being a job."

"Aren't we all?" Lewis said with a laugh.

"I think I'll stick to writing."

"How is that going anyway?" He looked genuinely curious.

"Well, I sent my agent the start of a new manuscript, which I'm in love with. But so far, not so great on the other two books."

He furrowed his brows. "Really? Did you send them to Warren?"

"Uh...yeah. Yep. We sure did," I said awkwardly, remembering the horribly worded rejection letter I'd gotten the day I first met him.

"And?"

"Honestly, they were kind of mean." I shrugged. "Rejection is part of the job."

"Huh. Well, shit. I'm sorry."

"It's not like *you* were the editor who rejected me. You don't even work in publishing," I reminded him.

Not that I knew exactly what he did, but I had a feeling that working with hedge funds didn't exactly mean he dipped his toes into the literature side of his father's fortune.

"That's true. Though I do love to read. You can't grow up in a publishing house and not love reading."

"Well, one day I'll get published, and the work will have been worth it. But for now, I'll continue working as a vacation home watcher and writing on the side. It's a strange life."

He laughed. "You think your life is strange? I can't imagine what you think of ours."

"It's definitely different," I said with a smile.

"Speaking of different," he said, sitting back up, "what's up with your friend Amy?"

I chuckled. "She's a lot, right?"

"I'll be honest, I've never had anyone turn me down for my money."

"That sounds like Amy."

"So, you're telling me that she actually prefers broke artists?"

"I mean, she might be happy with a rich artist if he was hot and looked homeless on occasion. Also, if he was really manic."

Lewis shook his head in disbelief. "That is the oddest thing I've ever heard."

"Well, money doesn't rule everything. Just because someone is rich doesn't make them more appealing, and her interests are very particular."

"That's fair," he conceded. "I've just seen so many clingy and money-grubbing people that you start to expect it. Someone like Amy…or like you is refreshing."

"As I enjoy first row tickets to a concert that I didn't pay for."

"Come on. That's not who you are. I can tell that accepting this makes you uncomfortable. I saw it on my yacht when we first met. It's not that you don't want to be here, but you don't want to owe anyone."

I stared at him in surprise. I hadn't thought Lewis was really paying that close of attention. It was like he'd stepped into her brain and read her thoughts.

"Yes, that's true. I'm not used to this for sure."

"Well, people who are trying to use you for your money aren't normally uncomfortable when people spend money on them," he said with a nod.

"That's just how I was raised."

"It's endearing," he said with his signature smile that lit up his face.

"I'm glad. Sometimes, I'm not sure if I really fit in with you all."

"Eh, I wouldn't worry about it. I love that you keep everyone on their toes."

"Just what I want to be known for."

He nudged me with his shoulder. "It was a compliment."

Then his eyes gazed past me, and he groaned. "Don't look behind you."

So, of course, the first thing that I did was whirl around to see what he was talking about. All I saw were two beautiful black girls. One was tall and thin with pin-straight black hair to the middle of her back. She had on a gorgeous black designer dress. The other girl was shorter than me with a sharp bob and an edgy leather dress that hugged her curvy figure.

"Friends of yours?" I asked conspiratorially.

"Yeah...my sisters."

"Oh!" I gasped. "Penn told me about them. Charlotte and Etta, right?"

"That's right. I knew they'd be here, but I thought that they had a box."

"I thought you were close with them. Penn said that they're basically family to him."

"We are close. But, if they see me at this show, I'll never live it down."

I laughed and then stood up, waving. "Charlotte! Etta!"

The girls turned to face me with quizzical looks. Then they saw who I was seated with and broke into laughter. They strode over to our seats with a drink in one hand and phone in the other.

"Brother, you are at a Chloe Avana show," the tallest girl said. "How embarrassing!"

Lewis vaulted to his feet, towering over his little sisters. "Charlotte, Etta, this is my friend Natalie."

"Natalie, this is Charlie," he said, pointing out the taller of the two, "and my youngest sister, Etta."

Charlotte shook my hand. "Any girl who can get my brother to a concert like this is a girl we like, right, Et?"

"Hell yes. Please take a picture with us, so we can put this on Crew later," Etta said.

We snapped a few shots. Most of the time, Lewis looked miserable.

"Okay, get out of here, you hellions," Lewis said, ushering them away.

"Message us later, Natalie," Charlie said. "We'd love to do brunch sometime."

"We can fit you into our social calendar," Etta agreed.

"Yes. Sure," Lewis said. "Bye now."

"We love you, too," Charlie said.

"Make sure to sing every word," Etta teased. "We know you know them all."

They left with a trail of laughter, and I decided that I loved them on the spot. It was the most *normal* familial relationship I'd encountered since being on the Upper East Side.

"They're amazing!" I cried.

"They are. Though they're also the worst," he said with a shake of his head that said he loved them fiercely.

"How old are they? They can't be that much younger than you. They look like supermodels."

Lewis chuckled. "Uh, Charlie is twenty, and Etta is seventeen."

"Oh my god!" I gasped. "Do girls on the Upper East Side just come from a different planet? Etta is Melanie's age, and she seems so much more grown up."

"You have to grow up fast to live here. Be glad that Melanie is still so young and innocent."

I still couldn't believe it. If Melanie dressed and acted like Etta, my dad wouldn't let her leave the house. What a different world.

"Also, that's quite an age difference," I noted. "Mel and I are seven years apart, but you guys are, what? Nine and twelve years apart?"

"Yeah. My mom and dad fell in love young. When my mom had me at eighteen, everyone said she'd never amount to anything. That they'd only gotten married because he'd knocked her up. Thirty years later, and she's the ambassador to the United Nations and the most incredible person I know. She waited to have Charlie and Etta until after her career took off, just to prove everyone wrong. She's pretty much goals for everything in life."

"Wow! She sounds amazing. Like someone you'd read about in a textbook."

He grinned, clearly proud of his mother and all she'd accomplished.

The lights flickered, announcing that the opening show was about to start, and the crowd erupted in applause.

"How long have Penn and Katherine been gone for to get that drink?" I asked. "They're going to miss the opener if they don't hurry."

Lewis leaned back again. "I'd get comfortable. They'll likely be gone forever."

I arched an eyebrow in question. "Why?"

"Katherine hates waiting before the show. Usually, she shows up right as it starts or waits backstage or in a lounge or something. I'd be shocked if we saw her again before Chloe comes on."

"Oh," I said, disappointed. I'd wanted to spend time with Penn. I'd thought we'd have the night together even if we were with his friends…and he hated the music.

"Oh boy," Lewis said. "So…you and Penn, huh?"

"What? No. Why would you think that?"

"You have that…look. Trust me, I've seen it a lot."

I frowned at that. "I don't know what you're talking about."

"You're together, right?" he asked, leaning away from me.

"We're not together. We're just, you know, casual."

"Uh-huh," he said disbelievingly as he rose from his chair.

I bit my lip and turned back to the stage as the lights faded completely. A minute countdown showed on the screen for the opener. Penn and Katherine weren't going to come back for this. They were going to stay out wherever they were. Alone. And I didn't know if something was going on.

"Can I ask you something?" I asked when I got to my feet.

"What's that?"

"Are Penn and Katherine…you know, something?"

He grimaced. "Define *something*."

"Together? Or have they been together?"

"You're asking this because you and Penn are so casual?"

"Ugh! Never mind."

"Look, Penn doesn't want Katherine," he told me. "They've been this weird thing for years, but if he wanted to be with her, he already could be."

That helped marginally. At least it mirrored what Penn had said.

"And Katherine?"

He stared down at me, and I could see that he didn't want to answer.

"Katherine only wants what she can't have."

"So…if Penn and I *weren't* casual?"

"She would be worse. So much worse."

Great.

Peachy.

Fuck.

PENN

23

Katherine lounged comfortably in the private room she'd dragged me into. I should have known better than to think she wanted to get a drink and then go back to our seats. She detested waiting. She was the kind of woman who always had to arrive fashionably late. Make an appearance.

I'd only come for Natalie. And I wanted to head back already.

Normally, she couldn't even drag me to this kind of show. She knew that I didn't really like mainstream music. Not that Chloe wasn't talented, but it just wasn't my normal music.

It wasn't like I was going to try to get Katherine to an acoustic show at a small venue. I knew that she would never show up for that. So, it was particularly painful that I had to be at this one. If Natalie hadn't seemed so excited, I'd still be back at the beach house, working on my book.

"Oh, don't look so glum. Just one more drink, and we can go," she said with an eye roll as she raised her hand for the bartender.

"Why are we even here, Ren?"

"I had to make it up to Natalie."

"Ah yes, calling her a project to her face probably wasn't your best move."

"I didn't *mean* it like that."

I snorted. "Yes, you did."

"Honestly, I didn't. I like Natalie," Katherine said, and it almost sounded sincere. "It was just fucking Camden."

"How is fucking Camden these days?"

She bared her teeth at me. "Don't get me started."

"Still as good in bed as ever?" I teased.

"If you consider hate sex good, then sure."

I shrugged. "It can be if the person you're hate-fucking isn't a devious, manipulative, downright evil son of a bitch."

She patted my cheek twice. "Ah honey, are we jealous?"

"Just don't understand how you put up with it."

"A lady never spills all of her secrets."

"Are you considering yourself a lady now?" I said with a grin.

"Don't mess with me, Kensington."

The bartender appeared then, and Katherine asked for another round. I finished off my bourbon with pleasure. I'd need at least another to make it through the show.

Katherine's hand landed on my knee, and I arched an eyebrow. She just grinned devilishly and slowly crawled her way up my pant leg. She was dangerously close to my dick. And goddamn her, she couldn't just let it go. She had to keep going.

I grabbed her wrist hard in my hand. "That's not a toy you get to play with, Ren."

"You never like to have fun anymore." She crossed her legs and let a creamy white leg spill out of the slit in her skirt. "I'm not wearing any underwear."

"That's great," I said hollowly.

She sighed dramatically. "So, how's it going on your end? Is she in love with you yet?"

"Guess you'll have to wait and find out."

"Well, that's a no. Are you even fucking?" she asked with an edge to her voice.

Our drinks appeared, and I watched her down nearly her entire martini. She was pissed. I relished in it. Upsetting Katherine was like watching a ticking time bomb without the countdown. You never knew when she was going to explode.

"I have an idea," I told her, ignoring her question. "Why don't we end this bet?"

"Excuse me?" she gasped.

"I'm being a gentleman here. The stakes are high for you. And you're going to lose. So, I'm offering you the chance to back out."

"No."

"It's a stupid bet. And you don't have to go through with it."

In all honesty, I didn't want her to. Things with Natalie were so natural. And that had nothing to do with the bet. I didn't have to be anyone but myself with her, and we enjoyed each other's company. Not to mention, the sex was incredible. Katherine was destined to lose this thing.

"Are you afraid you'll lose?" she scoffed.

"Hardly. I know I'll win," I said confidently. The competitive side of my personality reared its ugly head. I wished that I could control that part of my character, but things like this just set me off. "But I'm giving you a chance to get out of marrying Camden. I'm giving you an out."

Katherine leaned forward until we were mere inches apart and smiled provocatively. "You should know me better than that by now."

"I do. But I thought I'd offer."

"No need. I'm still going to win," she said confidently.

I leaned back and downed my bourbon. "Lark was right. We shouldn't have done this."

"Fine. Then *you* back out of the bet," she said hotly.

"You know I'm not going to."

"Jesus, Penn, do you actually like her or something?" Katherine asked, fury in her voice. "You seem almost upset that we won't back out. Who the hell are you, and what have you done with Penn Kensington?"

"You like her. You just said you did."

"Of course I like her. She's gawky and strange. She has silver hair. She speaks her mind. She's not afraid to be whoever the hell she is. She's hardly *competition*, Penn!" Katherine said in exasperation. "Who would ever look at her when we're in a room together?"

I would.

I didn't say it, but the urge to nearly ripped through me.

There was a difference between upsetting her and pulling the pin on the grenade yourself.

"But you...why would *you* like her?" Katherine asked with an eye roll. "She's nothing and no one. She's not special in any way. She's like a cute small-town girl who stumbled on a gold mine."

"That's an interesting theory," I said dryly. "Considering that your fiancé hit on her, Lewis finds her fascinating, and I'm fucking her. There's clearly *something* special about her."

Katherine narrowed her eyes. And I knew that look. It was a possessive, dangerous look that said I'd said the wrong thing. Maybe I'd kicked a hornet's nest, but I just couldn't bring myself to care.

"I'm going to head back. Are you coming with?" I asked.

She downed the rest of her martini, dropped two hundred-dollar bills on the bar, and then swept out of the private lounge in front of me. I chuckled under my breath and followed behind her.

The opener had just finished by the time we made it back to our seats. Lewis and Natalie were grinning like fools and laughing at whatever the other had said. It almost looked like they hadn't missed the two of us. I would have much preferred to be out here than dealing with Katherine's scheming. She was one of my closest friends, but she never knew when enough was enough.

"Hey!" Natalie said, whirling around. She had a half-finished beer in her hand, and her blue eyes were wide and excited. "You made it back!"

"Sorry about that," I said. "We ended up in the lounge."

"Lewis warned me. It's no big. We just had the most amazing time. The opener was hilarious. I only knew one of her songs, but we're downloading the rest and listening to it the entire way back to the beach house."

"Oh god, what fresh level of hell have I entered?"

She and Lewis both burst into laughter.

"You were right," Natalie said, clutching her stomach. "Look at his face."

"Classic," Lewis said.

"What?" I asked in confusion.

"Lewis said that you'd go crazy if I suggested us listening to this music in your car."

"Hopefully, this is a joke because this music does not belong in the Audi."

Natalie giggled. A flush heated her cheeks from the beer and the show. She looked so unbelievably beautiful in that moment. I didn't know if it was just because she was so relaxed and so jovial or if it was the aftereffect of dealing with Katherine who was so uptight. But I wanted her right here. I wanted more of that carefree joy in my life. I wanted her for all the reasons that Katherine thought Natalie wasn't special. For all the reasons Katherine was wrong.

I wrapped an arm around her waist and tugged her tight

against my chest. Her beer sloshed and nearly spilled over, but she'd forgotten it as she looked up at me. She seemed surprised and happy. As if she had been wondering where exactly we were around my friends. And truthfully, I hadn't figured it out until that moment.

I didn't give a flying fuck what anyone else thought. Or that she wanted this to be casual. Or that we were just supposed to be fucking.

Those red lips were calling my name.

I tilted her backward and planted my lips on hers. She wrapped one arm around my neck and kissed me back just as hard. I faintly heard whistles and catcalls at the show we were putting on, but I didn't care.

This was where we were meant to be.

She pulled away breathlessly and giggled as she tried to smudge the red lipstick off of my lips. "I seemed to have gotten some..."

"There's no point. I'm just going to kiss you again."

Her smile brightened the room. "That so?"

"Definitely."

"Can you two get a room?" Lewis called teasingly.

"Not a bad idea," I suggested.

Natalie disentangled herself from my arms. "Never a bad idea," she agreed. "But I do really want to see Chloe. And Lewis knows every word. So, we have to stay for his benefit."

"Don't go telling him my secrets," Lewis muttered.

It was only Katherine who looked put out by the whole thing. Natalie sank into a seat next to her and thanked her a million times over again for the tickets. I was pretty sure that Katherine was regretting this entire evening. I took the seat by Lewis and shook his hand.

"Thanks for hanging with Natalie while I dealt with Katherine," I told him.

"Hey, no problem. She's great. You got that all worked out with Katherine?"

"Honestly, I think I made it worse," I told him.

"You think? That kiss probably made her go nuclear," Lewis said. "Not your smartest move."

"Can't help myself around Natalie."

"Well, watch out for Katherine. When she gets mad, she fights dirty."

"I know," I said, glancing over.

Natalie and Katherine were talking as if they were old friends. All those nasty things Katherine had said about Natalie came to the surface, and anger coursed through me all over again.

"It's not too late to end this," Lewis said with a lifted eyebrow.

"I just suggested that, and she wouldn't bite."

"Eh, it'll all be over soon anyway," Lewis said dismissively.

"Yeah," I agreed and ignored the unease that shot through me.

Natalie turned back into my side just as the lights dimmed. "That was probably the hottest kiss of my life."

"Yeah?"

She nodded.

"How about this one?" I asked and then kissed her again. And again. And again.

Actually, the show wasn't so bad when I got to kiss Natalie on and off through the whole thing.

NATALIE

24

"Penn!" I shrieked.

I raced down the hallway and burst into the master bedroom. We'd moved my stuff in before the show, and I'd thought it would take some getting used to. But I already felt completely at home, living in this enormous master suite with Penn. I swore that it was larger than my entire parents' house.

"What's wrong?" he asked, appearing out of the bathroom in nothing but a low-slung towel.

I'd discovered he was the kind of guy who went for a run every morning and came back and showered. Apparently, I'd caught him at just the right time.

My jaw dropped. "Holy abs."

"I'm going to go out on a limb and say that nothing is wrong?"

"Sorry, you are incredibly distracting," I said with wide eyes.

"Am I now?" he asked, purposefully striding forward.

"Uh…yeah. Just look at you."

"Me?" he asked. "You're only wearing my T-shirt."

I glanced down at myself and laughed. "Oh, yeah. I forgot about that. But I couldn't find anything to wear when my agent called this morning."

"She called? What for?" he asked with excitement in his eyes.

"She read my new manuscript and wanted to gush on the phone," I said, bouncing up and down on the balls of my feet.

"That's great! Are you going to submit the new book?"

"She said that she wants to start right away. That she couldn't get enough and wants to read the rest. She thinks this is the one!"

I did a little jig, and Penn just laughed.

"You're adorable. This is huge news!"

"I can't believe it. I mean…it doesn't really mean anything. Just because my agent likes it doesn't mean that the publishers will. She liked the last two books and the sample of my road-trip book, but no one bit on anything. So…I don't know."

"Okay, hold on. Let's not sour this," he said, putting his hands on my shoulders. "Your agent loved your new book and thinks it's the one! That's a great feeling. We don't have to think about the next part of the process yet. Just revel in the fact that you are clearly writing in the correct direction."

"You're right." I let the negativity of future rejection fall off my shoulders.

My agent loved it. She wanted to shop it immediately. And she had only seen fifty pages. That was astronomical odds! I'd never gone out on proposal before. Super scary to think about, but I wanted to be happy.

"This is the best news I've had in weeks."

"Then we should celebrate."

I grinned and gestured to the king bed mere feet from us. "I have a few ideas for how we can celebrate."

Penn groaned. "I want to sweep you up right now and ravish you, but…"

"But?"

"I have to go into the city for a meeting."

"Really? Today?"

"Unfortunately, yes." Penn veered into the walk-in closet, and I followed, waiting for that towel to drop. I arched an eyebrow at the goods. "Getting a good enough look?"

"I wouldn't mind taking a good, long look with my mouth," I suggested.

His dick twitched at my words. "Maybe we have time for a quickie."

"Nope. You're just going to have to wait until after your meeting."

He moved into my personal space, backing me up into the closet wall. He was an Adonis sculpted out of marble and just as gorgeous. "Do I?"

"Well, you don't have to," I said as he stroked me through my thin panties. I tilted my head back and sighed. "I wouldn't mind."

"Tonight," he said with a cocky grin as he stepped back and started to get dressed.

"Tonight…what?"

"I'll be back tonight."

"You want to make me wait all day for you?"

He slid into a blue-and-white button-up. "I want to have enough time to celebrate your book and to celebrate you. If I took you now, it would be three hard thrusts and a kiss good-bye."

"I'll take both," I said, helping him with the buttons.

"And I'll give you both," he said devilishly. "Both tonight."

"Ugh! You're killing me."

"This tie?" he asked with a grin. He held up a navy-blue tie, and I nodded.

"Yes. Everything you wear is hot as fuck. Though I'm not used to the suits anymore. You're so relaxed here."

"Honestly, the suits are more who I am. It's strange, not having to go into the office every day in one. And we had to wear them all through high school as part of our uniform."

"Well, this is me." I gestured to my outfit and then remembered I was only wearing his T-shirt. "I mean...whatever. You know what I mean."

"I know who you are."

My heart melted.

He finished with his tie and then pulled on the black suit jacket. "I'll see you tonight. Don't wear anything you don't want to get destroyed."

"Guess I'll have to be naked," I said suggestively.

"Perfect. I will see you tonight, completely naked."

"Deal."

"You don't mind watching Aristotle? I can take him to the apartment."

"Oh no, Totle can stay with me."

Totle—who, up until this point, had been too busy lounging in the sun—trotted into the master bedroom to find out why we were saying his name. His tail wagged, and his ears were all floppy. I scooped him up into my arms and kissed him a dozen times.

"Just you and me today, buddy. You know what that means?" Totle licked my face. "That's right. All the treats you want, and your dad won't be here to tell me to stop spoiling you."

Penn rolled his eyes. "You two are trouble."

I gave him the most innocent look I could muster. "We'll behave."

"Only until I get back," he said with a wink.

His mouth dropped hard on mine in a lingering kiss that made me want to reconsider letting him leave. How important could this meeting really be? But Penn pulled away, looked back at me once regrettably, and then disappeared. I watched the Audi leave and sighed.

"Now, it really is just me and you," I told Totle as I let him out onto the back deck.

It ended up being a productive day without Penn. More like what I'd expected every day to be like when I first signed on to the job. I'd met with the decorator and seen the progress in the guest bedrooms. As much as I'd loved the feel of the house before, the decorator was a genius, and I hadn't even seen the end result. But everything was already so much more modern while still holding on to the traditional aesthetics of the place.

With the motivation from my agent's call, I managed to write two whole chapters on the new book. Totle and I took a good, long walk on the beach, and I even got in a swim. Thank god the pool was heated because the temperatures were dropping. I knew they'd have to close it down soon, and I wanted to get every chance I could to swim.

While Totle finally fell asleep on the bed, I took a luxurious shower and blew out my long hair. I didn't normally wear much makeup, but if we were celebrating tonight, I thought it would be worth it. I added the red lipstick he loved so much and then threw on his T-shirt and a pair of sweats while I waited. When I found out what time he'd get back, then I'd strip.

A thrill ran through me at the prospect.

I sent him a text to see if he had an ETA but didn't get a response.

I shrugged. Maybe he was driving.

My phone buzzed noisily, and I reached for it. My heart sank when I saw it was Melanie and not Penn.

"Hey, Mel. What's up?"

"Michael and I got back together," she unceremoniously told me.

"Wait, what? Why?"

Truly, I wasn't that surprised. Considering how she'd acted when he started texting her and their history, I'd had a feeling she'd go back to him. I just wished that she hadn't. That she'd been stronger and held him off.

"I don't know, Natalie. I thought about how I felt when I was in New York with you, but I can't stay mad at him. He regrets everything that happened with Kennedy, and neither of us is talking to her anymore. I've completely cut her out of my life."

She could do that to her best friend but not to the douche who had broken her heart on a whim.

"Are you sure about this? I mean, he did just toss you aside so easily."

"He said it was all Kennedy's idea."

I rolled my eyes. "You're not that naive."

"I know. I know," she said softly. "This is why I didn't want to tell you."

"Because I'd tell you the truth."

"Kind of."

I laughed. "Well, it's okay, Melanie. You shouldn't worry about talking to me about things. I love you. I just want what's best for you."

"I know. I really think that Michael is it. We've been together so long."

"I get it," I lied. Because I didn't. If a guy ever treated me like that, I'd throw him to the curb so fast that he wouldn't have even seen it coming.

I let Melanie talk it out. She really just needed someone to listen as she convinced herself that this was the right move. I wasn't super great at that, but I also knew that I couldn't change her mind. She was as stubborn as I was. And she didn't want me to tell her that she was making a huge mistake. Even if she was.

When I finally got off of the phone with her an hour later, I still didn't have a text from Penn. It was getting late. Already nine o'clock, and I hadn't heard a peep. Had he gotten stuck in the city?

I debated between sending him a text and letting it lie. He'd said he was coming back tonight and made the plans for us to celebrate. So, it wasn't like I expected him to stay in the city. But, if I kept sending texts, would I look like a nagging girlfriend? I sighed and decided against it.

Instead, I pulled my computer up and scrolled through Crew while chatting with Amy about Melanie and Michael as I waited to hear back from Penn.

An hour rolled past.

And then another.

No text.

"What the hell?" I grumbled.

I was irritated that I'd put makeup on to sit around the house. This wasn't how I'd thought tonight would end up.

I shot him another text to try to check in. At this point, I just wanted to make sure that he was alive. He wasn't the kind of guy who blew off plans and didn't text. Or at least…I didn't think he was like that anymore.

Before in Paris, I would have absolutely said he was that guy. But now? After the weeks we'd spent together, I'd actually been thinking he was an upstanding guy. He warred with who he was because of his past, but overall, he was actually one of the good ones.

So, maybe he had gotten into a car accident. Maybe he'd been taken to the hospital, and no one knew to call me. Maybe…

A million other horrible scenarios ran through my mind.

This wasn't about our missed night. We could have

another night. This was worry. That was all this was. Yep. Definitely.

I pulled my phone out and tried to call him. The number went straight to voice mail. I furrowed my brows. Did that mean it was off? Or dead?

Well, shit. I couldn't get ahold of him like that.

I scrolled through my phone and stopped on the two numbers that I had who *might* know where he was and if he was okay.

My finger hovered over Katherine, and then I thought better of it and pressed Lewis's number instead. If Penn was with Katherine, I really didn't want to know about it.

"Natalie?" Lewis answered. He sounded surprised.

"Hey, sorry about this. I know it's late."

"No, no, it's fine. You can call me anytime. What's up?"

"I just…Penn went into the city this morning for a meeting. He told me that he'd be back tonight, but I haven't heard from him all day, and his phone is off. Normally, I wouldn't think about it, but he definitely promised to be back. I'm kind of worried he might be hurt or something."

"Shit," he said. I heard rustling, as if he were moving around. "Sorry about that. That's my fault."

"Your fault?"

"After he finished his meeting, we went out for drinks. He told me he had plans, but one drink turned into a bottle. He's drunk, and his phone is dead. He's literally asleep on my couch right now."

"Oh," I said softly. "Well, I feel stupid."

A laugh escaped me. I'd really worked myself up to think that something was wrong. I should have texted Lewis earlier, and maybe I wouldn't have let this worry creep in.

"Hey, don't feel stupid. I didn't realize that his plans were with you."

"Yeah, well, no big. I'll talk to him tomorrow when his phone charges. Thanks for letting me know."

"Anytime, Natalie. Anytime."

I hung up the phone, feeling like a moron. We weren't dating. I wasn't his girlfriend. I was the casual sex that I'd offered him. He didn't owe me an explanation for why he was staying out all night when we had plans.

With a sigh, I grabbed the last piece of cold pizza we'd ordered in the night before from the place in East Hampton that I was now obsessed with. I ate it on the way back to the bedroom to snuggle with Totle…alone. Happy celebrating to me.

NATALIE

25

My arms viciously cut through the pool. I hadn't swam like this in a long time. Needing the release of diving into something and not coming up for air. Just me and the water. Slicing through the water, exerting my body to its max, racing my own thoughts. I'd be sore tomorrow, but I didn't even care. It was the only thing that really quieted everything down.

I was still disappointed about yesterday.

And irritated with myself for being disappointed.

I was the one who had started this casual thing. I had known it was a bad idea. I'd let Amy talk me into it. And then the sex had just been so good.

But I'd be stupid if I said yesterday hadn't proven just how much the casual thing did not work for me. I'd tried to rationalize. Truth was harder to look in the face.

Truth was…I was falling for Penn Kensington.

I was leaving in a matter of weeks, and I was catching feelings for someone I knew I couldn't have. Our worlds didn't connect. Our lives were so far from normal.

I didn't *want* to want this. I didn't want to want *him*.

It'd be easier if I didn't.

Easier if I hated him still. If I had never seen him as anything but the asshole who had left me in Paris. So, so much easier.

I came up gasping for breath and saw a figure in a black suit standing over the pool. His hands were in his pockets. He had stubble on his jaw. And he looked like hell.

"Morning," he said when I looked up at him.

"Nice of you to show up." I swam over to my water bottle and took a long drink.

"I'm sorry about last night."

I waved my hand at him. "Why would you be? You don't owe me anything."

"Well, I told you I'd be back last night. I made plans with you, and then I broke them. I didn't even let you know I was breaking them."

I shrugged. "It's not like we're dating."

"No," he agreed, "we're not dating. But I should have called, and now, you're mad at me."

"I'm not mad at you. I was worried about you. There's a difference."

I was mad at myself. Not at him.

I hopped out of the pool and hastily toweled off before hustling back inside to put on warmer clothes. Penn followed me as I put sweats back on, tugging a hoodie over my T-shirt and knotting my hair on the top of my head.

"Natalie," Penn said, reaching out and stopping me in my tracks.

"It's really fine." I stepped out of his touch. "You're safe. Lewis said he got you drunk. Your work meeting must not have gone that great if you had to get drunk after."

"Work meeting?" he asked.

"Yeah…you said you had work stuff."

"No, I didn't."

"Yes, you did," I said and then thought back on our conversation. It slowly dawned on me. "No, you didn't."

"I had a meeting with an old friend. I would have rather been working for how well the meeting went. Lewis and I went out after. I honestly thought I'd have one beer, but he kept me out."

"Oh. Who was the friend?" I asked before I could stop myself.

"No one important. Someone I knew from college. She said she wanted to meet with me about my book project but spent more time catching up." He rolled his eyes. "So, will you accept my apology?"

She. Hmm…I wondered who this mysterious old friend was. Not that it was anything I should wonder or care about. He was back and trying to apologize. I should just accept the apology and move on. I was really upset with myself for doing exactly what I'd told Amy that I'd do.

"Okay," I finally said.

"Will you let me make it up to you?" he asked, tilting my chin up.

"I'm really not in the mood right now," I whispered. "Plus, the decorator should be here soon."

"Tonight then," he insisted. "I'll be here. I'm not leaving. I'll make up for last night."

I should say no. I should say that he had nothing to make up for. I should tell him that we should stop doing this. But I said none of those things.

I just nodded. "Okay. Tonight then."

I felt like a sucker to my own heart. And the way he made it beat.

. . .

ANXIETY RACED through my brain as the sun went down, and the time was approaching to meet Penn. I'd promised myself I wouldn't get in too deep, and here I was. I'd known I couldn't make it happen. I should have listened to my instincts.

What was going to happen when I left after the mayor's election party? There was no future here for us. And I didn't know if I wanted one even if there was. I was falling for him, but could this ever be serious? I didn't know. And I hated thinking about it.

"Natalie?" Penn called.

I was standing in the bathroom, staring at my reflection. I'd gotten all dolled up last night for him. I'd been so excited for our celebration. But these worries made me wonder if I should end it where I stood. Make it easier on both of us. Even if it was the last thing I wanted.

"Nat?" He strode into the master and saw me standing in the bathroom. He looked gorgeous. Blindingly beautiful. Those eyes. Those magnificent blue eyes that seemed to see right through me. He leaned his shoulder against the doorframe and slid his hands into his pockets.

"Hey," I said.

"Everything okay?"

That one question, and I couldn't do it. I didn't want to. I wanted to be present. I wanted every moment I could get from him while I still could. Even if I went home later without him, I didn't want to regret a second now.

"Yeah," I said quickly. "Just deciding on lipstick. Red?"

He shook his head. "Wear the pink."

I furrowed my brows at him. I knew that he liked the red lipstick. Red was sexy and let his filthy mind work. Pink was soft and pretty. Not our casual relationship at all.

"I'll let you finish," he said. "Meet me out back."

I nodded and watched him disappear through the doorway. He confused me. Pink lipstick? Was it not that kind of celebration?

Hmm.

I applied a layer of the pink matte that was normally my go-to color. Then I grabbed a long cardigan with fringe at the bottom to ward off the cold and slipped into my moccasins before heading out of the bedroom.

I found Penn on the back deck and sucked in a shocked breath at the sight before me.

"Is that a telescope?" I gasped. "I love telescopes!"

He grinned devilishly. "I used to be mildly obsessed with the stars when I was a kid."

"Did you want to be an astronaut?"

"Didn't everyone?"

I laughed, letting all that anxiety fall off of my shoulders. This was Penn. If I'd realized anything in the last couple of weeks, it was that he had a knack for making me forget my worries.

"I also have pizza," he said.

He moved to the table, which I hadn't even noticed with the excitement of the telescope. He opened the box to reveal pepperoni and sausage from my new favorite place in East Hampton.

"Bribes now, huh?"

"Hey. It's not a bribe. It's an apology." He reached out for a bottle of wine and pulled the cork on it. "This too."

He poured each of us a glass of red. I gratefully took mine and sipped on it. God, it was smooth and just a little sweet. Perfect. Probably cost a fortune.

"Can I reiterate that I'm sorry about yesterday?" Penn said.

"You can, but you don't have to."

"With anyone else, I'd agree. It's never been me to care

about this sort of thing, but I have been trying to be better. Trying to reach a happier life. And breaking plans with you or making you worry does not make me happy."

"I see that this is an ethical dilemma for you," I teased.

"Of sorts. I care about your opinion of me. And I don't want to damage it."

"No damage done."

Penn searched my face as if he wanted to believe what I was saying. I thought for a minute that he was going to say more. As if he had something on the tip of his tongue that he needed to confess, but it disappeared completely.

"All right then."

We finished off half of the pizza before I all but dragged Penn to the telescope. I put my eye to the eyepiece and looked at the great field of stars before me.

"Orion?" I guessed.

"Well, I thought I'd start easy." He used a red flashlight to show me Orion's belt on a star map.

Boy had come prepared. It was hot in such a nerdy way.

"Please, let's try something better."

I consulted the star map before moving the telescope to a different point of reference. "In Greek mythology, there's a story that, when Mount Olympus was being attacked, Aphrodite and Eros fled by tying themselves together, changing into fish, and throwing themselves into a river. The act was commemorated by putting a pair of fish into the sky." I glanced back up at him and offered him my place.

Penn raised his eyebrows in surprise and then looked down into the telescope. "The fish. Pisces, of course."

"The very end of the zodiac. And not the best story if you ask me, but I claim it anyway."

"You're a Pisces?" he asked, glancing up at me.

"Oh, yeah. My birthday is February twenty-eighth. I fit it

a hundred percent. Water sign—swimmer, romantic, dreamer. What's your birthday?"

"June twenty-first."

"Summer solstice," I said in surprise. "On the cusp of Cancer or Gemini?"

He shrugged. "I always claimed Gemini."

"Yeah, you aren't much of a Cancer. But Gemini. Huh." I took his place at the telescope and began to maneuver it.

"What?"

"I just would have pegged you as a Sagittarius with your love of philosophy." I offered him the telescope again. "Here, take a look. Gemini has a much better story. The twins, Castor and Pollux, were the sons of the queen of Sparta. They weren't real twins really. Castor, the queen had with her husband, the king of Sparta, but Pollux was an immortal born of Zeus. When Castor died in the Trojan War, Pollux asked his father to make him an immortal, so they could live out their days as brothers for all of eternity. Instead, he put them both in the sky as twins truly."

"How do you know all of this?" Penn asked. His eyes were wide and speculating. "Here I thought, I'd be the one showing off my knowledge. Who knew that you would completely trump me?"

"Well, most kids get bedtime stories with fairy tales and nursery rhymes. I grew up on horoscopes and the stories behind the constellations."

"That's kind of amazing."

"Eh," I said with a shrug. "My mom is really into New Age stuff. Hence the ritual burning you unceremoniously walked in on. No matter what you do...some of it manages to stick with you. Plus, I aced my mythology class in college."

He laughed. "I bet you did. That actually sounds like such an interesting background. I can't imagine the things that you learned from her. Can you read my palm or tarot cards or a crystal ball?"

"Whoa there. Crystal-ball reading is serious work." I giggled as I watched Penn adjust the telescope for himself. "But yeah...I could probably read your palm, and it's been a while for tarot cards for me. People usually get mad when I read for them anyway. I predict a lot of death."

He snorted. "You're something else."

"Fact."

"Here, look at this one. I thought of you when I picked it out."

"What am I looking for?"

"A half-circle of stars like this," he said, pointing it out for me. "It's Corona Borealis and supposed to be a crown."

"Do you know the story?" I asked.

"I do. Do you?"

I grinned up at him. "Tell it to me anyway. I want to know why you picked it for me."

"Well, as much as I remember, when Theseus defeated the Minotaur, he ran off with the guy's daughter."

"Ariadne," I filled in.

"Yes. But Theseus leaves her, and she's left crying in despair. But a god finds her and falls in love. He presents her with a crown, and she threw it up into the sky when they were married."

"I do love happy endings," I said. "Not your typical tragedy. Is that why you thought of me?"

"I thought of you because of this." He removed a thin blue box from his coat pocket and tried to pass it to me.

"Um...what is *that*?"

Tiffany blue box. Holy shit. What the hell?

"Open it and see."

"Uh..."

"Here."

He pried the box open, holding it out for me. Inside was a linked silver chain with a circle on one end that read *Tiffany & Co. New York* with a toggle on the other end that connected to the circle. And dangling from the chain was a delicate silver crown.

A crown to match the constellation I had just found in the night sky.

NATALIE

26

"I can't accept that," I said at once.

"Yes, you can."

"If this is part of your apology, it's way too much."

"I'm not apologizing, Natalie."

Penn took it out of the box, scooped up my wrist, and attached it there. The crown dangled from my wrist, and it felt perfect. I'd never in a million years thought I'd own something from Tiffany. And I had no idea why I did right now.

"Then...why?" I managed to get out.

I'd been unsuccessfully trying to convince myself to dump him because my heart was in too deep. I couldn't fathom a reason for this.

"This isn't casual for me," he responded.

"It isn't?" I dragged my eyes up from the beautiful bracelet to his baby blues.

"No. It was never casual for me."

"But...I thought you wanted it to be casual."

"You suggested it after weeks of trying to avoid me. I wasn't going to say no. I went along with what you asked because I didn't want to scare you. But I don't want to pretend anymore."

"So…what do you want?"

"I want to be with you, Nat."

"You want…to be…with me," I said incomprehensibly.

"Yes. I messed up the first time around. I should have never let you go in Paris."

"Then why did you?" I gasped out.

I could barely understand what he was saying. It felt too surreal to me. There was a ringing in my ears. Something that told me this was impossible. Guys like Penn Kensington didn't want girls like me. No matter that we worked so well together. No matter that the sex was beyond incredible. No matter that we had matching interests.

I hated to admit it, but it made more sense when he'd abandoned me that day in Paris than that he wanted me now.

"I was a twenty-three-year-old idiot."

"Obviously," I said. "I mean…you had sex with me and then abandoned me. I was eighteen, and you took my virginity and then disappeared. Can you imagine how that made me feel?"

Penn's eyes rounded in shock. "Wait…what did you just say?"

"I was eighteen," I said, realizing that I had told him the thing I had sworn to myself that I wouldn't.

"You were a virgin?"

"I mean…"

"Natalie?"

"Yeah, I was."

"Why would you go back with me?"

"Hey, don't blame me!"

"I'm not blaming you. I just can't believe it. No wonder you were so mad at me all these years. What a way to end that night for you."

"Ha," I said humorlessly. "That was only half of it. You told your maid to let me out, and she called me trash and kicked me out on the street."

"I never told her to make you leave," he said in shock. "I didn't even see her before I left."

"Really? She made it seem like you'd told her to act that way."

"I have very little memory of that morning," he said solemnly. "Mostly just getting on a plane and rushing home."

"Why?" I waited anxiously for the answer I'd wanted all these years. It wasn't enough for Penn to tell me he wanted me. I had to get all of this out in the open. Without the truth, I didn't know if I could trust myself or him enough to do this. "Why did you leave that day?"

Penn glanced at the floor and rubbed the back of his head. He leaned against the deck wall, sighed, and then looked at me. "It was the day my father died."

My jaw dropped. "Oh my god."

"I should have woken you up and told you. But everything was a blur. I just jumped on a plane and left."

"You do not have to apologize for that."

My heart was racing as I restructured everything that had happened that night and processed it over again with this new information. It changed everything. Yes, he'd still been a dick for not waking me up and telling me he was leaving. It was a shitty thing to do. But…if my dad had died, I couldn't say that I would have thought to wake him up. I'd been so mad for so long. And now, it had all come down to this moment.

I released the anger. Released the mistrust. Released it all.

Then, I moved forward and kissed him.

He leaned into me, his lips soft and inviting. None of the casual playfulness we'd had for the last couple of weeks. This was deeper, better. A hundred times more intense.

His arms wrapped around me, dragging our bodies tight against each other. My fingers tangled in his hair. His dug into my back. My body responded instantly to his touch. To the soft caress of his tongue against mine. The way he moved it to tease my bottom lip and then drag it between his teeth.

I whimpered softly at the touch.

He pulled back and pressed his forehead to mine. "Does this mean you'll accept the bracelet?"

I laughed. "Yes, I guess I will."

"Good. Does it mean that we're no longer casual?"

"Were we ever?"

He nipped at my bottom lip and grinned. "Good."

Then, he lifted me up into his arms and carried me back through the house and into the bedroom.

"We couldn't have just had sex out there?" I suggested as he kicked the door closed behind him.

"Too cold for you to be naked." He dropped me onto my feet in front of the bed. "And I want you completely naked."

"You owe me at least twice," I reminded him.

"Oh, I remember." He tossed his jacket to the floor. "Slow and steady first. And then hard and fast. Just how you like it."

I raised my eyebrows.

"Don't pretend you don't like it hard and fast," he said, nuzzling into my neck and making my legs go weak.

"I do," I agreed easily.

"But not right now."

He spent careful time removing my moccasins and then my hippie cardigan before tugging my dress over my head. His hands grazed my body as he slipped my panties down my legs. But, before he could push me backward, I started in on the buttons of his shirt. Pushing each one through its hole and then finally slipping it off of his shoulders. I moved to his pants, dragging the zipper to the base and letting them fall off of his narrow hips. I was as anxious to get him naked

CRUEL MONEY

as he was for me. And I wasn't satisfied until I stripped him out of his boxers, leaving us both completely in the nude.

"You're so beautiful." He traced his thumbs over my nipples before dragging one into his mouth.

I tilted my head back and moaned softly at the feel of him. Everything was suddenly heightened.

My hand swept down to his cock. I wrapped my fingers around the base of him and then moved it up to the head. He sucked in a breath as he sucked in the other nipple, savoring the taste of me. I wanted to do the same.

I ran my thumb across the head and felt a bead of pre-cum wet the tip of my finger. He lengthened further in my hand, and, god, I just wanted to taste him.

Penn bit down on my nipple, and I arched back, achingly tender and wanting more. His hand moved from my breast to between my legs where I was already wet for him.

Before, he might have just scooped me up and buried himself deep inside me. Forgotten the world for a while as we lavished in each other's bodies. But not tonight.

He tried to ease me back onto the bed, but I stopped him. My hand was still on his dick as I dropped to my knees before him. He inhaled sharply and then gathered my long hair into his hands.

"Open up," he commanded.

My eyes drifted up to his, and he cocked an eyebrow. I opened my mouth, and then, with his hands still in my hair, he guided his dick between my lips.

I ran the flat of my tongue down his shaft before licking the tip. He shuddered slightly, and I took that as a good sign. I pulled him back into me, sucking his cock and enjoying the way his body reacted. The groans coming out of his mouth. The way he fisted my hair. The rock of his hips as he tried to get deeper into my mouth.

We'd done this before, of course. But this time was different. I could feel how desperately he wanted to take control. How he wanted to fuck my mouth and come deep down my throat. And I fucking loved when he did it. But right now, he was letting me take the lead. Something he rarely allowed. Something I rarely craved.

But this was powerful. It was seductive and made me delirious with need.

"Fuck," he spat. "Oh fuck, Nat."

"Mmm," I moaned on his dick.

He thrust into my mouth harder, losing control. I could feel his dick thickening, preparing to unload.

"Oh Jesus, fuck." He pulled me backward by my hair. "Fuck, wait."

"Wait?" I asked, looking up at him with hooded bedroom eyes.

"I want to fuck you."

"Can't finish what I started?" I trailed my finger down his shaft.

"I want you to come with me."

He hoisted me to my feet and then laid me back on the bed. I knew it'd pained him to stop. That he'd been so close. Just on the tip of the iceberg. But he had, and when he looked at me, it was one of desire. He wanted to worship my body.

His hands spread my legs wide. I was bare before him, like a feast at a banquet. And he wanted to devour me.

He leaned forward onto his elbows, gazing down into my eyes. His cock was poised at my entrance, waiting. I lifted my chin and pressed my lips against his.

"I want this," I told him, rubbing my hand along his jaw. "You."

"I have to tell you something," he said, suddenly serious.

I laughed halfheartedly. "Right now? Really?"

I pushed my pelvis up so that the head of his penis

pressed ever so slightly inside me. My eyes rolled back, and I invitingly swirled my hips.

"Open your eyes."

Mine fluttered back open, and I smiled. "What is it you wanted to tell me?"

He looked torn for a minute before saying, "You're the most beautiful thing I've ever seen."

My smile broadened, and I pulled his lips back down to mine. "Thank you," I murmured.

Then, he thrust forward. He was gentle at first, slicking himself with my wetness. Then he bottomed out inside me, and we both groaned.

"About that slow and steady," I said with a chuckle.

He responded by pulling out and slamming back into me. Hard and fast, just like I liked it.

"Oh," I gasped.

"Come here," he said. Then he hoisted me up into his arms so that I was practically sitting in his lap. He lifted me up and then forced me back down, driving himself deeper inside of me.

Our chests were pressed tight together. My arms were locked around his neck. There was nowhere else to look but deep into those blue eyes. And I was lost to them. Not to the sex we were having that was so much more than just fucking. But to his eyes and the story they told me as we slept together. The way they seemed to only see me. The window to his true emotions, which I'd thought were buried. And in truth, it was me who had hidden myself away.

Once he'd opened up, it had just unleashed from me.

He wanted this.

I wanted this.

Together, we were incredible.

I wanted this moment to last forever. To make up for those years we'd wasted with miscommunication. When I'd thought he was nothing but a conceited jerk and he'd been too wrapped up in his own problems to have something real and meaningful.

Penn's grip tightened on my hips, and I could tell he was close. He thrust up hard inside me, and I unleashed. My orgasm sparked his own. We came together in a blur of ecstasy, and I collapsed backward on the bed.

Penn dropped down at my side. His chest was rising and falling in time with my own. I rolled over and lay my head on his shoulder.

"Wow," I whispered. Because we'd had some great sex, but this was on another level. I hadn't known it could get better.

"Wasn't it?"

"Yeah. That last bit you did…just wow."

He kissed my head and stroked my hair. "You were magnificent."

"Mmm," I agreed.

"Shower?"

I nodded. "I think that's probably mandatory before round two."

"Hey."

"Hey," I replied with a sigh.

"What are you doing for Halloween?"

"Is that coming up?" I rolled over to look at him.

"It's, like, ten days away."

"A lot can happen in ten days."

"Yes," he said. "We can have a lot of sex."

"Well, then I am planning on having a lot of sex."

He laughed. "There's a party. I want to take you."

"Like a date?"

"Like a date," he confirmed.

"I could do that."

"Yeah? Good. We'll have to find you some lingerie."

I raised my eyebrow. "What kind of party is this?"

"Annual Lingerie & Ears party," Penn said. "Katherine throws it to raise money for animal hospitals and rescue shelters and sells out Club Marquee every year. It's the best event in the city."

"Aww," I said. I was surprised Katherine had a charity of choice. "That's great that the money is donated. But do I really have to wear lingerie and ears? Doesn't that narrow down the options?"

His eyes grazed my body, and he got a good, long fill. "Most definitely."

"Sounds like you wouldn't mind some lingerie before the party."

"I wouldn't say no," he said.

I felt his cock twitch against me, and my eyes widened. "Already?"

He rolled on top of me and grinned like a devil. "Imagining you in lingerie makes me want you."

"Everything makes you want me."

"Well good. Because I have every intention of fucking you all night."

PART IV
TRICK OR TREAT?

NATALIE

27

"Must we coordinate?" I asked Katherine as I stepped out of her closet.

She took one look at my ensemble and actually applauded. "Oh my god, yes, we have to coordinate. Look at you!"

She spun me in a circle to face the tri-fold mirror. I was currently dressed in a white corseted leotard with a white garter that held up my white sheer thigh-high leggings. Emmanuel had fixed my makeup so that I shimmered brightly and my hair so that I had a fluffy halo. He had even affixed white wings, which I had no idea how I was going to get off.

"My little angel," Katherine cheered. "These shoes."

She pointed out white pumps, and I slipped my feet into them.

"I feel ridiculous."

"But you look hot as fuck. And we match." Katherine moved to stand next to me in the mirror in her devil outfit complete with horns, a tail, and a small pitchfork.

I still didn't know how I'd ended up here, allowing

Katherine to dress me up again. After her project comment, I'd felt out of sorts, but when Lewis had told me that Katherine got really bad when Penn was into someone, it had me totally on edge. I'd kept that fact from her because I had no interest in knowing what *really bad* actually meant.

"Perfect timing, too. The limo should be here any minute."

She grabbed her blood-red bag and handed me a matching fluffy white one. I dropped my phone, small wallet, and the bracelet Penn had gotten me inside.

"So...things with Penn are heating up?" she asked as we strode toward the elevator.

"Oh...I don't know."

"You looked pretty into each other at the Chloe concert."

I shrugged dismissively. "Well, it's new."

"And it's not serious?" she asked with a secret smile.

"I mean...I don't know."

Katherine laughed and poked the bag she'd handed me. "Oh, come on. Spill the goods. A Tiffany's bracelet doesn't exactly scream casual to me."

I couldn't keep the smile from my face. Even though I'd promised myself I wouldn't say anything about us, I couldn't keep it in.

"Yeah, it's not casual. I'm not sure exactly what it is, but I'm excited."

Katherine squealed, "I am so happy for you two!"

"Really?" I asked.

Lewis's statement had made it seem like Katherine would go ballistic at the news. Not congratulate me.

"Are you kidding me? Of course I am! I want my friends to be happy. And you two are some of my closest friends."

I looked her straight in the eye. I waited for the sneer to follow. For her to show her true colors. For what Lewis had said to be true.

But it just honestly wasn't there.

Katherine looked actually pleased by the prospect of us dating. And maybe she was lying, or perhaps she was a phenomenal actress, but it made me relax. Made me stop second-guessing every interaction with her. I'd been prepared to have a horrible evening, but I wanted to have fun tonight. And Katherine was a guaranteed good time.

"Here's the limo!" Katherine said when we stepped out of the elevator and then out onto the street.

The driver opened the door for us, and I slid in behind Katherine. Lewis was seated at one end, dressed to kill in the *Black Panther* villain costume for Killmonger. He was in dark pants and a long black jacket that he left open to reveal that he was bare-chested, except for a gold necklace that looked like an exact replica of the one Killmonger wore. His face lit up when I entered, and I whistled when I saw him.

"Excellent choice," I said.

He winked at me. "I am not the only one."

I blushed at his assessment of my lingerie. Then I found the person I was really looking for. Penn was seated closest to the front of the limo in the sharpest-cut tuxedo I'd ever seen in my life. He hadn't told me who he was dressing up as, and now that I saw him, I realized it probably didn't even matter with how hot he looked.

Then he withdrew a small, hopefully fake gun from his jacket pocket and held it up. "Bond. James Bond."

My mouth watered at the sight of him. Hadn't I thought he looked just like Bond the first night I met him? And then again when I'd seen him at the beach house. It was hardly a costume on him. He was just that attractive.

"It suits you," I said, sidling up to his side.

He draped an arm across my shoulders and whispered in my ear, "I'm getting you out of this later."

"What do you think, I'm some kind of Bond girl?"

"If you are, your seduction is working."

I laughed and leaned back into him.

Katherine sank into the seat next to Lewis, and after saying hello to both of the boys, we drove over to where we were picking up Rowe.

"I don't know why he insisted on being last for pick-up this year," Katherine said irritably. "I'm always last. Because look at this costume."

"No Lark tonight?" I asked.

"She couldn't make it this close to the election. She's out, knocking on doors for the president or something," Katherine told me. "You should be glad you haven't seen her right now. She's sleep-deprived, food-deprived, and high as fuck on caffeine. She'd probably ask you if you'd voted and then manage to get all of us sick like last time."

"That sounds like a rough job."

"Yeah, she loves it though," Lewis said.

"And she's good at it," Penn said.

"We just wish we could have more time with her when she wasn't utterly manic," Katherine muttered right as we stopped.

The driver hopped out and opened the door for Rowe. But instead of Rowe, a long, bare leg stepped into the car. That leg was accompanied by a stunning body and a swath of glittery red dress and bright red hair. The gorgeous woman was clearly dressed up as Jessica Rabbit.

"Uh, who the hell are you?" Katherine asked.

"Amanda," the girl said, holding out her hand.

"I mean…what are you doing here?"

"That's my date," Rowe said as he slid into the backseat in a nondescript suit. He nodded his head at everyone. "Sup?"

"You didn't say you were bringing a date." Katherine rolled her eyes. "And I told you that you had to dress up."

"Uh yeah, I did," Rowe said. "Both accounts."

Amanda leaned forward, her perfect breasts almost

falling out of her costume. "He said he's dressed up as a philosophy professor." She ran her hand back through Rowe's hair. He looked uncomfortable by the whole thing. "I've never seen a professor this hot though."

"Oh dear Lord," Penn groaned.

"I'm Penn," Rowe told them easily. "Just look. Notebook." He held up a leather notebook. "And give me a second, and I can bore you all with useless philosophical ramblings."

Penn just shook his head. "You astound me."

"The ethical theory of life is happiness, and happiness is about right or wrong, which brings me to my conclusion that everyone must follow a set of rules to live a life of something, something," Rowe droned, sounding like the teacher from Charlie Brown.

Katherine and Lewis died laughing.

"Nicely played, my man," Lewis said, shaking Rowe's hand.

Even I couldn't help but giggle.

"I do not sound like that," Penn said.

"A little," I ventured. "But I like it."

Penn shook his head, but he was a good sport.

Jessica Rabbit unfortunately tried to carry on a conversation the rest of the way to Club Marquee. The problem was, she was utterly dull and kind of a moron. I had no idea what Rowe saw in her other than her amazing breasts. But... maybe that was enough for him. He seemed to tune everyone out well enough. At least he had that talent. Unlike the rest of us.

We pulled up outside of Club Marquee, and Katherine made her debut in her devil's costume. She dragged me next to her so that the cameras could see that we were a matched set. After a few minutes of short interviews about the charity event, she whisked us all inside.

Club Marquee was a huge multi-floored club in the heart

of the Upper East Side. Balconies overlooked the main floor, which was already packed with women dressed in scantily clad outfits and various kinds of ears dancing with men primarily dressed in suits. The three main bars on the first floor were all packed with people, but Katherine directed us to the open booth area next to the DJ. It was a prime location that overlooked the entire room...while also leaving us visible to everyone in attendance. Exactly how Katherine liked to see and be seen.

I stepped up onto the booth with Penn at my back and was surprised to find Camden Percy already in attendance. He was dressed as Clark Kent, complete with glasses.

"What the hell are *you* doing here?" Katherine asked.

"Hello to you, too, darling," he said, roughly gripping her and planting a kiss on her bright red lips.

She pulled out of his grip and rubbed her arm. "I see you haven't had enough to drink. You're still being almost pleasant."

"I'll be sure to be less pleasant later," he said and grabbed her ass as she scoffed and pushed past him.

I wanted to get far away from Percy, but Penn was staring at the man standing next to him.

"Fuck," he snapped viciously.

"What?" I asked.

"Penn!" Camden cheered, gesturing us closer. Anything that made Camden that happy could not be a good thing. "Look who I found in the crowd."

The man next to him was extremely attractive. Tall, dark hair, and a smile that could light up a room. He wore a custom-tailored suit that had to have cost a fortune and held a dirty martini glass to his full lips. He had his other arm slung around a woman in a silky red baby-doll dress and bunny ears. When the waitress handed her a glass of champagne, she passed her a hundred-dollar bill and told her to keep them coming.

Penn placed his hand on the small of my back, and I could feel the tension rolling off of him. But he didn't say anything.

"Where are my brother's manners?" the man with the martini glass said. He bent dramatically at the waist to kiss my hand. He looked up at me with baby-blue eyes I'd recognize from a mile off and a smile that screamed troublemaker. "It's a pleasure to meet you. I'm Penn's older and much more handsome brother, Court. Court Kensington."

NATALIE

28

I hastily withdrew my hand from his grasp. "Uh, it's a pleasure to meet you. I'm Natalie."

Penn was seething at my back. I didn't know their history. Or anything but that his brother was a train wreck. But even if I'd known nothing about Court Kensington, Penn's reaction right now was enough for me to realize that I should stay far away.

"I must say that your angel is stunning," Court said with a smile that mirrored his brother's to a T. It was a little unnerving.

"Well, thank you."

"And introduce your friend," Camden said. "She's a real charmer."

The woman next to Court finally looked up from her champagne flute and smiled at me and Penn. "Jane Devney," she said, holding her hand out. I shook her hand as she just barreled forward. "You look so familiar, Natalie. Have we met before? Were you in Paris last summer?"

"Actually, I was." I stared at her and tried to place her. But she had one of those faces that just didn't stick.

"I thought so. I was studying luxury fashion design and marketing at the French Fashion Institute while interning at *Vogue Paris*. I could swear that I saw you at a party held by Harmony Cunningham."

I opened my mouth in surprise. "I was at a Cunningham party. I worked for her mother for a time."

"I never forget a face," Jane said. "I met Harmony through Bishop McHugh, the British diplomat while he was in Paris."

"Honestly, I'm usually better with faces." In fact, I remembered everyone I met generally. I must not have been introduced to her or else it probably would have stuck.

"Of course. Well, Bishop and global environmentalist Marin Russo's daughter, Camilla—you know, she's an up-and-coming Italian fashion designer—are helping to back my new club. I'd hoped to get Harmony involved. Is she going to be here tonight?"

"I'm not certain," I said, staggering over how connected this girl was. "But congratulations on your club."

"We're just in the investment stage, but we're getting there," Jane said, finishing her drink and getting another one handed to her immediately. "Champagne?"

"Oh, yes please."

I got my own drink and tried to ignore the tension settling between Penn and Court. Neither had said anything while Jane and I talked about our chance meeting in Paris last summer. And I knew that anything that came out of Penn's mouth now would be far from pleasant. It would be better to extract us from this.

"Why don't we go dance?" I asked Penn.

"All right," he said.

"Wait, don't you want to do shots first?" Court asked. He snapped his fingers at the waitress. Actually snapped them. "Four tequila shots."

Camden smacked him in the chest. "One for me, too."

"Make that five."

"Oh, good. Tequila and champagne—the perfect mix," Jane said dryly. "Can't us girls skip out on this one?"

Court grinned down at her, and she seemed to melt in the same way I did when I looked at Penn.

"Do it for me, Janie. This is the first time you're meeting my brother."

"Ah yes, Penn Kensington," Jane said with a smile. "How are your classes? I knew Professor Friedrich Weber, who studied metaphysics back home in Germany. Of course, not what your focus is, but he certainly went off with a bang back home."

"Ah, Weber," Penn said, momentarily stunned by someone who knew anything about philosophy. "I studied him some in grad school. He's quite renowned."

"To be fair, his wife threw lavish parties that I attended with my family, and I know hardly anything about his work, except that he had exceptional taste in champagne, which I consumed rather frivolously."

Penn laughed, obviously charmed by Jane's demeanor. She seriously seemed to know everyone. "Well, metaphysics can be dull, so I don't blame you."

"Here you are," the waitress said, holding a tray of five tequila shots.

Jane sighed, and her wide hazel eyes stared back at me. "What do you say, Natalie?"

"All right," I agreed, taking the shot and lime.

Court held his glass up. "To lingerie parties on Halloween. May we all find out if the ears match the tails."

Camden snorted. Penn rolled his eyes. Jane and I giggled. And then we all tossed our shots back with ease.

"Whoa!" I cried, putting the drink back on the tray. My vision blurred for a second, and I teetered. I was really a terrible lightweight. "That was intense. Haven't done that since college."

"Well then, you really must hang out with me some more. I might even be generous and invite my Court," Jane said. She fluttered her eyelashes up at him.

"Yes, Natalie," Court said with a devious smile on his face. "Do come out with us more often. Any friend of Penn's is a friend of mine."

"Is that how you want to spin it?" Penn ground out.

Court just ignored him. "We're going to the back room later if you and that halo want to join," he offered me with a wink.

"Uh…"

Penn stepped between me and Court. "She's not interested."

"Court, leave them be," Jane said.

Camden cackled. "As if little Natalie would be into that."

Penn looked like he wanted to deck his brother, and I already knew he hated Camden.

"Come on, Natalie."

He directed me away from Court and Camden to where Lewis was dancing with some model in mouse ears. Rowe and his date were doing something that approximated dancing as well. Mostly Jessica Rabbit was throwing herself at him, and he appreciatively stood behind her.

"Trouble?" Lewis asked.

"Court," Penn growled.

Penn grabbed me around the middle and pulled me into him. His movements were slow and sexy to match the music. I could have gotten lost in him, but his interaction with Court was still caught in my mind.

"Hey, what was up with that?"

"Up with what? My brother?"

"Yeah," I said, wrapping my arms around his neck. "Why were you so upset with him?"

"I'm always upset with him. But you don't know him. You didn't even realize what he was suggesting when he invited you to the back room."

I arched an eyebrow in question.

"There are only two things my brother has any interest in—sex and drugs. Do you want to do either of those with him?" he snapped aggressively.

"No," I spat back. "But you don't have to ask me about it like that. Why would I have any interest in doing anything with Court? I know that you said he's a train wreck. I just didn't know that you actually hated him."

The anger dropped off of Penn's shoulders, and he sighed. "I don't hate him. We just…don't get along. We have a rich history of mistrust, and he has a constant need to make me miserable."

"Well, he's not going to ruin our night."

"He has the uncanny ability to do that without trying."

"Who knows? He might surprise you anyway. He seemed pretty into Jane. Is that normal?"

"Yes. He usually has some kind of woman who is infatuated with him. He destroys their life and then leaves them out to rot."

"Don't know anyone else who has ever done that before," I said with a pointed look.

"That was different."

"Maybe," I concede. "But only because we're together now."

"He's not a good guy," he told me. "And…he doesn't even care. He and I couldn't be more different in that regard."

"You struggle with your demons. Your philosophical notion of right and wrong. And I adore that about you. It makes you so real, Penn. But you came around to that, Penn. He could still come around too."

"Unlikely," he grumbled. His hands gripped the corset and then ran down to my ass. "Let's talk about something else."

"All right, just forget your brother."

"I take issue with these wings," he said.

"Why?"

"I want to turn you around, and they get in the way. Plus, I have a feeling, they'll be a problem later tonight. I was thinking of throwing you against a wall."

I laughed and stood on my toes to kiss him. "Sounds like you're going to make me lose my halo."

He smirked. "I'm a hundred percent sure that I will be the one to do that."

I swatted at him. "You."

He laughed and pulled me in for another long, sensuous kiss. Our bodies moved together in time to the music. Our hands drifted invitingly. I was half-tempted to grab him and drag him out of this party. I was in such little clothes, and he was taking full advantage of that.

"Penn," Lewis said suddenly. There was a note of something I'd never heard in his voice. Almost frantic. "Penn!"

"What?" Penn asked. He whirled to face Lewis in frustration. He'd almost effectively slipped his hand inside my leotard.

Lewis tilted his head to the side. Penn looked like he was going to question what the hell Lewis wanted, but then he froze. He sighed heavily and then turned back to face me.

"Can you excuse me for just a second?" he asked.

"Um…sure."

"I'll be right back."

"All right," I said warily. "What are you doing?"

"I have to talk to someone. Dance with Lewis until I get back." Then, he pointed at Lewis. "Watch your hands."

Lewis laughed and then sidled up to me.

"What's going on?" I asked in confusion.

"Nothing. Don't worry about it."

"You know, it's amazing. When people say that, I tend to worry."

"There's no reason to," Lewis tried to assure me.

But it was Katherine who gasped beside me. "Jesus Christ, when is Emily going to take a hint?"

"Katherine," Lewis ground out.

"Who's Emily?" I asked.

"Penn's ex-girlfriend," Katherine said.

She pointed to the front of the room. The thing about our booth was that we could see almost the entire first floor. And there, standing in the entrance to the club, was a girl with dark hair in a black patent leather cat costume that hugged her body like a second skin. Standing beside her with his hand on her arm...was Penn.

My mind reeled a bit at the news. I hadn't known that he'd had a girlfriend. When I'd asked about exes when we went sailing, he'd said there was no one important to talk about. And he hadn't even wanted me to say. I didn't know if that was a lie or if Emily really didn't matter. And if she didn't, then why was she *here*? And why had he rushed off to talk to her?

"There's nothing going on with them though," Lewis added quickly.

But my eyes were glued to him. I didn't know what he was saying. And from a distance, it was impossible to read his expression. Except that they were speaking intently, and his head was tilted down toward her. His hand was still on her.

And then they were kissing.

My jaw dropped, and I whipped around, so I didn't have to watch. Didn't have to burn my retinas with that display.

My stomach was churning. My head ached. Suddenly, I desperately wanted to be out of this room. Out of this party. Away from these people and this miserable world.

"Fuck," Lewis growled. "Natalie…I…"

"Get me out of here."

"Natalie, maybe just talk to him?"

"Please," I asked with wide eyes.

"God," Katherine said, putting her hand on my shoulder. "I'm so sorry. I thought his meet-up with her last week had ended things. I thought that's why you were finally together."

My head snapped to the side so fast that I got a crick in my neck. "*That* was who he met with last week? When he stayed in the city all night?"

Katherine opened and closed her mouth. Her eyes were full of sympathy. "I'm sorry. You didn't know that?"

I wanted to throw up. That tequila shot and champagne felt like fire in my throat. And at any second, I might hurl. I was such a fucking idiot. Why hadn't I seen it before? Because he'd said he was sorry and showed me the stars? Dangled a Tiffany's bracelet in front of my face?

Of course he was covering something up. Fucking fuck, fuck. I felt so stupid.

"Now, Lewis, will you get me out of here? You offered to let me stay at your place once. Will you do it again?" I pleaded. I wouldn't cry. Not here. Not in front of all of these people. Not when Penn was doing whatever the hell he wanted with his ex-girlfriend.

"Okay," Lewis said finally with a sigh. "Okay, I'll take you."

I nodded, unable to get the words out, and followed him through a back exit and out of the club.

PENN

29

I grasped Emily by her shoulders and shoved her away from me.

"What the fuck do you think you're doing?" I asked.

I couldn't believe she'd fucking kissed me. What the fuck was she thinking?

"Kissing you," she said, batting her long lashes. "Haven't you missed me?"

"No!" I snapped. "What the fuck would give you that idea? I thought I'd made myself perfectly clear when I was in the city last week. We're through. We've been through for a long time. And I'm not going to deal with any more of your bullshit."

"Wait, what?" Emily asked. Her eyes so dark, almost black, turned from seduction to confusion. "Katherine called and invited me to her party. She said that you'd had a change of heart."

I seethed at that comment. This fucking bet was ruining everything. I needed to end it. I needed to cut Katherine to ribbons and make her see reason. This whole thing was stupid. And bringing in Emily? That was low, even for her.

"I have no fucking clue where she got that delusion. But I don't want this or you."

"Fine," she said, squaring off with me, as she so often had. It was something I'd admired about her, and now, it just drove me crazy. "Say what you want."

"You should go, Emily."

"You don't control me, Penn Kensington," she cried. She yanked her arm away from me.

"There's no reason for you to be here anymore."

"This is the biggest event in the city. I'm sure I can find *someone* to entertain me."

"Yes, I'm sure there are plenty of men here you've already *entertained*," I said dryly. "Most of them while we were dating."

"I cannot believe I thought of giving you another chance," she yelled at me. "You will never get over that."

"No, I won't," I said evenly. My eyes were dark and dangerous.

I needed to get away from her. If she wasn't going to leave, then I could have one of the security guards escort her out or something.

"Excuse me," I said, waving one of the guards over.

"What are you doing?" she gasped.

"Katherine Van Pelt requested that this woman be removed from the premises. She came in on a fake name and wasn't invited," I said harshly.

"Yes, sir."

"Penn!" Emily shrieked.

I shrugged and turned my back on her. Now to deal with Katherine Van Pelt, who had started this whole mess.

I rushed back to the booth Katherine had reserved for her event and found it surprisingly half-full of strangers. It looked like Camden, Court, and Jane had gone to the back room. Probably to do cocaine or whatever latest thing Court was into. Rowe and Jessica Rabbit were making out in a corner. Katherine was entertaining a posse of her minions. But no Natalie. No Lewis.

What the hell?

I strode up to Katherine and whirled her in place. "Why would you invite Emily here?"

A slow, dangerous smile spread on her face. "Oh dear Lord…is Emily here?"

"Don't bullshit *me*, Ren. It's *me* after all. She told me that you sent her here. Why?" Then I looked around again, and it dawned on me. "Where's Natalie?"

"She might have seen you and Emily kissing."

"We weren't kissing," I ground out.

"Sure looked like it from our angle." Her smile was triumphant.

"Where. Is. She?" I snarled at her.

I didn't care that I was playing into her hand. That this was exactly what she wanted. She'd engineered this entire thing, and I'd walked right into it like an idiot. I should have known better.

"I think she went home with Lewis. Maybe he isn't really on your side," Katherine said with a laugh.

"The bet is over, Katherine. It's done."

"Is it now?" she purred.

"Forget about it. This isn't fucking happening anymore. You can leave your games behind. I'm not going to play them anymore. I only did this, so I could spend uninterrupted time with Natalie in the first place. Now, I don't give a fuck what you think."

"A bet's a bet," Katherine said with a shrug. She stroked my cheek. "If you want to quit, I'll be happy to collect early. Say tonight? My place?"

"That's not happening." I swatted her hand away. "It's over. I'm going to go make things right with Natalie."

"Well, I suppose I could tell Natalie the truth then."

I froze. "You wouldn't."

"I mean…if you're going to back out, then I think she probably deserves to know how you've manipulated her."

"I never manipulated her."

Katherine laughed. "Yeah. Sure. Why don't we tell her and find out?"

"I'll tell her myself then," I said, seeing my opening.

"Or we can wait until the bet is over. We'll find out who wins, and no one has to be any wiser."

I'd underestimated Katherine. Of all the people for me to underestimate, this had to be the worst. I had known what she was capable of. I had known the measures she took to win at all costs. I should have said no. I wished I could go back to that pool when it had suddenly become serious and just laughed and thrown the whole idea aside. But it was here now. We were too far in. And any way I looked at it, I was fucked.

But right now, it wasn't my biggest concern. The fact that Natalie had seen Emily kiss me. That she'd left with Lewis. I needed to talk to her. To explain.

"Whatever, Katherine."

"Happy hunting," she said cheerfully.

I pulled out my cell phone to text Lewis and saw I already had a message from him.

You're such a fucking idiot.

Yeah, thanks, man. I jotted out a text back.

Don't I know it? Is she at your place?

Yeah, but I don't know if she wants to see you.

Be there in ten.

I stuffed my phone back in my suit pocket, rushed out of the building, and hailed a cab to go make this right.

NATALIE

30

"Here," Lewis said. He handed me a glass of amber liquid. "Scotch. It should help."

I didn't question his judgment. I just downed a large gulp of the stuff. I coughed repeatedly as it burned its way down my throat. "Smooth."

He grinned at me and then plopped down beside me. "You have to get used to it. It's the good stuff though."

"It tastes like fire."

"But it feels like forgetting your life," he said, holding up his glass to mine. "Cheers."

I clinked it and downed another large gulp. It wasn't as bad as the first drink, but, man, it wasn't easy either.

"So…Emily, huh?"

He winced and then took another drink. "Yeah, that's Emily."

"When did they break up?"

"I really don't think I should be the one to tell you about this." He stood and reached for more scotch.

"Yeah, well, the one who *should* have told me about this was making out with her."

"They weren't making out," Lewis said. "It was one kiss, and we don't know what it means. You just left. You didn't even ask him."

"What would I ask exactly? *Why did you lie to me? Why are you kissing some other woman that I don't know anything about? How much of this is just a game to you?*"

He shrugged his shoulders. "It'd be a start."

"I'm too angry for his fabricated answers right now. Just tell me the truth."

"Natalie, why don't we talk about something else?"

I finished off my scotch and passed him the glass. "I met your ex-girlfriend Addie. We could talk about her."

"Are those my only options?" he asked with a wince. He rubbed the back of his neck and checked his phone.

I sighed and flopped backward on the couch. I'd already had Lewis remove the stupid wings attached to my back and flung off the thousand-dollar shoes I was borrowing from Katherine. I kicked my white-stockinged feet up onto Lewis's lap and held my hand out for my drink.

His eyes roamed my scantily clad body for a heartbeat too long before he passed me my drink. I'd forgotten that I was still just in a corset, garter, and stockings. My cheeks heated.

"Sorry," I said, straightening.

"Hey, no, you can lie back down. It's fine," he said, but he had to clear his throat to get the words out.

"Tonight is so fucked."

"I think you should talk to Penn. You'll feel better."

"Yes, I know what you think."

But would I feel better? Knowing more about Emily. Knowing *why* he'd kissed his ex-girlfriend and not told me he'd met her the week before. I didn't really think so. But then I remembered the bracelet tucked away in my purse, which I'd hastily discarded as soon as we entered Lewis's posh penthouse. The crown that dangled from it and the constellation it symbolized. Maybe I owed him a conversation.

"Fine. I'll hear him out, but I'm still staying here."

He shrugged. "There's a room for you if you need one."

"Thanks for this, Lewis. I do really appreciate it."

"Anything for you, Natalie."

His eyes met mine, dark and comforting and honest. He smiled in a way that said he was sincere. And for some reason, I believed him. That he might actually do anything for me.

Then there was a ding of the elevator.

Our moment of silence was broken, and Lewis scrambled to his feet as if he were the one who had done something wrong. Instead of being the white knight who had whisked me away from disaster.

I sat up and set my drink on the coffee table. I'd just straightened up in time to see Penn blow into Lewis's living room like a tornado.

Lewis cleared his throat. "I'll just...give you two a minute."

Then he disappeared into what I had to assume was his bedroom, leaving me alone with Penn. The knot of his bow tie was undone and hanging around his neck. He'd unbuttoned the first two buttons on his shirt. His eyes were a mixture of anger, pain, and confusion. I'd never seen him look like that before.

"You just left?" he demanded.

I raised my eyebrows. "You just kissed your ex-girlfriend?"

"I didn't *kiss* Emily."

"Oh, and now, I'm blind, too?"

"*She* kissed me. There's a difference. If you'd stuck around long enough to see, I stopped her and had her thrown out of the party. Because I have no interest in Emily."

"I don't know why you're yelling at me," I said, raising my voice. "You're the one who saw her last week and lied to me about it. You're the one who never mentioned an ex to me, even when I asked. You're the one who went to her tonight as soon as she showed up. What the hell am I supposed to think, Penn?"

He backed down at my comment, coming forward to stand in front of me. I could see the fire had left his eyes. All that was left was guilt and sorrow.

"I'm sorry," he said. "I don't know what I was thinking, coming in here. None of this is your fault, and you had every reason to leave that party."

"I know," I said, sinking back into my seat on the couch. "I know that much. I just don't know what the hell is going on with you, Penn. You say you don't want things to be casual between us, but then you treat us casually."

"No, no, I didn't. I don't," he corrected. He dropped into the seat next to me. "I only went over there to tell her to leave. That was also the reason I saw her last week."

"Why wouldn't you just tell me that?"

"Emily is complicated. She's a nuisance and a liar and my past. She's not someone I like to think or talk about. And it had nothing to do with you and everything to do with me."

I sighed heavily and looked away from him. I could still see his lips on another woman, and it hurt. No matter how I wanted to shield my heart from him, he'd ripped everything wide open. There was no going back. I was vulnerable now.

"It's not you, it's me," I said softly. "Original."

"Look, you want the whole story? Here's the story," Penn soldiered on through gritted teeth. "Emily and I met at Columbia. She was a law student. We knew each other vaguely through our families. We hit it off. We dated for a year and a half. Then one day, I came home and walked in on her. Fucking Court. In my bed. There. That's it. That's the story."

I gasped. Shock hit me like a tidal wave. What the fuck was wrong with her that she would do something like that? What was wrong with Court? Jesus, no wonder he hated his brother so much. No wonder they didn't get along, and he had been so defensive when Court talked to me. With that history...anyone would have been defensive.

"That's horrible. I see why you can't stand being around Court."

"Among other reasons," he said. "But can't you see now that I want nothing to do with Emily? We broke up at the beginning of the summer, and she kept trying to fix things with us—showing up in the city and at events I was at, begging me to come to her place, and generally being infuriating. I wanted her to know it was completely over and done with. That I was never going to entertain her bullshit again. I wanted it done before I talked to you."

"And you didn't think I'd understand?" I asked softly.

Because I did understand. And I hurt for him. Even while I was so angry with him for what I'd seen. He'd clearly felt deeply for Emily if he dated her for over a year. I'd only ever dated one guy that long, and the breakup had been brutal.

"I wouldn't have been *happy* you went off to see your ex-girlfriend, but if you'd told me..."

"I know," he said. "I should have told you. But, at the time, I didn't know if you really wanted anything more from me. You wanted a month of casual sex, right? No need to bring exes into that equation."

"But you clearly wanted more since you asked for more *right* after seeing her."

"I did...I do want more. And I had to clear things up with her before starting something with you."

I nodded. That at least was admirable. If it hadn't resulted in her kissing him in front of me tonight and ruining everything. Toppling my already-shaky trust in him.

"I asked you about exes point-blank, and you said there was no one important enough to mention. Emily seems pretty damn important."

He ran a hand back through his dark hair. "That was the truth. She wasn't important enough to mention because she's nothing to me."

I sighed and buried my face in my hands. "I don't know, Penn. She doesn't seem like nothing."

He stood and paced the room. "I don't know what else to do to prove to you that we're over. Do you want to call Emily or go find her wherever the security guard dumped her after I kicked her out of the club? Do you want to find out the truth from her? Or at least whatever her version is? Because I'll do it. She'll tell you that we're done. That we have been for a long time. And I'll tell you…that I only want to be with you."

I stared up at him, pacing and irritated. As if he couldn't believe he'd managed to fuck all of this up within a week. That Emily had shown up and he'd dealt with it all wrong. I'd never seen him lose his cool so completely. Normally, he was this put-together guy with his Upper East Side flair and his philosophical chill. But right now, he actually seemed… scared that he'd lose me.

"Penn, sit down." I patted the couch next to me. He took the seat next to me. "I need to know if there's anything else I should know. Any other girls in your closet? Waiting to jump out at you and kiss you. Katherine maybe?"

"Katherine?" he asked in surprise. "Dear god, no. There is absolutely nothing going on between us."

He had such conviction in his voice. Such earnest calm that he seemed to come back to himself at my question. As if he couldn't even believe I was asking about Katherine.

"I think she's in love with you."

Penn laughed and shook his head. "I'm honestly not entirely sure if Katherine has feelings. And even if she did, it wouldn't matter because I feel nothing for her. I never have. Not like that. The only person I want…is you."

He reached out and placed his hand over mine. When I didn't immediately pull it away, he threaded our fingers together and rubbed his thumb down mine.

"Can you forgive me?" he asked.

I didn't pull away, but I remained silent long enough that I could tell he was worried. And it made it all the harder to say no to him when I could see that he was being honest. That he was worried about losing me. And it might be stupid, but I wanted him, too. I didn't want this to come between us. But at the same time, I didn't a hundred percent trust him either. And I hated that.

"I think I need some time," I told him honestly. "I can't erase the anger and hurt and betrayal I felt tonight."

"Right."

"I need more than the last hour to process."

He brought my hand to his lips. "I understand that. But can I convince you to come back to my place with me? I can grovel some more if you'd like."

I laughed softly and shook my head. "You don't have to grovel. I'll come back with you. I just need you to be honest with me from now on, okay?"

His eyes drifted away and then back to mine. I didn't know what that look meant, but he then nodded. "Okay."

NATALIE

31

Everything excellent is as difficult as it is rare.

Ever since Penn had brought his big philosophy brain into my life, I'd started reading daily quotes from famous philosophers. Most of them I read, deleted, and moved on from. But this one from Spinoza's *Ethics* stuck. It resonated. It sang symphonies in my brain and let the words just pour out of me.

And right now, it felt like a hit to the head with a two-by-four.

Because Penn and I were excellent together. I knew that for certain.

But *difficult* was hardly a strong enough word.

Still, I knew what we had was rare.

The way our stars had aligned to bring us to this moment. How effortless we were when we were together. The ease with which we fit together like a diver landing in the water without a splash. And yet we felt like a tide being pushed and pulled by some unseen force that just didn't let us fucking *be*.

And I wanted us to be.

I didn't want my prediction to Amy to come true.

Still, I was quiet on the way back to the beach house the next morning. I wasn't even upset that Penn had seen Emily so much as he hadn't told me he did. We weren't dating at the time. Though things had obviously been heating up. And I understood that he wanted to have closure in regard to her.

I just hated the lying. How easy it had come to him. How he'd been able to say he was going to a meeting and let me assume it was for work. Then say he was visiting a "friend." As if that *friend* wasn't his ex-girlfriend.

Totle bounded up the stairs ahead of me as we exited the Audi and entered the beach house. I let him out back and watched as he ran around before doing his business. I heard Penn's footsteps behind me. His hand rested on my back.

"Nat."

"He's so happy. Carefree and happy."

"He is," Penn agreed. "You've been quiet."

"Just thinking. Curse of a writer. Always stuck in my head."

"Do you want to talk about it?"

I turned and looked up into his gorgeous face. Those big blue eyes and that strong jawline and perfect lips. But there was no smile. Only a furrow from worry between his eyes and concern in his baby blues.

"You know, not really."

"Okay," he said evenly, taking a step back. "Well, I think we should talk about it when you're ready. But in the meantime, the guest bedrooms are finished. You could always move back into your old room. Or I could take a different bed if you want. That way, you have your own space."

"No," I said at once. I was even surprised by my immediate resistance. I didn't want to move out of the master. I wanted to stay where he was. I didn't want this to *ruin* everything.

"No?"

"I don't want space. Not from you."

"I don't either."

"You made a mistake. You owned up to it. I don't want to move backward with you, Penn. I just want forward."

That beautiful smile returned, and he retrieved that step he'd taken backward. "Good. I didn't really want you to leave my bed."

I playfully swatted at him. "So, this is all about sex?"

"You know it's not," he said, pulling me closer.

"I do know." It was the reason that I was even saying this. Because it wasn't just sex with him. It was so much more. And I knew that I had trust issues, but I didn't want it to crumble us. "I'm only here for ten more days. Then I'm going home to Charleston."

"I don't want you to leave," he told me.

"I know. But my contract is up for the house. I planned to go home for the holidays and look for another home-watching job for the New Year. So, I think we should make the most of this."

"You don't know what's in store for the future."

"That's kind of part of the job."

"I meant with us." His hands slid up into my silvery-white hair, and he gazed down at me with a look of adoration.

"Can we take it one day at a time?" I asked helplessly. Because if I thought too far forward, the prospect got scary. Did we work long-distance? Did I try to get another job in New York? He couldn't leave Columbia, but I couldn't afford the city.

It was all too complicated. And with the issue of trust still hanging precariously between us, I didn't want to deal with it right now. So, I grabbed him by the collar of his shirt and kissed him before he could respond one way or another.

Penn didn't need any more encouragement after the last twenty-four hours. He pressed me back into the wall. His hands moving freely down my body. His lips hard against mine. As if he could kiss away our problems. Use his tongue to make me forget what we were going through. And honestly, it worked.

My brain shut down. There was just him in this moment. I craved his touch, his lips, his everything. I wanted him to claim me. Remind me that I was his and he was mine. And what had happened wasn't real.

It was irrational. Our problems would still be there when we finished. But I still cared for him. I still wanted things to work between us. I still wanted him so desperately. Just like I had that night in Paris.

It didn't change how I felt. Even though how I felt complicated my entire life. Because Penn Kensington was a game changer.

I knew it. And was helpless to the fact.

I'd been so upset all those years ago because I thought I'd known even then. We'd connected so deeply, so fast. I'd told him things I'd never really told anyone else. I'd thought it would be a fairy tale. Now, I was *living* that fairy tale. And I refused to let it go.

Penn's hands pushed under my dress, sure yet impatient. He found the edge of my thong and yanked it down my legs. They fell to the floor, a casualty of our desire.

I fumbled with his belt, button, zipper. Tugged his pants over his ass. He never relented on my lips as he hoisted one of my legs around his hip. His body pressed against me. I knew exactly what he wanted, and I wanted it too. I wanted last night to not have happened. I wanted to forget.

My hand moved into his boxers, and I stroked his dick. He was already hard at my touch.

"Please," I pleaded against his lips.

He groaned and lifted me up completely. I squeaked slightly at the sudden movement, but then his cock was in his hand, and he lowered me onto him. Slow at first, easing himself deep inside me.

My eyes fluttered closed, and I gasped at the feel of him. The pure strength of holding me against the wall as he filled me. My legs were tight around his waist, arms on his shoulders, but he was the one doing the work. He was the one lifting me off of him and slapping me back down into place.

Up and down.

Harder and harder.

He rocked into me, driving up into my body as he leveraged me securely against the wall. And I just wanted more. More of him. More of this. More of us.

I knew that we had issues. That, together, we were both a daydream and a nightmare, but I couldn't help it. I couldn't go back to how things had been. Not when I knew what was right in front of my eyes.

"Come with me, Natalie," he commanded.

Our eyes locked, and something crashed down between us. Joy and ecstasy and sweet, sweet relief. Climax hit us both at full force. He dropped his head into my shoulder, and I nearly cracked my head open on the wall behind me.

Then he pulled out of me and released me to my feet. We were both panting. Our chests heaving. I felt like, at any minute, I could collapse into a puddle of goo. Still, I dragged his lips back to mine and kissed him, tender and sweet.

"Maybe we should have make-up sex more often," I joked.

He chuckled and shook his head. "All sex is good sex with you."

"I think we're disproving your hypothesis," I said cheekily. "Perhaps the standard view *is* best for your happiness."

"You're best for my happiness, Natalie Bishop." He kissed me thoroughly. "Just you."

NATALIE

32

*T*en days.

    Sometimes, a minute felt like a lifetime.

Sometimes, time flew.

Like a butterfly.

And when you tried to hold on to it too hard, you crushed its delicate wings.

Day one, Penn took me sailing. Not just him sailing, but he actually made me do it. I was abysmal. Truly. I had some upper body strength from swimming, but it was hardly what it once had been. He didn't mind that I failed. He helped, and then he made me do it again. I almost got the hang of it by the time we were out in the bay that afternoon, having a picnic on the water.

Getting the boat back into the dock was another story.

Day two, we ordered my favorite pizza, crowded into the library, and wrote all day. My new story flowed out of me like a sieve had opened in my brain. I still wouldn't let him read it. But the book was on submission. Any day now, I could hear if someone wanted to buy it. From experience, it usually took months before everyone said no. I didn't get my hopes up.

The third day was a Saturday, and Penn insisted he take me out on a real date.

"Let me spoil you," he said with a charming smile that I found impossible to say no to.

I got dressed up as best as I could with the little clothes that I had. But he didn't seem to mind that I was wearing a recycled dress he'd seen a dozen times this fall. His eyes lit up, and I could tell he was reevaluating whether or not we should leave the house.

"Come on," I said with a laugh, ushering him toward the door.

He opened my car door and helped me inside before driving me into East Hampton. He chose a fancy seafood restaurant with an ocean view. The prices were astronomical, but he told me not to look at them.

Growing up broke hadn't prepared me for that decision, and I skimped. He ordered extra on top of my order, giving me a look that said he knew I'd done it. And he was right, the food was the best I'd ever had in my entire life.

A pianist played classical music on a grand piano. At the end of the night, Penn held out his hand, and just like that perfect moment in Paris, he swept me out onto the small dance floor and twirled me around the room. I felt like a princess in my cheap dress and knockoff heels. More beautiful than I'd ever felt when Katherine played dress-up with me.

It was that look in his eyes that did it.

Day four, we woke up late. Really late. We'd had a late night that included a bubble bath and most of the surfaces in the house.

After we ate brunch, Penn grabbed a fleece blanket, his notebook, and a threadbare copy of *The Great Gatsby*, and he insisted we head down to the beach. I took my own notebook and followed him with interest.

I laid my head in his lap. The sea breeze kissed my skin. The waves lapped up to the edge of the beach. Penn read to me about Daisy and Gatsby's great love. Fitzgerald's incredible prose in Penn's mouth was like having sex for a lover of words.

On the fifth day, I had to deal with the decorators as they rushed to the finish line for the mayor's party on Saturday, which coincided with my last day of work. I was in a daze of happiness, even as we stood on a precipice. The halfway mark. There were now fewer days together than apart.

I fell asleep in his arms with *Versailles* playing in the background, and he didn't wake me. Just stroked my hair until the episode ended and carried me to bed.

Day six, election day.

Penn had voted early, and I'd voted absentee in South Carolina. So, we sat around the living room and halfheartedly watched the election results come in. I was no lover of politics, except in the instances in which certain issues were life or death for me. Penn had grown up with a mother in the political sphere, and Lark had been working on campaigns for years. His interest ran deeper than mine, and it was actually interesting, hearing his side of it.

We popped open a bottle of champagne when it was announced that President Woodhouse had won reelection.

The day after the election, I woke up in a tangle of limbs. My head pounded from all the champagne we'd consumed the night before. I took a long, hot shower and blew my hair out before Penn even surfaced from the bed.

"Morning," he said, kissing my cheek and then disappearing for his own shower.

I tugged on yoga pants and a sweatshirt before brewing a

pot of coffee. Penn gratefully took his cup and drained it, piping hot.

"You're insane."

He grinned. "For you maybe."

I finished mine without scalding myself, and then he put Totle on a leash and dragged me outside for our daily walk on the beach. Our fingers were locked. Totle bounded along, taking in every sight and sound. Sniffing and peeing on everything. The little ball of energy nearly pulled Penn's arm out of its socket as he tried to take down a bird on the beach.

It was brisk, and we hustled back inside the house, trying to keep up with the puppy and get warm. Penn unleashed Totle and let him fly inside. But he grabbed me around the middle and tugged me close. My cold nose grazed his. Our lips met.

I was already trying to sneak my cold hands under his jacket. He was squirming to stop me from freezing him.

A voice cleared behind us.

Our heads whipped to the side in surprise. No one was supposed to be here. The decorator wasn't due until that afternoon.

And then my jaw dropped.

My stomach with it.

"What exactly is going on here?" Mayor Kensington asked.

NATALIE

33

*P*enn and I jumped apart as if we'd been burned.

"Mother," Penn said in shock. "What are you doing here?"

"What am *I* doing here?" Leslie Kensington asked. She straightened her shoulders and managed to look down on her son who was a half-foot taller than her. And she did it with ease. "I think the correction question is, what are you doing here? Aren't you supposed to be teaching a little class or whatever it is you do over at the university?"

He gritted his teeth. "I'm on sabbatical to finish a book."

"And you thought diddling the help would be a better use of your time?"

I winced at the statement. That must have been exactly what it looked like to her. I hadn't thought about Penn's mom at all. She was my boss, and I hadn't considered what would happen if she found out about us. Mostly because I had never even met the woman. We'd never even spoken.

"That is not what is happening here," Penn said defensively.

"Oh, you're not screwing the help…*again?*"

"It's not like that with Natalie."

She shook her head in dismay. "Where did I go wrong with you and your brother?" Then her eyes darted to me as if she had remembered someone so insignificant was in the room. "And you..."

"I am so sorry, Mayor Kensington. I didn't know that Penn was going to be staying at the house while I was here. I see now that I should have reported that information to you," I said reluctantly.

"Well, I'm sure I know why. The way he was groping you before."

I bit the inside of my cheek. "We actually know each other from a few summers ago. It wasn't a whim."

But it was. And the look of anger and revulsion on her face made it all come into sharp clarity. I was trash. Dirt under her feet. Just the help. And she would never accept that I was anything more to her son than a phase.

"This was not how I wanted you to find out about me and Natalie."

"How did you want me to find out?" the mayor asked. "Should I have walked in on you humping?"

"We're together. We're dating."

Mayor Kensington actually tilted her head back and laughed. "I have never heard something more absurd."

"I'm remembering why I didn't tell you," Penn said with a bite in his tone. "Why I don't tell you anything. Why you're not even a part of my life."

"Yet you'll take my money and house without a second thought."

"I don't need your money, and I stayed here to get away from you."

"Not this old business," she said on a sigh. "Must we discuss your poor little rich boy routine again?"

I felt like backing into the wall and disappearing entirely.

No wonder Penn had never really discussed his mom. After seeing Court and hearing about their history, I hadn't known what to expect with his mom, but this...this was just cruel.

And she was so popular in New York. She'd worked as a judge and then a state legislator for years before becoming mayor two years ago. Her approval rating was through the roof. She was tough on crime and an excellent leader. I didn't know what the people of New York would think if they saw her now.

"Talk about whatever you want," Penn said. "But Natalie is not some passing fancy. She's not just some girl who happens to work for you."

"She's white trash from nowhere," the mayor spat at him.

I cringed at the hate-filled words.

I hated them more because they were true.

Penn's eyes rounded in horror. "You have no right to speak to her like that."

"I'm telling you the truth because, doubtless, she's lied to you about her upbringing."

"What is *wrong* with you?" he asked.

"I checked her out before the job. We did a thorough background check. She's a poor girl from Charleston. Her father is military, and her mother runs some kind of magic shop." The mayor shuddered.

"Natalie never lied to me about anything. I already knew all of that."

"Well, the only reason she's even in this house is because of her recommendations. You deserve someone better than that."

"Someone like what? A society girl? A brainless, shallow idiot who only cares that I have the right last name and the right amount of money? I don't know how to say it any more plainly, I would never be interested in someone like that. So, what I *deserve* in your estimation doesn't matter to me."

"Not every woman of class is a brainless idiot. You just like to slum it."

My jaw dropped. "You don't need to keep insulting me!"

"Telling the truth is insulting you now?"

When she fixed her eyes on me, I knew that it wasn't a good sign. I'd remained quiet through most of the conversation. Too in shock to know how to respond to his mother's abuse. But I couldn't let her keep going on like this.

"Mother, can we just speak in private about this?" Penn asked.

"We have nothing further to say to one another," she said flatly. She seemed to realize that she wasn't getting anywhere with her son. They'd likely had the same argument over and over again. A lose-lose situation at its finest. "And you." She pointed her finger at me. "You are in breach of contract."

"What?" I gasped.

"You're sleeping with my son!"

"Mother, you know that has nothing to do with Natalie's work," Penn said plainly. "You're only upset because of me. Let's talk about this reasonably."

"There's nothing reasonable about you anymore, Penn. You're not my employee, but she is. So, stay out of this."

"I assure you that all the work has been done to your standard. I've been here the entire time. I've made every appointment. I've hit every deadline. The decorator should be here in a matter of hours to discuss the final plans for the deck. You might not like that I have been with Penn, but I still got the job done."

The mayor narrowed her shrewd eyes. "Pack up your things and get out of my house."

"But—"

"You're fired," she said flatly.

"Mother, why are you doing this?" Penn asked in anger.

She just kept her eyes on me. "Now."

I swallowed and fought back tears. Fired. I was…fired. Oh my god. Oh my god. Oh my god. I didn't know what to do, what to think. I could just stand there and stare at the mayor in horror as those words rang over and over again in my mind.

"You'll get no recommendation from me. In fact, I'm going to contact the agency and request that you be removed. I'm sure other people would like to know what kind of person they're hiring."

Tears welled in my eyes at her words. Harsh, horrible words. Not just cutting me out of this job. Cutting me out of…all jobs,

"You don't have to do this," Penn said. "She only has a few more days left."

"Haven't you done enough?" his mother said with cold, furious eyes.

I didn't wait to hear his response. There was nothing I could do here. No point in arguing because it was clear that the mayor had made up her mind. She hadn't become such a successful lawyer, judge, and politician by wavering in her decisions. This was over. I was fired. And I had to pack up and leave now.

I turned on my heel and all but ran to the master bedroom.

Raised voices filtered toward me, but I couldn't exactly hear what was being said. I assumed it wasn't pretty. That it was a fight they'd had a lot, and this was just icing on the cake.

Speaking of icing…

I was going to need to pick some up.

Icing fixed everything. A whole tub full.

I swallowed back the tears at that thought and grabbed both of my suitcases out of the closet. I opened them on top of the bed and began to furiously pack my measly belongings into them.

I didn't even waste my time trying to fold it all to my usual standards. I just haphazardly tossed things inside and hoped it would close.

Fired.

I was fired.

My hands trembled as I dug my shoes out and threw them into the bag. Then I couldn't stop it. Tears. Fuck, I didn't want to be this weak. To cry over a lost job. But, god, it was a job I was good at. And it gave me the room to write when I wanted and see exotic places. It got me out of Charleston and away from my family. It was the perfect job while I waited and waited and waited to catch my break in writing.

Now, it was gone.

And I felt something snap inside me.

Suddenly, I was on my knees in front of the bed, the suitcases splayed out before me. Tears rolled down my cheeks in rivers. Sobs racked my body as I let it all out. My hands clutched the duvet cover.

I wanted to scream and scream and scream some more. But I couldn't do that with the mayor still down the hall. I wouldn't give her the satisfaction.

The world wasn't ending. I knew that. I rationally knew that I could figure out what to do from here. But it felt so grim. I'd just fallen off a cliff at the edge of the world, and I was spiraling down. The terror wasn't in the landing; it was in the free fall. In not knowing where I was going to land.

And right now, I was tumbling over and over again with no end in sight.

Suddenly, I felt arms around my middle, and a soft voice in my ear said, "Shh."

He turned me into his arms and held me pressed against

him as the tears continued. He kissed my hair and rubbed my back as he rocked me back and forth.

"It's going to be okay," he murmured placatingly.

"You don't…know that," I said through my hiccups.

"I do. I know that you will be. That everything will be okay."

"I just…lost my job. I lost…everything."

He kissed my hair again. "I know. I'm so sorry, Nat."

"I don't even…have a place to stay."

"You can stay with me," he said easily.

"Won't your mom be…mad?" I asked, trying to gulp in oxygen as I felt hyperventilating coming on.

"I don't give a damn what she thinks." He pulled back enough to look into my red, puffy face. He wiped away the streaks of tears and planted a kiss on my lips. "I want you to come back with me. We can figure this out together."

PART V
SOME THINGS ARE BETTER LEFT UNSAID

NATALIE

34

I had two suitcases to my name.
A name that now meant nothing.
Absolutely nothing.

It had meant a lot of things over the years—military brat, prized swimmer, star university student, elite vacation home watcher—and now, it held no value. Because just as with all of those other cloaks I'd put on, I had to take this one off too. Had it viciously ripped off. Leaving me naked and struggling to remember who I even was anymore.

The one cloak I wanted to wear—writer and acclaimed author—was still such a distant, impossible thought that it was nothing but a shadow. Not a real thing at all. Just a dream for a silly girl to cling on to when everything fell apart. And even now, it felt far-fetched as I stood bare, hoping to steal another cloak.

I stumbled into Penn's apartment on the Upper East Side, pushing one of the suitcases in front of me. He was carrying the other one while holding Totle's leash. We'd barely spoken on the drive over. He'd turned on music from one of his playlists on his phone, and I'd drifted through delirium as I stared out the window.

My tears had dried up. The dizzy feeling of pressing anxiety remained. And something else was clogging my throat and holding me under.

I dropped my suitcase in the living room, peeled my jacket off, and fell face-first into the couch. "My life is over."

Totle's tags jingled as he rushed across the room and jumped onto my back. Then he crawled forward and licked my face.

"Yes, yes, you. I know. I'll love you." I squeezed him into my side until he flopped his head down on the couch and huffed.

Penn stood with his hands on the back of the chair. "Your life isn't over."

"It feels like it."

"We can fix this."

"We?" I asked with an arched eyebrow. I released Totle and sat up. "There's no fixing this, Penn. This is all over. I have no job. I have no place to live. I have *nothing*."

"We can get my mother to come around."

I snorted. "Your mother is *not* coming around on this."

"Well maybe not on your job, but we might be able to get her to not call the agency. Then you could still get another job somewhere else," he said hopefully.

For a realist, Penn was being unbelievably optimistic.

"She's probably already called. It's over." Anger bubbled up inside of me. "Everything I've worked for in the last eighteen months is just gone. Poof!"

"I know. I'm sorry. I didn't expect this to happen."

"Of course not. Why would your mother even come out to the beach house?"

He frowned as if he hadn't even thought about that. Fury

crossed his features and then dissolved. "I don't know. She wasn't scheduled."

"Do you think, if she was scheduled, I would have let you even *stay* today?" I snapped.

"Hey, I'm trying to help. I want to figure this out. Figure out a way that we can salvage this."

"*We* can't solve this problem, Penn. I have no leverage to fix this. And you can't do anything to help," I told him. "This isn't a problem you can throw money at."

His eyes rounded. "What exactly is that supposed to mean?"

"You know exactly what it means. As much as you might have tried to get away from your roots, you are still money and used to using it to get you in and out of everything. You can take the boy out of the Upper East Side, but you can't take the Upper East Side out of the boy." I waved my arms around the room as proof, letting my anger fuel this argument.

"That has nothing to do with this."

I jumped to my feet. "It has *everything* to do with this! You want to fix this. You want to make it all better. But you can't. You can't make any of this better."

"Natalie…"

"Money fixes your problems, Penn. But it only causes mine."

I picked up the closest thing to me, which happened to be a coaster, and hurled it against the wall. It thudded noisily before dropping to the floor.

"It's just cruel…cruel money," I said, my voice going shallow and fierce. "I'm seen as the help, white trash, a project. Whatever, but I'm not like you. I'm not one of you. As you said before…I don't belong here."

"You belong with me."

"Do I?" I asked with wide, conflicted eyes. "No one else seems to think so."

"I don't care what anyone else thinks." He stepped forward, taking my hands in his. "I only care about us."

I wrenched my hands free and listlessly paced around the room. "Of course you only care about us. Because you have never had to consider what all of this means to someone without. What did your mother say? Diddling the help again, Penn? Again?"

He sighed. "Yeah. That was before."

"Before what? You tried to become all enlightened?"

His jaw clenched. "You know that I've changed."

"But is it really that different?"

"Yes. Of course it's different. We are different, Natalie."

I shook my head and tried to hold it all in, but I couldn't. I felt so helpless. So utterly useless. I'd put all of my eggs in one basket, and someone had shattered them.

"Why are you trying to pick a fight with me?" he asked.

"Because this is my fault. I should have never let you stay that day. I should have done something else. Should have turned you away."

"And where would we be now?"

"I'd be employed!"

"Is that more important than us?" he demanded. "You don't need a job right now or a place to stay. You can stay here with me for now."

"I don't need your charity," I hissed.

"Natalie, it's not charity!"

"You have no idea what it's like to have nothing." I gritted my teeth. "If you did, then you'd know charity when you saw it."

"You're right," he said, holding his hands up. "I have never been in this situation. But I am only doing this because I care for you. I want to make this right the best I can. And if I have to use my resources to do that, why does that have to be a bad thing?"

I yanked my jacket off of the floor and tugged it on. "It's not a bad thing. It's a great thing," I grumbled, striding back toward the elevator.

"Natalie, where are you going?"

"I need some air. Some space to think."

He reached out and brought me to a halt. "Please don't run out of here like this."

I tugged my arm away from his. "I can't think straight right now, and if I stay, I'm going to say something else that I regret. So, just…let me go."

"Okay," he said softly. "I'm going to try to figure this out."

"Go work your magic." I stepped into the elevator.

"We'll make this work," he tried to assure me.

As the doors closed between us, I realized that I wasn't sure if he was talking about my job or…us.

NATALIE

35

I strode aimlessly through Central Park. With nowhere to go and nothing on my mind to see, I got lost while wandering the park and managed to run into the Boathouse. I grabbed a hot dog and bottled water before meandering back around the lake. Bethesda Fountain loomed up ahead, and I remembered us coming here with Melanie and Amy. How different that day had been. Before Penn and I had even started this liaison. I'd predicted that I'd leave brokenhearted. The more I thought about it, the more I really, *really* didn't want that to happen.

My temper cooled as I walked up the steps that led to the Mall. I passed the park benches that were in a dozen movies and then turned back toward Penn's place. I'd been unfair. That much was obvious. I'd just been so angry. So frustrated that this had all happened because he had moved into the beach house with me. I hadn't wanted him to, but he'd done it anyway. I could have gotten another job. Picked a different household to work for. They would have been less desirable, but it would have been an option.

Instead, I'd stayed. He'd stayed. And neither of us had

looked back. I wouldn't trade our time together, but we only had three more days! It was wrong that we were here with so little time left.

I tucked my hands into my jacket and finally walked out of Central Park. My legs were tired, but my mind and soul were exhausted. Today had been a roller coaster. I needed to talk to Penn and decide what to do from here.

I wasn't prepared to give him up.

But I had no idea what I was going to do for work or where the hell I would stay. That was a scary prospect in a place like New York City.

I was glad that I'd gone for my walk even if Penn and I had argued before it. The cool weather and time away from it all had settled me. I wasn't better. I didn't know when I would be again after being fired like that. But I was functional at least.

My mind was still so far up in the clouds that I didn't even realize someone was saying my name until I had almost reached Penn's building.

"Natalie!" Katherine cried, darting forward.

Oh great, just what I needed.

"Hey, Katherine. You know...now is really not a good time."

"God, I'm sure, Natalie. Penn told me what happened at the beach house. I am so incredibly sorry."

I shot her a half-smile. "Yeah. Thanks. I don't really want to talk about it."

"I wanted to stop by and check on you."

"I'll be fine," I said as short and curt as I could manage.

Katherine had been nothing but kind to me during Halloween, telling me how excited she was to hang out again at the mayor's party, but I honestly did not want to talk to anyone. Just Penn. Just to make it right.

"I could come up and make you some tea."

"I said...I'm fine," I snapped.

Her spine straightened, and her eyes widened. "I'm just trying to help. I could not believe it when Penn told me."

I sighed. Of course, just trying to help. "I'm just going to go upstairs and see Penn."

"Oh, he went over to Lewis's, I think, to talk to Lark."

"What is Lark doing at Lewis's?"

Katherine shrugged. "She apartment-hops between the four of us when she and Thomas are fighting."

"Does that happen often?"

"More often than she'd admit to," Katherine said with a sad sigh. "Lewis is helping Lark with boy troubles. Are you sure I can't come up and help you with yours?"

"I don't have boy troubles. I have unemployment troubles."

"Oh," Katherine said in surprise. "Well, we can fix that."

I rolled my eyes. "I don't need anyone else's help finding a job. What I need is icing."

"Icing?" Katherine asked.

"Never mind." There was no way that Katherine could understand that particular habit. "I'm just going to go."

"Well, I don't think that you should be alone." She stepped forward to follow me inside.

I wanted to bite her head off for being so presumptuous, but I just didn't have the energy. "Fine."

Katherine smiled brightly and then whisked me inside. We took the elevator upstairs. Totle was pleased to see us at least. He kept running around our feet, begging for attention. I finally settled onto the couch with him in my lap under a blanket.

"I cannot believe he just gives that dog the run of the house," Katherine said. She was true to her word and making me tea.

"Try to stop him. It's impossible."

"True. At least he's cute." She brought the tea over and set it on the coffee table. Then she went back for her own cup. "It's good for the soul."

"I'm usually more of a coffee person."

"Drastic times," she said.

I took a sip of the tea and was surprised it was good. Katherine didn't seem like the kind of person who had to do much for herself.

"Thanks for this," I said, tucking my legs up underneath me.

"Of course. What are friends for?" She smiled. "So, how are you feeling about all of this?"

I shrugged. "Horrible. Pretty much horrible."

"Ugh! I could imagine. Penn said that you two had a blow-up fight."

"Yeah," I said, taking another sip. "I just kind of lost it. I need to talk to him. Make things right."

"Natalie..." Katherine said. Her eyes darted to the ground and then back up at me. "I really need to tell you something."

My stomach dropped at the way she'd said those words. *What* could she possibly need to tell me?

"Do you?"

"This whole thing with Penn...I really don't think it's a good idea."

My brain froze. Was she *really* trying to pull this right now?

"Oh, yeah? Why do you think that?"

"He's just...he's done this sort of thing before, and I don't want to see you get hurt."

"What sort of thing? Dated the help?"

Katherine furrowed her brows. "Well, yeah. I mean, he's slept with the help before at least. Led them on. But he's really not what you think he is."

"Katherine, you should stop. I don't need to hear this right now."

"I mean, I hate that all of this started over a silly bet."

I narrowed my eyes and tilted my head. "A bet? What bet?"

"It was stupid," she said with a halfhearted laugh. "Penn swore he could get you into bed and make you fall for him. We tried to talk him out of it, but, well...he wants what he wants."

My mouth went dry. This couldn't be real. Who actually *bet* on things? Let alone on whether or not you could sleep with someone? We had already slept together. What kind of prize was that? It didn't even make sense. That was something dumb jocks did in high school or maybe college. But we were...adults. The whole thing just sounded absurd.

"I'm really sorry. I felt like you should know."

I finally looked back up at Katherine. Really looked at her. That sad, sympathetic routine. The light in her eyes that didn't match her expression. Her mouth that tilted just slightly in the corners.

She wasn't concerned. She *wanted* me to believe this. She wanted me to fall into her trap.

What had Lewis said? If Katherine knew we were dating, she would do anything to keep us apart. She would be worse, so much worse.

Had she been hiding her true character? Was this the depth of her deceit?

"I don't believe you," I said, my voice low and even.

"Natalie, it's true!" she gasped.

"You would do *anything* to keep us apart," I spat in her direction. "Anything. You are clearly in love with Penn and cannot stand the fact that he would pick me, a nobody, over you. Well, your lies are not going to change my mind about him."

"I swear. It's true. If you don't ask Penn, then ask the rest of the crew. They were there that night. They'll tell you it's true."

Suddenly, I couldn't hold back any longer. I was laughing. A manic laugh. This was not real. This was not real life.

"Get out," I told her.

"Natalie…"

"I said, get out!" I yelled at her. "I don't want to hear another word out of your mouth. You aren't my friend. You aren't Penn's friend. You're a leech, a disease, a fake, and a fraud."

Katherine straightened. "We'll see about that."

When she left, I collapsed back into the couch. My breathing was uneven. My fury returning in force. A bet? Was she out of her mind? Was that the best that she could do?

Then for a fraction of a second, it hit me. I wondered, *Could it be true? Could all of this be a result of some stupid bet?*

I bit on my lip. I didn't want to give credence to Katherine's tall tale, but maybe I should find out…just to be sure.

PENN

36

When I entered Lewis's apartment, he and Lark were sitting in the living room, watching some detective show. They both glanced up at my entrance and then went back to their show.

"Hey," Lewis said.

Lark put her hand up in a form of a wave.

"Hey." I wanted to just dive into this conversation. After what had happened with my mother and Natalie, I needed to actually figure out how to make this right.

But then I sat down and saw Lark's eyes were red and puffy. She had a box of tissues at her side and was curled up in a ball in sweats.

"What happened?"

"Nothing," Lark said at once. Her voice was a mess.

I shared a look with Lewis. Thomas had happened.

"Another fight?" I asked.

Lark shrugged. "It was nothing. I just need a place to crash for a day or two."

"But it's *your* apartment," I argued.

"Easier than asking him to leave." She sniffled and then

blew her nose. "It doesn't help that I'm sick from the campaign. It looks worse than it is."

"I'm sorry."

She shrugged again.

"I hate to do this when you're not feeling well, but is there any chance that you could talk to my mother?"

Lark arched an eyebrow. "Because of Natalie?"

"I told her," Lewis said.

"Yes. She fired Natalie because of me, and I need to find a way to make it right. She's not just firing her. She's trying to ruin her chance of getting any other job after this." I sighed and ran a hand back through my hair. "It's to get back at me. She said, if I came back to work for Kensington Enterprises, that she wouldn't call. But I can't do that."

"You can't negotiate with her," Lark said. "That would be like me going back to work for my parents because they threatened me."

"I don't want to negotiate. I won't come back and work for her. Even if I did, I doubt she would hold up her end of the bargain. I just need her to see reason from someone she trusts." I pointedly looked at her. "You're her right hand."

"I'm flattered you think so. But I'm really not."

"We both know that you're important to her organization," I said. "If you could just talk to her…"

"Penn, it might not be the right time," Lewis said.

"I know. But…"

"I'll do it," Lark said, coughing into her tissue. "At least… I'll go see her and find out where her head is at. I can't make any promises. You Kensingtons have an irrational streak about you."

"Thank you, Lark. Thank you so much," I said, jumping to my feet.

"Don't thank me yet." She stood uneasily. "Just let me change, and I'll go."

Lark was only gone for ten minutes before she appeared again in a business suit and her hair slicked back. She waved good-bye to both of us and then left.

"That is not going to work," Lewis said.

"I know," I said. I flopped back into the chair and tilted my head up. "But I have to do something. She's furious over what happened, and how can I even blame her?"

"Well, you can't. But you can probably blame Katherine. This has her stink all over it."

"I already called and yelled at her. I don't care what she does to me, but getting Natalie fired?"

"Is right up her alley?" Lewis asked.

"Yeah."

"You shouldn't have entered into that stupid bet."

"Yeah, I'm seeing that. I tried to get out of it, but Katherine won't drop it."

"Of course she won't. She wants to sleep with you."

I put my head in my hands. "This is all so fucked up. Even for us."

"Well, so was the last bet. You didn't seem to give a shit then."

"This is different, and you know it," I growled.

Lewis shrugged. "Because you fell for Natalie?"

"No. You know why. And that shit in the past doesn't even matter." I sprang to my feet and paced the window overlooking Central Park. "She's pissed because she was fired. She blames me and herself. But it's not her fault it's mine. I never would have pushed to stay there if we hadn't had the bet. I thought it was harmless. I could fuck her and win the bet. I thought it would be a joke, and now…"

"It's not funny?" Lewis asked with an arched eyebrow.

"Not even a little." I slid my hands into my pockets. "What would you do if you were in my position?"

Lewis breathed out heavily. "Not get in this position in the first place."

"I'm serious."

"So am I," Lewis said. "Natalie, she's…special. She's not like other girls out there. She has a mind of her own. She's funny and sweet and smart. You'd be an idiot to let her go, man."

I nodded. I would be. That much was vividly clear to me. I'd spent so much of my life trying to be a better person, and then the one person who had come into my life that I actually cared about…was throwing that all into question. Would an ethical person make a bet like this? I couldn't figure out how the one person I thought made me a better person also made me a worse person. The conflicting sides of my character tore at me like a real-life angel and devil on my shoulders. And anything I did to fix it all…could only make it worse.

A buzz drew me out of my deep thoughts.

Lewis pulled his phone out of his pocket. "It's Natalie."

I froze. "Calling you?"

He shrugged. "Looks like it."

"For what?"

"I'll put it on speaker, but you need to stay quiet."

"Fine."

Lewis answered the phone. "Hey, gorgeous!"

He pressed the speaker button and placed the phone on his coffee table. He put his finger to his mouth, and I nodded.

"Hey, Lewis," she said. Her voice was shaky. She sounded like she had been crying again. "Is Penn still with you?"

"No, he just left," Lewis lied.

"Okay, good," she said with a sigh.

I pursed my lips in anger. She was *glad* that I wasn't there while she was on the phone with Lewis. What the hell?

"What's going on? I heard you two got in a fight, and I'm sorry to hear about your job."

"Yeah. Yeah, we did. I probably need to talk to him about that. I said some things that I shouldn't have."

Lewis looked up at me and raised his eyebrows. "That sometimes happens in arguments."

"Anyway, that's not why I'm calling." She took a deep breath.

I could tell that whatever she was thinking was eating at her.

"Are you okay?"

"Yes. No. Maybe. I don't know. Katherine came by," she said softly.

I jumped to my feet and cursed softly. Lewis glared at me and waved his hand to tell me to sit down and shut up.

"What did she want?"

"Well, she claimed she wanted to comfort me. I think she thought Penn and I were breaking up, and she wanted to gloat. I remember what you said at the concert about her being worse if Penn and I were together. And then she said something that was just…ludicrous." Her breath hitched. "Just so ridiculous that it couldn't be true. She was just trying to force us apart by whatever means necessary. But she said that, if I didn't believe her I could ask any of you…and you'd tell me the truth. So…can I ask you?"

My eyes locked on Lewis's. We both were frozen in place, as if we knew exactly where this train wreck was going but had no way to stop it.

"Of course. What did she say?" Lewis asked.

"She said that I was just a…bet." Natalie slowly breathed out.

"A bet?" Lewis asked with his eyes on me, as if to ask what I wanted him to say.

But I didn't know. This wasn't how I'd wanted her to find out, but fuck, I couldn't keep lying to her.

"Yeah...she said it was a bet to sleep with me and make me fall for him."

Lewis arched an eyebrow, and I finally slowly shook my head.

"There was no bet, Natalie. That's Katherine trying to get in your head."

"Oh," she said with a big sigh. "Oh okay, good. That's what I thought. But I just...I had this voice in my head, saying that I had to check. And I knew you'd tell me."

Lewis narrowed his eyes at me. "Anytime. Hey, I have to head out now. Do you need anything else?"

"No, I'm okay. I'll just wait for Penn to get back. Thanks, Lewis."

"Anytime, Natalie."

He hung up the phone and then vaulted to his feet. "You have me *lying* for you now!"

"How is that different than any other time?"

"She asked me point-blank, and I told her it wasn't true." He spread his arms wide in anger.

"It will all be over in three days!"

"Are you that blind and stupid? Katherine will never let this go. Natalie deserves to know."

"I know. I know, but it's not the right time."

"It's never the right time," Lewis spat at me. "You did this. You can't keep stringing her along."

"I'm not stringing her along. I care about her, and I don't want to hurt her. I just want this whole thing to be over with."

"You are *un*believable," Lewis said. He shook his head and stormed away from me. "You have this girl. This amazing, beautiful, confident, funny, brilliant girl. A girl any guy would die for, and you're just going to sit there and say, *Let's* *wait three days and hope it all goes away*. News flash: it's not going to go away."

"Jesus, Lewis. Since when do you even *care*?" I demanded.

I was staring at my best friend and hardly recognized him. For all the years we had known each other, Lewis had always had my back. He'd been the one to egg on my antics. To amp everything up to make it worse. To be there when things went south. And now, this?

"Because you don't deserve her," he roared at me from across the room. He clenched his hands into fists, breathing deeply. Then he released them as the tension seemed to leave him. "You don't deserve a girl that amazing."

"What the fuck does that even mean?" I demanded. Then I saw what I hadn't seen before. This couldn't be reality. "Do you…like her?"

"Just now catching on?" Lewis asked sardonically.

"What? How? When?" I stammered.

"I thought she was gorgeous the moment she walked into the beach house and yelled at you. Then when she drank straight out of that whiskey bottle and held her own against us. Totally out of her element and totally alive. And then a million moments since then. But it was her words…" Lewis held his hands up, as if he could barely get it out. I hardly recognized him. I had never seen him like this. "It was her books that really won me over."

"You've *read* her books? She won't even let me read them."

He shrugged. But his next words were chilling. "You need to tell her about the bet….or I will."

"You're not serious."

But looking at him…I knew he was.

He really was.

I HAD TO TELL HER.

I stared at the elevator that led up to my penthouse and wondered how the hell I was going to break this to her. I'd lose her. She'd been shaken when she called Lewis. Me confirming it…that would only break her. One more thing on top of everything else.

But I still had to do it. It was the right thing to do.

I took the elevator upstairs and waited for Totle to come attack me. I scratched his head. "Okay, Aristotle, make this easier for me, man. Help me out."

I kissed the top of his head and then followed him inside.

But what I found when I entered was Natalie sitting on the couch, sobbing.

"Natalie?" I asked, striding toward her and enveloping her in my arms in one big rush.

"The…vacation home agency…called," she gasped out between sobs.

"Oh shit, really?" Guess Lark hadn't gotten to my mother in time. Fuck!

"They said that…I was terminated. They're removing my account and sending…final payment."

"I am so sorry, baby. I'm so, so sorry."

I rocked her back and forth in my arms, as I had back at the beach house. One punch after another just kept coming.

"No, Penn, I'm sorry," she said, swiping at her eyes. "I shouldn't have said those things to you. I was just mad. And now, this. I don't know. I can't keep it together."

"Hey, you have *nothing* to apologize for. Nothing."

"You sure? Because I was pretty mean. I shouldn't have said those things to you."

I tilted her chin up to look me in the eyes. "Forget about it. I'm just sorry about the agency. I tried to get Lark to talk sense into my mother, but she must not have gotten to her in time."

"Well, thank you for trying. It was kind of inevitable

anyway." Natalie's shoulders shook one more time. "And then Katherine was here, being a total bitch."

"What did she want?"

"Ugh! Nothing. She acted like she wanted to help me out, but I really think she's in love with you and trying to break us up."

Her blue eyes looked up into mine, so trusting, and I knew then…I had to do it.

"Natalie, I…need to talk to you for a minute."

"Okay," she said uncertainly. She wiped at her eyes again. "I'm kind of a mess. This has not been the easiest day."

"No, I suspect not."

"What is it?"

"I…" I opened my mouth to tell her. To get the words out. But they wouldn't budge. "My…my mother did this because of me. Not you."

"I mean…I know she said that, Penn, but you don't have to blame yourself."

"No, she said she'd give you your job back or at least not talk to the agency if…if I went back to work for the company."

"Well, that's awful!" Natalie cried. Her eyes were angry again. That sadness replaced by fury. "She can't do that to you. That's blackmail. How dare she use your affection for me against you."

"But…I should have done it," I said out loud for the first time. "It would have saved your career."

"At what cost?" she gasped. "The loss of your career and life and passion and *soul*? No, Penn, that is not an even trade. And if you think that I'm going to blame you for this, you're wrong."

"There's more," I said cautiously.

"What?"

I needed to contradict her. I needed to tell her the real

reason this was my fault. But that look. That look of adoration in her eyes. I couldn't break this. Even if it was an illusion. I couldn't break her heart along with anything else.

"I want you to stay here," I told her.

She nodded. "Okay. I'll stay until my flight on Saturday."

"No, Natalie." I took her hands in mine. "I want you to move in with me."

"Penn, it's so...so soon."

"I know. I've never done anything like this before in my life. But for you, Nat, it's real. Move in with me. Stay in New York. Let's work this out together. Here."

"No," she said softly.

"What?"

"I'm sorry, but...no."

"No?" I asked, dumbfounded. My jaw hung open in shock. I'd never thought that she would say that. Not in a million years.

"It's too soon for us to move in together. We've only just begun. I need to go home. To go back to Charleston and figure out my next move. I can't stay here and do that. But...I don't want this to be the end for us." She took my hand in hers again. "I know it won't be easy, but we'll figure it out."

"You really won't stay?" I asked, still in shock.

"No, I won't."

NATALIE

37

I'd said no.

I still couldn't believe that I'd actually said the words.

I'd been shocked. Penn Kensington asking me to move in with him. It had been a dream. And I'd wanted to say yes so bad. So, so bad. But…I couldn't. Not with my entire life hanging in the balance.

And I didn't know how I was going to say good-bye.

Penn pulled his Audi into the drop-off lane at JFK International Airport. My flight home left in two hours, but I liked to be early, to Penn's dismay.

He put the car in park, hopped out, and went to get my suitcases out of the trunk.

I kissed Totle's head and then hugged him to me. "I promise, promise, promise that I will come back and visit you, cutie. You're my little man, you know? Have to take care of Penn while I'm back home. But don't let him skimp on treats. Be good." I kissed him again. Tears welled in my eyes. I hated leaving him so much. "I love you."

Then I moved him back into the passenger seat and

closed the door. I heard his whimper as I walked away and faltered. Ugh! Leaving him was almost harder than Penn. Totle, who had no idea why I was leaving. Who wouldn't understand about long distance and trips to visit. He was just this cute, defenseless, little puppy that I'd come to adore. And I just wanted to take him with me.

"Are you sure I can't steal your puppy?" I asked Penn from the curb next to my first suitcase.

"I am certain you cannot steal Aristotle." He dropped the second suitcase next to the first. "What other leverage do I have to get you to come back?"

I laughed. "I can think of a thing or two."

"Can you?" he asked, tugging me in close and kissing me until I was breathless.

"Well, with that kind of send-off, I most certainly can."

"I wish you didn't have to go."

"Me too," I murmured.

"You could stay."

"I know, but I can't."

He nodded. "Yeah, I know. You'd think, if you were going to change your mind, you already would have. Now, I'm stuck going to this party solo."

"I can't even believe you're going to your mother's party. After what she did to you and how she tried to blackmail you."

He sighed and then lifted one shoulder. "It's the one party every other year that I'm expected to attend. It would be worse for me if I didn't show up."

"Well, I hope the house is beautiful. Send me pictures of it all decorated for the event. I was looking forward to that much."

"I'll be sure to do that."

"Just…drink lots of booze and try to ignore your mother."

"It'll be hard, being there without you. I can't imagine

looking at that house and not seeing you in every corner, on every surface."

"Are you picturing me naked now?" I asked, trying to lighten the mood.

"Always." He kissed me again. "I'm going to miss you."

"I know. I'm going to miss you, too." I tried to pull away, but he just held on harder, kissing me so long that I was sure someone was going to make us leave.

Finally, he reluctantly released me, tucking my silvery-white hair behind my ear. "Text me when you get there."

"You too."

He smiled that charming smile that had won me over time and time again, but I saw the sadness in it. I grabbed my bags and left before I changed my mind. Because if I had to look at that smile one more time, I might stay.

We'd had our ups and downs. We had our differences. We came from different worlds. But at the end of the day…we fit together.

And I loved that about us.

With my heart in my throat, I strode into the airport. I waited in the outrageously long line to check my bags in and made it past the security check. Then I maneuvered around the large airport until I found my gate. I checked the time and groaned.

One hour and nineteen minutes until takeoff.

I could have sworn it had taken longer than that to get to the gate. I plopped down in my seat and pulled out my headphones to drown out the noise. Then I took a selfie of me waiting and sent it in a text to Penn. He responded with a picture of Totle in the passenger seat of the Audi. A text came in right after it.

He misses you too.

I snapped a picture of me pouting and then rested my head back against the chair. This was going to be nearly impossible. Like seriously impossible.

Another text came in, and I glanced down at it but was surprised to see it was from Amy.

You're really coming home today? After that boy asked you to move in with him? I cannot believe you're really doing this.

Me either.

Because I honestly couldn't believe it. What was I even thinking?

We said two scenarios, Nat. You catch feelings. He doesn't. You come home brokenhearted. OR you have a fling with no feelings and come home and get in a relationship. Neither of those is happening! You got the scenario we hadn't even pictured. You both caught feelings. He wants you to stay...

I know, Amy. I know.

Another text came in from Penn. It was him pouting this time with a text that said:

Come home soon.

Where's home?

Amy interrupted our conversation again.

If you know...then why are you coming back? Stay with him!

I can't. I know we didn't predict this, but we also didn't guess I'd lose my job. Plus, even though I care for him, I don't even know if I trust him.

And that will get easier with a thousand miles between you?

No...

You've been given the opportunity of a lifetime. I love you to pieces, Nat, but this is stupid.

I didn't respond. I didn't know what to say.

I'd had all these reasons when I told Penn that I couldn't stay. I wanted to be independent. We'd only known each other for a short time. I didn't know if I could trust him with everything we'd gone through. We came from two different worlds. I still needed to figure myself out before I could figure *us* out. But as the call for boarding came through, I couldn't seem to think of any of that. Just that I was leaving.

My phone dinged, and I realized that I'd ignored it. I had a half-dozen more messages from Amy that I ignored and opened Penn's response to my question about home.

He'd sent a picture of us at the beach house that we'd taken one day while we were lounging around. I was in the infamous white dress that we'd first met in. He was in khaki shorts and a polo. I was laughing like a fool while he kissed my cheek and snapped the shot.

There was only one line beneath it.

Home.

I jumped out of my seat. "Oh my god, I'm an idiot."

The woman next to me looked at me as if I were actually insane. But I ignored her, hauled my bag and purse up onto my shoulders, and ran back out of the terminal. I darted through the exit and back out onto the area for departures and arrivals.

I hailed the first taxi I could find and jumped into the backseat.

"Where to?" the driver asked.

"East Hampton."

My breath was coming out in puffs from my sprint out of the airport, and my luggage was going to go to Charleston ahead of me, but I didn't even care. The taxi was pulling away, and I was on my way to the beach house. Because I couldn't leave. I couldn't leave New York without telling Penn the truth. Without telling him how I really felt…that I loved him.

PENN

38

By this time, Natalie was probably on her flight, about to head home.

I'd actually let her slip through my fingers. Just like that, she was gone. She'd said that she still wanted to work on things. That we'd video chat and visit, but it wasn't the same. And we both knew it. She had already started pulling away as soon as she said no. I didn't want that good-bye at the airport to be enough, but I'd royally fucked up. And I was only going to make it worse when I told her about this insufferable bet.

Maybe we could salvage it. At least, I hoped that we could.

I'd figure it out after this damnable party.

A few hours here, and I might want to fly to Charleston tonight. I pulled into the driveway of the Kensington Cottage, as I had done over and over the last two months. It looked the same, and yet I knew that it was empty. She wasn't in it.

Every inch of this place reminded me of her. I wasn't sure I'd ever be able to set foot inside without seeing her here. All the hours we'd spent together, writing, joking, brooding, fucking. This house now belonged to her in my mind.

I leashed Totle and then entered the house. Totle took off at a bound. He was so excited to be back. He looked around at all the strange people and seemed to be looking…for her.

"What are you doing with him at this party?" my mother accosted me.

"I couldn't just leave him," I told her flatly. "I'll put him in a bedroom, and he'll be fine for the evening."

"I hope you're going to behave at this event, Penn. This is important for my career."

I leveled her with a blank gaze. "Sure. I'll *behave*."

Then I shouldered past her and went back to the master bedroom. It would be occupied later, but for now, it was where Totle was most familiar, so I'd leave him here. I shooed him inside and then closed the door behind him.

I couldn't be this Penn anymore tonight. I had to be aloof, placating, devious even. I needed my Upper East Side mask. The one I wore to fit into these crowds that I'd once owned. And to care about the bullshit they spewed. To not embarrass my mother at this important event where nearly every politician in New York was in attendance. Even though that was all I wanted to do.

But I had been raised in this world. Slipping back into that skin was second nature. As easy as breathing.

Natalie wasn't here, so nothing was real.

Not even me.

I strode around the room, shaking hands and kissing babies—metaphorically, of course. I charmed housewives and smirked at daughters. I did what was expected of me. What I'd always done. What I was good at. But there was nothing enjoyable about it. Not even the three glasses of bourbon I'd guzzled down to deal with these unbearable sycophants.

Three phone numbers, an offer to disappear down to the beach, and a suggested affair with the wife of a state senator, and I'd had enough. I tossed the numbers and reached for another drink.

"Ah, little brother is back in business," Court said. He was leaning against the counter in the kitchen and smirking at me deviously.

I narrowed my eyes at him and didn't respond. I just poured my drink and took a good, long sip.

"Where's your new girlfriend?" he asked. "Thought she'd be making an appearance with you, or have you already blown through another one?"

"I really don't want to discuss Natalie with you. Believe it or not."

"Ah, Natalie! That was her name," he said as if he'd just remembered. "She was smoking hot. Little angel. Was she a devil in bed?"

I ground my teeth and ignored the impulse in my brain telling me to beat the shit out of him. "Whatever, Court."

Jane Devney strode into the kitchen then. She had on a nondescript blue dress and heels. Her ash-blonde hair was pulled up into a twist.

"Hello, pet," Court crooned at her.

She smiled at him. "Ah, there you are. I was just talking to Senator Cumberland about that new initiative he's working on in clean energy. But I just *knew* that I'd find you in here."

He pulled her into his side and grinned down at her like a fool. My brother…a fool for love? I was imagining things. Jane was probably a means to an end or, at the very least, a short-term lay that he hadn't dismissed yet.

"How do you deal with him?" I demanded.

Jane glanced back at me. "Hmm?"

"Ignore him," Court said. "Just jealous."

I snorted and raised my glass to them. "To the day that I'm jealous of my brother. May I be six feet under."

Court's eyes narrowed in warning, but I was already exiting the kitchen. Antagonizing Court was never a smart idea. He liked to push buttons. He didn't like to be on the receiving end. Go figure.

I turned around and ran smack into another gorgeous, young blonde. But I realized that I recognized her.

"Anna English," I said with a broad grin.

"Penn Kensington."

Anna was Lark's best friend from law school. She was a hundred percent LA, and it was obvious in this crowd of pale people in drab black garb. Thank god that there was someone here that I didn't desperately need to avoid.

"Did Lark invite you?"

"Yes, I happened to be in town and could get away."

"What are you doing again?"

"Celebrity publicity. Business is good."

"That's excellent. And you got married recently, right?"

She grinned. "Yes, over the summer. It was a small wedding."

"Understandable when you marry a movie star like Josh Hutch."

She laughed and waved her hand. "It's no big deal. He's just Josh around here. But anyway, it was nice playing catch-up, but I think Lark was looking for you. She said that they were meeting in the library. I hope that means something to you."

"Yeah, it does. Thanks for delivering the message."

"Anytime. Just going to go find some more booze," she said, raising her empty glass and striding into the kitchen where I'd just left my brother. Good luck to her.

I extracted myself from the party and headed down to the

library. No wonder I hadn't seen any of my friends floating around. They must have been holed up in here the entire time. Not that I was particularly looking forward to this conversation. But I knew what was coming.

And I entered at my own risk.

Katherine was lying out on the chaise by the window with her long, lean legs bare as her dress fell off the side. She looked arranged, like a portrait. Lewis had his nose buried in a book he'd probably grabbed off of one of the shelves. Rowe was seated behind the desk, staring intensely at the computer. It was Lark who looked up first from her spot near the entrance.

"Hey, you made it," she said.

"I've been here awhile. I just didn't know you were all back here."

"I'm sorry about…not being able to help, you know?"

I held up my hand. "Not your fault. Don't even worry about it. How are you and Thomas?"

She chewed on her lip. "Well, he couldn't make it today. He got called into the office. I was going to head over after this. I think things will be okay."

"Good."

"Can we move on to the main course?" Katherine trilled from her seat. She lifted her arms overhead, stretching her body out long and invitingly.

Lewis snapped his book shut and looked up at me. We hadn't spoken since that day. I hadn't told Natalie about the bet, and I could hardly look at him, knowing he had feelings for her, too.

"So, where is she?" Lewis asked testily.

"She's not here," I said.

Katherine's laugh started out as a titter, small and breathy, and then turned into an almost maniacal cackle. "She isn't even…here?"

"No, she left. She's on a plane right now back to Charleston."

Lark frowned. "Oh Penn, I'm so sorry. I know how you feel about her."

"Well, that settles it, doesn't it?" Katherine said. She tilted her head to the ceiling, grinning like a Cheshire cat. "I win."

"She fell for me. That was the bet," I spat.

"No, the bet was that you bring her *here*, and then we get an impartial judge to say whether or not she really fell for you." Katherine kicked both of her feet off of the chaise and stood. "She's not here. No one can judge. You. Lose."

I opened my mouth and then closed it. She was right. Damn it. Natalie had to be here for me to win. "But you *told* her about the bet. That was against the rules."

"Actually, there weren't any rules. If you wanted them, you should have stipulated," she purred.

"And didn't *you* tell her anyway?" Lewis asked.

"No," I said through gritted teeth. "There was so much going on, and she'd just lost everything. I didn't want to break this to her too. She was already leaving to go home. I'm going to tell her, just…not the day she lost her livelihood."

"Pathetic," Lewis grumbled. He stuffed the book he'd been reading back into its place. "You couldn't even do that right."

"Look, that's none of your fucking business."

"What is going on with you two?" Lark asked.

"Do you want to tell them, Lewis?"

Lewis glared at me. "It doesn't matter."

"Well, I'm intrigued," Katherine said. "Did you two get into a little spat?"

I was prepared to spill his secret. But as I looked at his pleading eyes, at my very best friend, the guy that I'd grown up with my entire life, I couldn't do that to him. Even if he could do it to me.

"No," I yielded. "He just gave me some good advice that I didn't take. He's right to be pissed at me."

Lewis's eyes widened, as if he couldn't believe I hadn't ratted out his feelings for Natalie. But even I wasn't cruel enough to spill that to the likes of Katherine.

"Truthfully, I'm a little disappointed in you, Penn," Katherine said. She glided unhurriedly in my direction. "I was expecting a harder challenge. I thought you'd show me the dark Upper East Side of your nature. That bad boy underneath that you keep trying to push away with stuffy lectures about right and wrong."

"That Penn is dead," I told her.

"Everyone in this room knows that's a lie. You're still there. Hiding down deep. I'll claw it out of you." She trailed her finger down my chest. "All night tonight."

I swatted her hand away. "Enough."

"You guys," Lark said, glancing anxiously between us. "Maybe we should drop the whole thing. It was stupid anyway."

"It didn't happen how either of you expected," Lewis chimed in. "And all it does is hurt the group."

Everyone jumped in at once to argue their point of all of this. If only we had been this thoughtful two months ago in the pool.

"The bet was set," Katherine yelled over everyone. "If you'd won, I would have married Camden. No complaints from me."

"Yeah, right," I spat.

"I won, so I get to fuck you." Katherine shrugged. "That's the bet. That's what I get for going darker than you, Penn. Maybe, next time, you'll really play."

"You bitch…"

"Enough!" Rowe roared, shocking us all into silence. "The

bet happened. We all agreed on it that night. You can't argue your way out of this, so stop trying. I'm fucking tired of it. Natalie isn't here, so we can't judge if she fell for you. So, by the rules, Katherine won. Can we all shut up now and move on?"

NATALIE

The cab ride took forever and cost a fortune.

But I didn't even care as I bounded up the stairs and into the mayor's party. It was packed full of politicians and their friends. All dressed the same, as if they were going to a funeral. And here I was in a white dress and sandals with my hair in a topknot. No makeup. And nothing but my one bag and purse to my name. I probably looked like a hobo who had wandered into their midst.

Luckily, the mayor was nowhere around. I excused myself at the door and hurried through the living room. It was really beautiful, the way the interior decorator had finished everything. Not that that was my mission here.

I needed to find Penn. I had to tell him the truth.

I stumbled into the kitchen, keeping my eye out for him. I saw a man I recognized. I took a deep breath and then pushed forward.

"Court?" I asked.

He glanced over at me and frowned. "Are you lost, love?"

"I'm Natalie. We met briefly on Halloween. Have you seen Penn?"

"Oh right. Penn's little girlfriend. And here I thought, he'd ditched you."

"Uh, no. But have you seen him?"

"He was harassing me earlier."

I nearly rolled my eyes but held it back. "Do you know where he went?"

"Think he ran toward the library. But don't hold me to it. When he ditches you later, feel free to look me up." He winked.

I shook my head in disgust and pushed past him. He seemed every bit as dastardly as Penn had described him. Especially since I was pretty sure that his own girlfriend had been standing only a few feet away when he hit on me. Charming.

The library was around the corner and down closer to the master bedroom. I knew the layout by heart and rushed to open the door. My hand was on it when I heard raised voices from the other side.

I froze for a second. Who was yelling? And what about? Maybe Penn wasn't in there at all, and Court was sending me into some kind of trap. I'd walk in on someone having sex or in the middle of a huge argument and make a fool of myself. I released my hold on the doorknob and then pressed my ear to the door. Better find out before I make something worse.

"The bet was set!"

I furrowed my brows at those words. That was definitely Katherine. Who was she yelling at?

She continued, "If you'd won, I would have married Camden. No complaints from me."

My eyes bulged. Married Camden? No one thought Katherine would actually do that. It was a stupid, arranged thing that she hoped to put off long enough to find someone better.

Then someone said something too low for me to hear.

"I won, so I get to fuck you."

My stomach turned at that. Oh god, I had a feeling I knew who she was talking to. No, no, no.

"That's the bet. That's what I get for going darker than you, Penn. Maybe, next time, you'll really play."

My stomach dropped even further. Penn. She was…definitely talking to Penn. The bet was real. The bet Katherine had warned me about was true. And the terms…that was what Katherine had been spewing. Marry Camden or fuck Penn.

"Enough!" Rowe roared. "The bet happened. We all agreed on it that night. You can't argue your way out of this, so stop trying. I'm fucking tired of it. Natalie isn't here, so we can't judge if she fell for you. So, by the rules, Katherine won. Can we all shut up now and move on?"

I didn't think.

Didn't take time to process.

Didn't control the initial impulse that raced through my body.

Just thrust the library door open and strode into the room. "Wow, so the bet *was* real."

Five sets of eyes turned to me all at once. Katherine's jaw dropped open. Lewis took a step toward me. Lark covered her mouth in shock. Rowe actually looked surprised. But it was Penn. It was Penn that I stared at. Who looked both shocked and overjoyed. Like he wanted to wrap his arms around me and demand to know what I was doing here. Kiss the breath out of me and get me away from this horrible moment.

"Natalie, what are you doing here?" Penn asked. He brushed past Katherine and moved toward me.

"Don't!" I spat. I held my hand out. I was on fire. Anger flooding my veins, searing my body. "So Katherine was telling the truth. Wow. And I refused to believe her because I couldn't think you all were petty and stupid enough to go through with something like this." I laughed once. "Guess I was wrong about that. You are that stupid."

"Natalie…"

I glared at him with the fire of a thousand suns. "Just so we're clear, Penn didn't lose. I'm right here. And I clearly cared for him enough to abandon my flight home and call a cab to tell him how I felt. Like an idiot."

Penn's face contorted in pain. But I had no sympathy for him. He'd done this to himself.

"So, there. Bet over. And you can all go fuck yourselves."

I whirled on my feet and stormed back out of the library.

PENN RACED out of the library behind me. I could hear his footsteps as he caught up with me. I was making a scene as I rushed through the house. I didn't even care that people were staring at us. Or that the mayor had just appeared, looking aghast. I didn't care about any of it. Just that I'd actually done this incredibly stupid thing. And it had all backfired in my face.

"Natalie!" he called as we stormed through the living room.

"Leave. Me. Alone!"

I shoved some socialite out of my way and yanked the door open. I tried to slam it in Penn's face, but he grabbed the door and hurried out after me.

"Natalie, please, let me explain."

He tugged on my arm to get me to stop. I turned around so fast and slapped him hard across the face. The sound rang out into the silence. His stunned look was enough for me.

I yanked my arm away from him. "Don't touch me. Don't ever touch me again."

"I deserved that." His eyes were wide and pleading. Full of that devotion I'd enjoyed as a lie for two months.

I hated him in that moment. Hated him for that look. And how it made me weak in the knees.

"Yes, you did."

"Please, let me explain."

I glared at him. "Explain what exactly? That you played me? Again? A-fucking-gain, Penn?" I nearly shrieked at him. "That this is all a lie? Some fucking game to you. My life is not a game! I'm a human being. You don't get to toy with me like a puppeteer, tugging on my strings."

"I wasn't. I swear. It wasn't like that with you."

"You entered a bet! You actually bet on whether or not you could fuck me and get me to fall for you. That is playing with people's lives! My life. And what did I get out of it? A few weeks of sex and then a lost job, a lost place to stay, a lost *life*."

"I did not expect any of that to happen."

"You never expect it! Because nothing bad ever happens to you. And none of you give a fuck that you're ruining other people's lives! That girl Addie even tried to warn me," I said with a shake of my head. Disgusted with myself. "And I was too dumb, too stuck up your ass to see it."

"Natalie, I am so sorry for what happened. But I'm glad that we had those months. I didn't know that we'd fall for each other. That we'd end up here."

"Do you even hear yourself?" I shook my head in exasperation. Then I turned and started walking down the driveway.

"Natalie, stop."

"No, you stop! Stop talking to me! I don't want to hear anything else that comes out of that mouth of yours. You can't make this right. In Paris, you lied and manipulated me. That is *nothing* compared to this. Fool me once."

"It was all real. The bet was stupid. Just a pretense for me to get close to you. But how I feel, that's real," he tried to assure me.

"You didn't need a pretense!" I screamed at him.

I stopped in place, looked up at the sky, the beautiful blue sky that was such a lie today when everything else fell apart. I couldn't stand this. Couldn't handle this anymore.

I turned to face him. Not with tears in my eyes, but anger. No heartbreak, just emptiness. This was the end. It was over. Penn Kensington had done everything he could to ruin what was left of the romantic in my soul.

My voice was calm when I finally spoke again, "You spew all this shit about ethics. But you can't tell that betting on someone's life is wrong? That *this* is wrong? You research and study and teach what is happiness, what is the good life, how to live an ethical existence. But you don't live it."

"Nat…"

"You're not ethical, Penn. You're a hypocrite. A fraud." I swallowed back the pain welling in my chest. "You think you're so above everyone else on the Upper East Side, but really, you're just a wolf in sheep's clothing. Pretending to be one of the good guys when you're no different than any of them."

"I wish I could take it all back."

"Wish upon a star." I unclasped the bracelet at my wrist and threw it at his feet.

Then I turned and walked away.

"Natalie, please let me at least drive you."

I kept walking. "I don't need any of your *help* anymore. We're through. Don't try to contact me."

I walked down the driveway that led to the road beyond and to the city beyond that. I walked and kept on walking. And I left Penn and the Upper East Side and all of New York and the in my rearview.

EPILOGUE

ONE YEAR LATER

"Can you help me with this painting?" Amy asked.

I glanced up from my computer to see her struggling with some massive piece of artwork for her new show at the gallery. I hopped to my feet and helped her maneuver the thing into place.

"Shouldn't you use your actual help to do this?"

"Hey, you're here!"

"Yes, and I'm trying to work."

"Psh, you don't need to work!"

"Whatever, Amy. I still have to write another book. The publisher won't be happy with just one."

"I think you should just milk it for a while."

I rolled my eyes at my best friend and went back to my computer where I stared at the blank page that was supposed to be my next book. Not that I'd been having any luck with writing anything.

My phone buzzed noisily and I glanced down at it. "Hey, Ames, it's Caroline. I'm going to take this."

"Okay!" she called from behind another painting.

"Hey, Caroline," I said with a smile as I stepped out of the gallery and onto King Street in Charleston. Home sweet home.

"Natalie, darling. I'm glad I got ahold of you. How are you feeling?"

"Well, you know, fine. Jittery. Worried about the release next week."

"Everything is going to be fine. I wouldn't worry about it," she said in her strong Northern accent. "I spoke to Gillian, and she said the preorder numbers are out of this world."

As soon as I'd come home from New York, I'd gotten a call from Caroline. I had an offer in from Hartfield for my latest proposal. A big offer. And then another offer came in. And another. And then the book went to auction where all the publishers could bid on it. Thirteen publishers in total.

I'd actually fainted when Caroline came back with the final offer in the seven-figure range. Warren Publishing had won out, and I'd signed on the dotted line for my first book deal with Gillian editing.

It had been a dream and a nightmare.

Because of course, it had to be this book.

The one I'd written while living in that house with Penn for two months.

"So Warren wants to throw you a release party here, in New York. They're inviting everyone who matters and early readers who adored the book. I have your ticket and hotel situation all lined up. The publisher said they'd handle everything. You'll get a tour of Warren and a meeting with the higher-ups. I'm sure they'd love to hear what you're working on next. Nothing official, just an elevator pitch."

Caroline droned on about the party and my meeting with Warren, and I froze up. A party. In New York.

"Caroline, is there any way that I can...skip New York?"

"Are you kidding? Of course you can't skip. And they've already made the arrangements. It's important."

"Okay," I said softly.

"You can bring your friend Amy, too. We can get her a ticket if it makes you feel better."

"Yeah, that'd be great actually."

"Then it's set. I'll see you next Tuesday in New York City as the world gets your debut novel, BET ON IT."

Caroline talked for a few more minutes before hanging up. But I was left with a sense of panic. New York. I was finally going back to the place that had broken and remade me. I probably had nothing to worry about.

New York was a big city.

Millions of people lived there.

What were the chances that I would run into anyone that I knew?

To Be Continued

ACKNOWLEDGMENTS

Cruel Money was three years in the making. And it all began with a dream about a couple sitting on a park bench in Paris. I tried to start writing Penn and Natalie's story so many times. Finally, it came to me exactly where to start them, and the transformation they made along the way is one of my favorite stories. There's more to come, of course. I couldn't leave them so soon when they have so much to say.

But as always, thank you to all the people behind the scenes that made this book such a success. I couldn't have done without you. Day in and day out, you see the struggles and make it a little easier to create these stories come to life. Including—Rebecca Kimmerling, Anjee Sapp, Katie Miller, Rebecca Gibson, Polly Matthews, Diana Peterfreund, Jennifer Barnes, Danielle Sanchez, Staci Hart, Jillian Dodd, Kimberly Brower, Jovana Shirley, Sarah Hansen, Ashley Lindemann, Alyssa Garcia, Anthony Colletti, Chelle Bliss, Corinne Michaels, Yasmine Kateb, Lauren Perry, and so many more.

But especially my husband Joel for his unfailing dedication to me. And my puppy Riker, who was the inspiration for his likeness in this story, Totle. Finally, apologies to my other puppy Lucy for not writing you into a book yet. Love you all!

ABOUT THE AUTHOR

K.A. Linde is the *USA Today* bestselling author of the Avoiding Series, Wrights, and more than thirty other novels. She has a Masters degree in political science from the University of Georgia, was the head campaign worker for the 2012 presidential campaign at the University of North Carolina at Chapel Hill, and served as the head coach of the Duke University dance team. She loves reading fantasy novels, binge-watching Supernatural, traveling, and dancing in her spare time.

She currently lives in Lubbock, Texas, with her husband and two super-adorable puppies.

Visit her online at www.kalinde.com and on Facebook, Twitter, and Instagram @authorkalinde.

Join her newsletter at www.kalinde.com/subscribe for exclusive content, free books, and giveaways every month.

CPSIA information can be obtained
at www.ICGtesting.com
Printed in the USA
FFHW021554040119
50036313-54814FF